Ovum

Gideon Masters

TSL Publications

First published in Great Britain in 2021
By TSL Publications, Rickmansworth

Copyright © 2021 Gideon Masters

ISBN / 978-1-913294-96-0

Cover images:
https://pixabay.com/illustrations/angel-mystical-gothic-fantasy-wing-4706175/
https://pixabay.com/illustrations/skeleton-mysterious-cemetery-4986586/

Heartfelt dedications to:
Deb for her love and forbearance.

Anne for her patience, hard work and belief in me, and in a work alien to her interests.

Casting off

With Ben at the wheel, the *Ark* heeled over and struck for open water. Eve stood alone at the prow. Tendrils of spray-soaked hair whipped unattended about her face. Sucking in lungfuls of salt wind she sighed with the sheer pleasure of leaving the troubled world far behind.

They'd had five wonderful days getting the boat seaworthy, and the *Ark* now ploughed a furrow into a new and unpeopled future ... Four hours out, Eve had Ben help her to mount the prow gun, and another in the stern. She took great pleasure in his look of boyish delight, as she handed him a missile launcher and told him to find a handy place for it. The need to hide her lethal horde was long past. On this voyage, he was her trusted companion. "Pirates won't find us easy pickings this time Ben." Smiling broadly, he shouldered the weapon and headed amidships. "Ben? I've been looking at the charts. We can be in deep and fairly unpopulated waters by nightfall. Right now, it's calm, and visibility is excellent, so no one is likely to surprise us. I think we can afford to relax a little. I'm for a swim and some lunch. How does that sound for you?"

"A warm shower and a hearty lunch will be waiting my Lady." Having escaped the weight of responsibility that had confined him these long months, he was flushed with excitement and exhilaration at the prospect of embarking on another lone adventure with the mistress he so idolised and worshipped, and was more than eager to attend to her comforts.

"Still calling me Lady; can't you just say Eve, Ben? We are friends now, aren't we?"

"Always Lady Eve, but it wouldn't be proper."

"You know my history Ben. You know that I was once a man, so that epithet is not really very appropriate."

"I was a man too Lady Eve, but things are different now. We are different."

"Oh! Ben, I am so sorry I didn't mean to taunt you."

"Taunt all you wish my Lady. I deserve it all. I am better now than I ever could have been, had you not punished me so. And I know you will make all well again, if, and when, you think me worthy."

Eve grabbed his shoulders and fixed him with a searching look. "I can't give you your balls back Ben."

He returned her stare with a searching look of his own. "What lesson do you teach me now my Lady, with your denials? I know I am heavy with sin, and perhaps I can never pay my debt, but I will always serve you faithfully, and hope that you will continue to restore me."

"What are you talking about Ben? Continue? Continue what? Restore what?"

"I don't understand why you want me to tell you what you must already know. By your grace Lady Eve, my balls are re-growing."

Eve sucked in a deep and awkward breath, and held it for several seconds, whilst she contemplated her response. "I hate to disillusion you Ben but that is impossible. It's just wishful thinking."

"After all that has happened. All the great things you have done, you still do not really know who and what you are. Did you not regrow your own face?"

Eve's intended response froze on her lips. She began to muddle her words. "Th, that is diff...different; you know that I am nn... not like other people Ben."

"Yes..." He just looked at her. After several tight-lipped moments and an incomprehensible expletive, Eve spun on her heel, and stormed off below deck to look in on Zeus.

She bent to pat his head then prepared some warm milk and bread, and brought it to him. He lapped at it slowly. It seemed he had never gone far from the reed beds, where she and Ben had left him and the other dogs. Eve suspected he had been guarding the boat. She had been spooked on the first night when she'd heard a whimpering and rubbing alongside the hull, and had dashed out, gun in hand to look into the dark water. And there he was, swimming pathetically around the boat. He hadn't fared well. He had a gunshot wound in his rear leg and was barely able to stay afloat. His muzzle was even more scarred than when they last saw him; but he was able to yelp for assistance when he saw Eve. She pulled him out, fixed his wound, and had been nursing him since, and, thank God, he seemed to be recovering. In fact, given his condition, he seemed to be recovering far better than anyone could have expected. Ben's uncharacteristic exclamation on seeing him, had secured him his name.

Eve rapped on the door of Ben's cabin, and shoved it open with juddering force. "Show me!" she demanded.

"Show you what my Lady?"

"Your balls dammit! I want to see for myself this marvel of regeneration." He calmly stood, and dropped his trousers. Oblivious, she got down on her knees for a closer look. "Come on, it's no time to be coy. I've not only seen this before, I bloody well mutilated it. Now, lift what's left out of the way. This is more important than you can possibly know." She scrutinised his sack closely; and after some hesitation, informed him that she was going to physically examine him. He was now looking at the ceiling but managed a stiff shrug. She prodded tentatively at first, then …

"Ah fuck it!" she reached her fingers up behind and probed with her thumbs. Ben became restless and fidgety. Eve suddenly snatched her hands away and stood up quickly. "Jesus Christ Ben! Can't you keep control of yourself for one minute … I'll be on deck. Do whatever you have to, to get rid of that!" She pointed at his erect member. "Meet me up top. But wash your bloody hands first." Taking her own advice, she washed her own, patted Zeus again and went on deck to think … Could they be tumours? They were like soft jelly and a little bit small; but two perfectly formed testis-shaped growths was one hell of a coincidence. And clearly his ardour had returned, if it was ever absent? She would ask him about that. What did this all mean for her, and for all those close to her? Should she tell Freddy; and what of Soames? He'll probably want to kill me again. He'll definitely insist on more regular examinations. She was muttering now. "And why the fuck haven't my ovaries regrown too? God, even out here in the middle of the ocean there is no escape from all the shit that is happening to me; and around me."

"Pardon my Lady." Eve whirled around to see a diffident and red-faced Ben, maintaining a safe distance and fumbling his hands together in a wringing motion. "Oh for God's sake Ben! I'm not angry or disappointed with you. Like I said, I was a man myself once. I know how it is. I should have known better. I am happy for you, but I am deeply shocked and confused. And I need you to enlighten me in great detail, about your condition, right back to the time you first recovered from my castration of you. When was it that you were first able to gain a full erection, and has there ever been any previous discharge or ejaculation?"

Ben shifted uncomfortably from foot to foot, and responded with continued diffidence. "First time today my Lady," he mumbled. "For both."

"Oh shit! I can't deal with this. I'm going for that swim. You should too, dampen your ardour." So saying, she dived off the boat and swam several hundred yards in seconds, and then duck dived straight down. As before, she felt her abdomen pushing her lungs high up into her chest, and her body adjust to the environment. This was disconcerting, but she continued to swim down, and sank fast, barely noticing as the colours faded; then everything went dark. She looked up and could see only a watery midnight blue. She twisted and turned and looked in every direction and saw nothing but the same. Black panic dilated within her, withering her self-control. She kicked wildly, desperate to return to the surface and fresh air. Her efforts began to pay off. It was getting lighter. She fancied she saw a shimmer of sunlight. Struggling to resist her body's imperative to breathe, her strokes became frenzied. A shadow froze her movements. A huge shape clouded her vision and brought back the dark. Eve's eyes had adjusted now, and she saw several other shapes circling above her, and cutting off her escape to the surface.

Wrestling with her fear, she forced control into her wild move-ments. Taking smooth long strokes, Eve tried to put distance between the sharks and herself, whilst angling up towards the life-giving air she so desperately sought. Too late! She saw it from the bottom of her eye. It had come unnoticed from directly below and was almost on her. Its nose was already up! With gaping eyes, she looked into its fleshy, yawning mouth. There was no escape. Kicking hard, Eve turned to face it. She nursed the vain hope that her head might float free; and her last moments be remembered outside of its stinking gut. She contorted her arms, pincer-like, to gouge at the eyes of this mindless beast who would consume her.

At the last she screamed. The water rushed in. The world went black. And she failed to see the shark veer off, and circle her sinking body several times, then repeatedly butt her toward the surface. A while passed. She was vaguely aware of being buffeted, and that she was still well below the surface. As the light grew brighter, so her senses returned. She swam a couple of experimental strokes, and then felt a winding blow in her side. A grey wall thrust between her face and the endless blue, and she looked directly into the black and soulless orb of a great white. A jolt of recognition almost overcame her, and it.

There was no coherent thought in this creature, but it knew its mistress, and it would obey; if she only knew how to command it. Increasing ambient pressure alerted her that she had started to sink again. Before she could assimilate this, she was butted again, hard in the abdomen, and thrust violently upward. Her limbs flailed in the turbulence of her wake, and her scrambled thoughts fought for focus. A picture of Ben panicking on the deck of the *Ark* elbowed its way into her mind. Zeus was with him, looking pathetic and howling. The huge creature now swam ponderously beneath her, sliding its dorsal fin along her body. It circled and repeated the action. Her dulled senses got the message, and she took hold. After several minutes she broke surface next to the *Ark*. Zeus was barking like crazy with his head over the rail.

Then she heard Ben. "What is it boy?" His head poked out next to Zeus's, and he was over the side on a line, in seconds. Unthinking of his own safety, he straddled the back of the shark, and heaved her over the rail, Zeus dragged at her sweat top to take some of her enormous weight. As soon as Ben's feet were off, the shark was gone, but it circled back. There were moments of frantic scrabbling, whilst Ben got clear of the thrashing jaws ripping along the gunwale. Eve was too busy retching sea water, and gasping for air, to know much of what went on. Ben managed to manhandle her into the cabin and get off her wet clothes (she made a token resistance, and then let him get on with it). He towelled her dry and put her to bed. Zeus managed with Ben's help, to get up onto the foot of the bunk, where he growled and bared his teeth at Ben until he left.

Within minutes, Eve recovered, but was exhausted and desperate for sleep. She felt safe with Ben in charge and began to drift away ... then jerked upright, with an exclamation. "I was breathing underwater for fuck sake! BEN! BEN!"

Ben came crashing in. Zeus barked and growled but was shushed by Eve. She coiled the covers around her and ushered Ben into the galley. Ducking into the head, she looked in the mirror, poked out her tongue, and saw flaps of skin receding down her throat, settling back into the seamless, normal, and unruffled shape she was familiar with. She got a full account of Ben's perspective of everything that had happened. "I was hoping to have a break from the others Ben, but I think we have got to bring them in on this, and on your ... your testicle situation. Trouble is I'm not happy about telling Soames. Apart from anything else, I know the bastard will have any transmission on our radio tracked, and I don't like him knowing our location."

"Jackie put new mobile phones in our packs Lady Eve. We could phone any one of the others without him tracking us, although some of them might be protective enough to try and do likewise."

"It's good you are here Ben. My mind is so befuddled with intrigue, I totally missed the obvious. And Jackie would be the best one to contact. You, you don't mind my talking to her about you, your ... Fuck it! Your bollocks?"

He couldn't contain a chuckle at her awkwardness. "I'm the one who should be embarrassed my Lady, and I suppose I am. She is only a young girl, but she is the right one to contact, and my feelings are of small import."

"Christ Jackie. I've barely put to sea and I've got all this crap to deal with. I was hoping to have some time to relax, take stock and recharge." The line went silent. "Are you still there Jackie ...?"

"Yes Eve still here. You know this couldn't be better. This is proof certain that you cannot only communicate with sea creatures, but can have command over them. We could have spent months trying to achieve this and ended up in failure. There is now the possibility that we can actually communicate with whatever it is down there. This is a huge burden lifted Eve. You must have been worried sick about how to proceed. And Eve, you can dive deep, and breathe under water for Christ sake. It's too much to say we're halfway there, but you have to admit to have come so far at this early stage is miraculous."

Eve started to splutter. "Breathe under water? Dive deep? I was shitting myself Jackie! You probably think the shark was the most frightening thing. It wasn't. It is cold and dark, and … nothing, nothing anywhere, and even that is not the worst. You find yourself praying that nothing disturbs the silent dark, because you know, there is something invisible out there … somewhere, and it is gargantuan, and will drag your soul into torturous oblivion. And we are talking about a lot, lot deeper in the Sargasso. I can't do it Jackie!"

Jackie's tone softened. "You may not have to Eve. There's a whole sea load of creatures out there that will do your bidding. Whales can talk across an ocean, so why not to the bottom of it. And Eve, I hesitate to mention it … it is such a long shot, but so many strange things have happened, and hope is what we live on isn't it? It … it would be such a prize as would make anything; any risk, worthwhile … But I have said too much. I must speak with Soames and Freddy, but please have faith."

"Not Soames, Jackie!"

"Trust me on this Eve. I will be as discreet as I can, but this is too momentous."

"What Jackie? What is so momentous?"

"I'm sorry I can't tell you now. It would be too cruel if I am wrong. I need to do some research. I need to bring in Soames and Freddy. Just know there are possibilities. I have to go."

"Jackie don't. Jackie? Answer dammit. Ah shit!"

"You told her everything?"

"Yes Ben, and she just hung up."

"You can trust her Lady Eve."

"I know that. She must have a reason. She always does. And if she thinks Soames and Freddy need to know before I do, I guess there must be some good reason for that too, but it is bloody infuriating, and …"

"And what?"

"This is hard to say, but I really needed her reassurance and comfort, and encouragement, and there just wasn't enough of any of it."

Ben looked abashed. "I'm here my Lady."

"Oh, I know Ben." She placed a hand over his. "And you are always a comfort. Just knowing you are around makes me feel better, but sometimes …"

"You just need a female shoulder to cry on."

She paused and thought about that. "Well, yes, I guess I do. Isn't that strange? But you'll do Ben. You ride the backs of sharks to rescue me, and that goes a long way to filling the void." Eve yawned. "I think I'm for bed Ben." She rose, and absently bent to kiss him on the forehead before heading to her cabin. Zeus followed her and managed to gain the foot of her bunk without help. She kissed him too, crawled into the top end, and crashed.

She awoke to the sizzle and smell of bacon. Zeus knew not to be around just prior to her waking up. She washed and went to the galley. Zeus was happily wolfing down the scraps Ben threw his way.

"Saw a group of three boats a while back, a long way off, probably just a flotilla group. To be safe I put on some sail and left them for dead. I doubt if they even saw us, something to be aware of though." He shoved a steaming plate towards her.

"Perfect timing Ben, you always know when I'm up and about."

"Not hard when you do that fitting workout thing, about ten minutes before. Anyway, it's the only time Zeus leaves your side. What do you think happened to the rest of the pack?"

"All dead I'm afraid."

"Did he tell you that?"

"Not in so many words, but yeah in a way."

Ben put two cups of coffee on the table and sat opposite. "Probably terrorised the local farms, tends to bring out the farmers' violent side, when a couple of their goats are mauled or eaten."

"Ah he's just a big softie." She ruffled Zeus's neck.

"To you maybe, but then so are sharks … Jackie sent a text."

"What! You could have said. Why didn't you wake me?"

"You needed your sleep, and besides, it was sent to me. She said not to worry. Soames is still in the dark about where we are headed and what we are doing. She has told him nothing about your underwater adventures, although Freddy had to be told some."

"That's odd, after her talk about how momentous it all was, and couldn't be kept from him."

"She said she did have to tell him about my healing though."

"Shit! What is her fucking game? That was the bit I least wanted him to know about, just when we had achieved a reasonable working relationship. He'll probably want to hunt me down and kill me now. I wouldn't be surprised if those boats were his."

"She guessed you would say something like that, and said to not worry. He's actually quite excited about the whole thing and is going to work closely with Freddy on it. She also said you should try and relax as much as possible during the voyage, and to get in the sea as much as you can. See just how far you can attune yourself to whatever abilities you have there."

"Callous little cow! Oh well, better get about relaxing then; any ideas?"

"Well ... That rock where we had our encounter with the pirates isn't too far off. Nice little beach. Bit risky maybe, as it's their patch, but they're scared shitless of you, and if they do pluck up the courage, I reckon we out gun them now. Could be fun, and just the satisfying type of adrenalin rush we need; if they don't show, we get to have that little holiday you promised last time."

"Yeah; why not? You are a clever bastard Ben. You always seem able to produce what I need, just when I need it. What are you going to cook?" Grinning, Ben went off to set the course and check the boat's radar. Eve grabbed the journal she had started to keep (at Jackie's suggestion) and started to sketch and annotate her recent experiences. She felt the boat yaw over as Ben altered their course, and spent several happy hours dawdling her way through her thoughts and ruminations.

Eve was daydreaming with her feet up, and her hands clasped behind her head, when she heard the anchor chain clattering into the shallows. She stretched, sighed, and went up to join Ben on deck. The sun was high and hot, and the sky cloudless. She helped Ben get what he needed onto the beach. Zeus managed the short swim to the shore, and she took him for a walk to the highest point, whilst Ben got on with the cooking. She checked his wounds. His recovery was remarkable. Eve squatted and looked into his eyes. He was always a good listener. "So Zeus, it seems on top of everything else, I am also a healer, albeit an unconscious one. And that is amazing, but no more so than all the other things that have happened. Why is it then, that Jackie is getting so fired up about it? And why risk telling Soames when she knows how he feels about my regenerative abilities? If it were anyone else, I might doubt their reasoning, but Jackie never does anything without a good reason, and she is loyal to a fault." She pushed her thoughts to one side, and wandered down to join Ben.

Eve picked meat from between her teeth with a fingernail, and patted a full belly. "You really do have a talent Ben. That was delicious." She laid back on the sand to soak up the sun, and closed her eyes. Ben slapped a Post It note on her head. "What the fuck are you playing at now Ben?"

"Relaxation. When was the last time you did anything recreational? So, twenty questions, who are you?"

"Well if that's the case you've got to do one too. Gimme them Post Its."

"Who the fuck is Irma La Douche?"

"Oh, some prostitute in a cowboy with Clint Eastwood."

"Who are these people? I know you are into ancient shit, but does everything have to be from before I was born?"

"Oh yeah, you mean like the Lochness Monster. He's only been around since yesterday I suppose."

"At least everyone's heard of it, and who says it's a he? Don't they call 'her' Nessie? I reckon that's got to be a forfeit, and another one for Irma La bloody Douche."

"Okay you got me, but if it's anything personal, I'll break your arms. What you got in mind?"

"Well, I reckon you've just fallen off a horse, or a shark if you prefer, and Jackie's right, you need to tune your abilities. I think you have to get back in the sea, as soon as ... and maybe try and call in a few sea creatures, see what happens."

"You had to spoil it didn't you? But I suppose you are right, I feel sick at the thought of going back in, but if I don't do something soon, I never will. Okay, I dread to ask; what's the other forfeit?"

Ben grinned. "Target practice!"

"What do you mean?"

"Those three boats, they may be harmless but I'm not sure. They blipped up on the radar when we were a few miles short of here. I doubt if you've ever used those weapons I helped you mount, so they should be tested, and there are some rocks out to sea that would be great for range testing; blow the bastards out of the water."

Eve wasn't sure whether he meant the rocks or the boats, but she supposed it didn't really matter. "Okay you bloody psychopath, I suppose it pays to be prepared. You go get the guns ready, and I'll take a dip. Calling sea creatures though is a bit of a tall order. But, in for a penny ..."

"What?"

"Don't worry, just a saying, another thing from before you were born, and no, that does not mean another forfeit."

She walked into the water and swam out to where the sea changed to a deeper blue. She hesitated, and this time, did not duck dive. She just let her weight take her down, slowly finning to reduce her speed. At thirty feet she arrested her progress, looked around, and tried to call in her mind, to whatever was out there; filling her mind with the more endearing sea creatures, dolphins, seals, penguins, and the like ... nothing. She tried to quell her fears but a sickening uneasiness was surging through her. She tried to empty her mind and leave only the desire to communicate ... still nothing. She let her mind idle, and a memory slid in under the wire, of another time in the sea, when she had dived down and communicated with a dolphin, and the image took over her thoughts as though she was there. She stopped finning, and unknowing of her predicament, began to sink. The gathering dark alerted her, and she kicked for the surface, and then stopped. She was breathing water again! And her eyes, she now realised, could see clearly, even though she wore no face mask.

She began to relax, swimming with effortless long strokes, and undulating her body like a dolphin; no! Not a dolphin, more like an eel, or that's how it felt. It was a strange feeling; her body didn't really have the mechanics for it. She looked down at herself. Everything looked normal, except for the subtle undulations that propelled her efficiently through the water. When she finally registered her surroundings again, she found herself swimming in the midst of a small pod of dolphins. She stopped, and they swam around her. She broke the surface, and they leapt over her. She duck-dived, and paused again; they fanned out, facing her. One came forward and pressed its beak to her forehead. A barrage of clicks and whistles assaulted her senses. Eve could not have translated their meaning, though she understood perfectly. They were more about feelings than coherent thought, and yet they revealed so much information about the history of the pod, the currents of the sea, and the dangers in the sea, but not this sea. Somehow she knew they were informing and warning her about the Sargasso.

Nevertheless, they exuded a lightness and happiness that buoyed her spirits and swept away her fears. She found herself laughing. Two of them came alongside and allowed her to take hold of their dorsal fins. Eve played with them for a blissful hour; then remembered Ben. He would be worried.

She arrived back at breakneck speed, one foot on each of the backs of two dolphins. Ben fist pumped the air and whooped at her approach. She stepped off, nuzzled each in turn, and they left, arcing in and out of the water by way of goodbyes.

"Atta girl, I ... I mean I knew you could do it Lady Eve." He moved on quickly. "And now; target practice. I've set everything up my Lady." Even in her current state of euphoria, it dawned on Eve that until now, Ben had not used the phrase "my Lady" much today, and had for the most part, adopted a much more familiar mode of address. She wanted friends not worshippers, but she wasn't entirely sure how she felt about that. Their relationship had always been a complicated one, a miracle that they had one at all when she thought about it. After all, it had been her original intent to kill him. And his plans for her had been equally sinister, or worse in her books. What was that phrase that Isaac had once used, "God and the Devil nurture their own I suppose." It seemed like a million years ago now, but which camp was she in? Soames would probably say the Devil's, Ben too for that matter. She sighed and followed Ben to the prow. She looked out at the rocks he'd decided to decimate.

"Hey! There's one missing, you started without me shithead!"

Ben looked sheepish for a moment. "Only three shots Ma'am. One to test the range, and I can tell you, it's long, and two to obliterate the smallest rock. I don't think pirates could get near enough to cause us any bother, and if they did, there's always the missile launcher, but I left that one well alone, can't waste our limited stock of shells."

They spent thirty minutes blasting chunks out of the several remaining rocks, and then Ben called a halt. Eve had to admit she was saddened. It had literally blown the last of the cobwebs from her mind, and she was left feeling flushed and excited. To maintain the mood she ducked below and scrabbled around in the cupboards.

"Ah there you are m'beauty." Eve had stashed a bottle of rum when she had taken delivery of the boat as homage to the folklore of pirates and mariners, past and present. It was a mascot really, bought on a whim. She had never intended to drink it, but now she had a craving for alcohol. It seemed the perfect way to end a perfect day. She grabbed two glasses, and invited Ben to join her. Somewhere, about three-quarters of the way through the bottle, they had got to talking about what if they just cut and run, and took to the life of pirating the seven seas? They traded stories, and sang pirate songs, and told pirate jokes, which ended with Eve singing a particularly disgusting sea shanty she had dredged up from somewhere, while Ben tried to do the hornpipe dance. Eve got up to join in, and they finished by doing a conga around the deck. Eve stumbled and Ben fell on top of her. She had an uncontrollable fit of the giggles, then she felt the bulge in his shorts pressed against her. Reacting without thought, she threw him across the deck, and he hit his head on the mast. He lay still for a moment, then groggily probed the wound on his head, and looked at the blood on his hand.

"Ben, I'm sorry, I didn't mean to … I just reacted. I wouldn't hurt you ever, not now. She found her eyes were leaking, and a knot of fear was twisting her stomach. She had to turn her face away. "I … I love you Ben, but not like that. Like a brother, or maybe a … a son." She felt him flop down beside her.

"You did what was right my Lady. I don't love you that way either, and I never would have tried anything, it's just this damned testosterone. I can't help myself when I am close to you. Christ! I can't even help myself when I brush past the ship's rail. I'm like a rampant adolescent on a hair trigger. Touch it and it goes off. I wish they had never regrown. Say the word Lady Eve, and I will cut them off again."

Eve grabbed his hand. "No! Never say that. There was a time when there may have been some justice in that, but not now. I want you whole. I want to see you married one day with a hoard of kids. And I speak from experience, when I tell you your urges will become more controllable as time passes. We'll just be a little more careful in the meantime." She rose, and Ben got to his feet too.

"You can always throw me over the side and drag me behind the boat like you used to." He grinned. "I miss those times."

She chuckled and grabbed his hand again. "Come on, let's finish up the bottle. We'll stick a message in it to all would be pirates, 'beware the *Ark* and its murderous, and slightly insane crew', and throw it in the drink, then we can turn in ..."

Eve had got up early, cleaned and dressed Ben's wound, and insisted that he take things easy for a bit. By 6 a.m. the *Ark* was under full sail and heading for the trade wind that would take them to the Sargasso.

Leviathan

They were becalmed. Eve was cooking breakfast. Ben wandered in from the head. "What's cooking Mum?"

Eve threw the tea towel at him. "Christ Ben! I finally get you to stop saying 'Lady' and you start coming out with this crap."

"Well, you said you thought of me like a brother or a son, would you prefer Sis?"

"Probably, but neither would be nice, why not just Eve?"

"Nah that doesn't work, it wouldn't be proper."

"But you think mum is okay?"

"Think about it. You will be the new mother of humanity, so everyone should be calling you mother, or maybe Gaia, mother of all ... No that wouldn't be right either, she's been around a long time, and you are new. Besides, with a slight deflection of me cockney accent missus, it could sound like ma'am, which puts us back where we were before, pretty much."

"Mother of humanity has a better ring to it than the antichrist, I'll give you that much, but I am not, and never will be, the mother of anything, and again, what the bloody hell is wrong with Eve? Wasn't she the original mother of humanity?"

"Well, if you're likely to smash my head against the mast again if I refuse, I guess I had better try. Eve it is, from now on, but not in company, or if I think I need to tug your string, Mum."

"At last; and talking of tugging strings ...?" Eve looked at his crotch and nodded her head.

"Lots of wet sheets ma'am ... er, Eve, but if I keep up with the laundry, I think I'll manage."

"Good!" She slapped two plates on the table, and they ate in silence. They took time over coffee, and then Eve started to pull on a wet suit. She was drawing it out, and Ben picked up on her mood.

"How deep are you going today m...m ... Eve?"

"Fucking deep Ben and I'm crapping myself. I'm not sure if there is really any point, I'm never going to make the bottom. This bloody sea is three miles deep in places. I might as well jump into a black hole, it's just about as dark as one down there, and God knows what's in it. You know, I'm starting to hate Jackie for coming up with this idea. Maybe it wasn't her idea at all. Maybe Soames dreamed it up to get rid of me. It's definitely his MO."

"I'd feel better if you took a marker line down this time, at least I would know you were on the end of it."

"No point Ben. If anything happened there is nothing you could do, and I can always find my way back to the boat. Just track me with the sonar, I'll hear it, and if not, I'll hitch a ride, although I'd rather not think of what on, surprisingly small amount of mammalian marine life around here, or maybe I just haven't seen any yet, I haven't really seen much of anything yet."

"Why don't you get Soames to send out a submarine, or a bathysphere or something?"

"Nah! I don't think even they can get that deep, and I think Soames may be even more dangerous than what's down there. We need to think laterally here. If my experience in Fadil's dreamscape is based in reality, then Afsoon seems to think he can communicate from the other side of the sun. He evidently has greater knowledge, but I reckon proximity counts for something, so I will see how close I can get. I reckon I'm pretty much at my limit though."

"Jackie's thoughts about whales seemed good."

"Yeah, maybe it's time to try communicating with one."

"Be careful."

She nodded, then went on deck and let him help her on with her fins, before slipping over the side and plummeting.

Ben watched her vanish into the depths and tried to track her on the sonar system. After a few minutes, he noticed the wind had started to pick up, and there seemed to be a slight current. He had to engage the motor to maintain position. He increased the ping speed of the sonar, as the agreed danger signal to Eve. She was the only thing down there, and he checked her depth, seven hundred feet or so and still diving. And now a shoal of something came up on the monitor, moving fast in her direction. He started throwing tins and anything heavy over the side, hoping she would see them and come back up, but had to stop, to monitor wind and current, and hold position. Zeus was padding around nervously on deck. Ben increased engine speed to compensate for the current. Zeus started to bark frantically, with his head over the side. Ben looked over and saw something in the depths, coming up fast, something fucking big!

There was a thump on the hull, and the boat tilted over to leeward, then back to starboard, giving Ben a view of first one side, and then the other, as the boat rails dipped below the water line. He managed to grab Zeus, before he went over the side. The area of the sea for metres around the *Ark*, was a boiling mass of eels. The centre of the mass to starboard erupted, throwing eels in every direction, many now writhing across the deck, and dropping into the stairwell to the galley below. A monstrous creature burst from the centre, and a thick tendril threw a gasping, and somewhat transformed Eve, sliding across the deck, before it disappeared back into the depths. Although recognisably Eve, she seemed almost serpentine, and was unable to raise herself onto hands and knees on her fin-like limbs, which were reverting before Ben's eyes. She gasped out instructions, between regurgitating lungfuls of water: "Get us the fuck out of here Ben, and get Soames on the transmitter as fast as you can!"

Eve recovered whilst Ben was still sorting out the rigging. She grabbed the transmitter and was already sending out a distress call. "Soames, get a helicopter, or whatever the fuck else you can muster, out to us fast." She gave co-ordinates, even though she suspected he could track their location. "I reckon you'll be the quickest, but I'm sending out a general distress call too. We are in deep shit here … Mayday, Mayday."

She helped Ben trim the rigging, and to get the *Ark* under way. They fought the rising wind and current for two hours. Waves were now thirty feet and rising. The gusting wind and spray was threatening to tear them from the deck. Eve's acute hearing caught the whumpf, whumpf, whumpf of the helicopter before they saw it. And then it appeared out of the mist, a huge double-bladed thing, already trailing a rescue line and rescuer. Eve refused to leave the boat until Ben and Zeus were safely aloft. The rescuer then did three passes, but still couldn't get close enough. Eve leapt and caught the line, and watched the *Ark* vanish into the baleful eye of a dark and terrifying whirlpool, as she was hauled aloft.

The copter fought buffeting winds, sleet, and giant air pockets, for twenty minutes, then broke clear into a glorious sunset. Their rescuer, who had vanished up front as soon as Eve was back inside, now came back to talk to them. "Weirdest weather conditions I've ever seen, name's Hank." He proffered a huge hand. "Helluva leap lady, thought we'd lost you. Shame about the boat, looked like a beauty. We'll be landing on the USS *Fairweather*, would ya believe, in around 45 minutes." He passed them a couple of old flight suits. "Probably best if you get out of your wet clothes. I'll go up front and give you some privacy. There's a flask in the rack over your head, good coffee, with a shot of rum. I find it kinda helps."

Captain Baker was leaning over the shoulder of an officer, studying a computer screen. On seeing them he waved them over and dismissed the escorting officer.

"Scary business, how are you after your ordeal? Feel able to talk about it?" He didn't wait for an answer. "Felix, get over here and take some notes ... Thank you Doctor and Mr Gabriel for that detailed account of the freakish conditions you experienced. We'll get that filed and sent to our scientific team ASAP. Research holiday, you say? Not much of a holiday in these waters. But I suppose if your son's thesis is on the life cycle of eels, it kind of makes sense. You are lucky we were here. You wouldn't have made it out otherwise. Damn near lost you both, and a very expensive helicopter, and highly trained crew in the process. We wouldn't normally have got involved. There were at least two ships a lot closer than us who had picked up your signal and were motoring hard in your direction. And no one could have known just how quick and bad conditions were going to get. We were going in the opposite direction, and we certainly would not have scrambled a war craft, but when you get a direct order from the Pentagon, you know you had damn well better act, and fast ... Anything you'd like to add to your account Dr Gabriel? Perhaps something about your son's research ... No? I have assigned you both quarters and you have the freedom of the ship, excluding restricted areas of course, that's anything below the top two decks, and the bridge and command centre. Don't stray. Is there anything you need?"

"Possibly. How about questions?"

"If you keep it short. Go ahead."

"Can I get a message out?"

"I'm afraid not. We are on communications shut down. Basically, we are in stealth mode."

"How about incoming? Anything about us?"

"We're filtering and monitoring specific data only, so unless we get another direct order from the Pentagon, you can take it as nothing received. You may be informed if that changes."

Eve digested this. "How long before we are clear of the Sargasso Sea captain?"

"We're staying around to make some observations, maybe four to six days ... I think that's enough questions for now, unless you can enlighten me any further on your circumstances, and what happened out there ... No? I didn't think so. I'll get someone to show you to your quarters." He turned to Lieutenant Felix. "See our guests are directed and instructed as to our expectations of them during their stay please Felix."

"Captain! You asked if we needed anything. I do."

He turned back with a weary look. "And what is it that you need Doctor?"

"Use of a decompression chamber and a very strong sedative."

A look of bewilderment fleetingly grazed his face. He sought to retrieve equilibrium with a bland response. "I'll consider your request."

Eve spoke over her shoulder as they were escorted away. "Any delay would be regrettable Captain, unless you can airlift me out of here very soon."

"What do you make of Dr Gabriel and her feral son Felix?"

"The son's a scary individual Sir."

"What makes you say that?"

"Looks as though he'd cut your throat if you as much as winked at his mother Sir, and is probably capable of doing it."

"How do you mean?"

"Don't know Sir. He's as supple as a rattle snake and has a look that says he's just about as deadly."

"And what of the Doctor?"

"Most beautiful woman I have ever seen sir, and ..."

"Spit it out Felix!"

"Well, I reckon she might be more deadly than her son, Sir."

"Yeah I know what you mean. Looks like butter wouldn't melt ... but there's an air of power about her that is almost tangible when she chooses to show it, like that not so veiled and enigmatic threat, when she left. Make sure she's watched day and night, but keep it discreet, and don't let her bring that brute of a dog any-where near the command centre again. In fact, apart from some exercise a couple of times a day, she can keep it confined in her quarters, and make sure she cleans up after it. That'll be all for now lieutenant."

Hank knocked on the door to Eve's quarters.

"Come in Hank. I'm glad it's you." Hank ducked his head and manoeuvred his large shoulders through the door opening. "I haven't had a chance to thank you for your heroism in saving our lives. I'm afraid I can't even offer you a drink, but you have my friendship and gratitude if that is any consolation."

"More than I deserve ma'am, just following orders." The Amer-ican accent made it sound more natural, but Eve still pulled a face at being addressed that way.

"Yeah, so were most of the holders of the Victoria Cross, but I think they did a little more than just follow orders too. And please, I will be more than a little distraught if you don't call me Eve."

"Sure Eve. Where's your son?"

"Oh he's next door. I told him to get some rest but he knows you are here and will be on high alert. He's not the most trusting soul, and I love him for it."

"Glad to hear it Eve, but I reckon old Zeus there would be a pretty fearsome adversary if anyone tried to harm you. As for the drink ..." He produced a flask. "Forgot to add the coffee this time I'm afraid, but I find it still tastes good." He raised his voice. "Hey Ben, will you join me for a drink?"

Ben was already halfway through the door. "With the man who saved my mother's life, you bet I will."

"And your life too Ben," she bent to ruffle Zeus's neck. "Not forgetting our mangy friend here. He's family too."

Ben nodded at Hank and smiled, taking the proffered flask and downing several mouthfuls. "Good stuff this."

"About the dog ..."

"Yeah I know, exercise only and clean up. Are you here to watch us Hank?"

"And to show you around, but I reckon I'd like to get to know you too, if that's okay with the three of you?"

"Of course it is Hank. Someone was going to do it and who better than a friend who risked his life for us. You were a wise choice."

"I hoped you would say something like that. Do you want the tour? Not that there is a lot you are allowed to see. Bring Zeus along, he hasn't been exercised today."

They were in the loading bay, where a few of the women personnel were practising basketball. Hank called them over for introductions, and they seemed eager to meet her. A tall willowy blonde with a southern accent wiped her hand on her shorts and stuck out a sweaty palm. "Hi, I'm Freya, that's Jodie, Sara, Jane. Heard about your rescue, jeez, musta been real scary out there. Spooky stuff, but hey, Hank says you can jump. You're not that tall, but if you can jump as good as he says, we could sure use you in a match we've got against the guys tonight." There was a chorus of objections from the others.

"Jesus Freya, leave the poor girl alone, she's just escaped a near death experience!"

"But she's here isn't she? Alive and looking pretty healthy, and we're the guys who turned a whole ship around to go to her rescue, and even Hank here helped a little bit." She batted her eyes at him. "And, I don't know about you guys but I'm sick of doing the men's chores, because we've lost the last three challenges against them. And they are so fucking unbearably arrogant. Come on Evie you'll help out the sisters, won't you?"

"Of course, I owe you, and anyway it'll help to blow the bloody cobwebs away."

"Whoohah! Love that British accent." She high fived the rest of the team, put a long arm around Eve's shoulders and guided her to the basket. "See if you can put one through." She thrust the ball hard and fast, at close range, into Eve's chest. Eve snatched it easily, spun on her heel and put one through the basket from standing. She got a few whoops and a round of applause. "That's real good honey, but we still haven't seen you jump." She thrust the ball at her again, harder, faster and closer. Eve snatched it just as easily, bounced it under Freya's left arm as she tried to block her, ducked low under Freya's right – chest thrusting – arm, passed behind her, and picked up the ball, now bouncing off, away from Freya's left rear; then slam dunked it into the basket. She was suddenly mobbed by the other girls all screeching their approval. Freya was left scratching her head. "Well, I guess that'll do. Reckon we might just make those grunts eat crow. I owe you a fifty Hank, never seen anything like it."

When the guys arrived for the game, there were catcalls and insults. "Hey Freya: you recruiting dwarves now? We'll try not to tread on her. You might as well give up now. Give you time to wash and press the pile of shirts we've been saving."

"Yo Jodie. Guess what? I've been given another latrine duty. Know you loved the last one. Have to warn you though, Josh has been on the beer again, real bad stomach, so you maybe want to wear a gas suit." Freya wasn't happy with Eve staying up the home end, but she soon realised it was the best place, when a seven-foot giant came hurtling down the wing, received the ball, and took a mighty leap that took him above the basket. The slam dunk never happened. Eve was up there first, snatching the ball from his thrusting hand, then raced up the opposite wing to feed Freya for a basket. Eve couldn't be everywhere, and the boys put up a good fight, but the girls were pretty good, and with Eve's help, they maintained a slight lead. The boys actually drew level at the three-quarter stage, but Eve did a spectacular basket, weaving up the court and dodging the defence. The guys were getting really pissed with her, and tried to barge her down, but she was heavier and stronger, and they came off worse. With the game over, the insults were flying the other way.

"Hey Gary, you can clear up your own shit, and Josh's too, and guess what, we've saved a pile of laundry for you, and you know how, when girls get together for a long time, they kinda sync their cycles? Bad time of the month Gary, real bad."

"Up yours Jodie."

Captain Baker had wandered in for the last part of the game, with

Lieutenant Felix in tow. He called over. "Dr Gabriel, see me in my quarters in two hours please." Eve almost lost the instruction, as the girls were hauling her off to the mess for a celebration, with the captain's full permission. As he left, he threw a bottle of Jack Daniel's at them, which Freya deftly plucked from the air.

"Have one on me, but don't get drunk. I want you all combat ready first thing."

Captain Baker sat half perched on his desk, facing Eve and Ben. "That was a helluva game Doctor. Some of those guys have played professionally."

"Why am I here, Captain?"

"Mainly because we rescued your arse from certain death, now call me naïve, but I reckon that entitles us to some answers. You are obviously something special, so who are you? And what the hell were you doing out there? You weren't following any eel migrations. And what do you want with a decompression chamber and a sedative?"

"About that Captain, have you got them on standby? Because time may be getting short. How are the sea and the weather acting at the moment? Has there been any communication regarding us yet?"

"Explain yourself Doctor, and then maybe we'll get around to answering some of 'your' questions."

"Okay, well my guess is that the sea and the weather are acting unusual at the moment. I also suspect that the real reason you are having trouble with communications is because of some strange atmospheric conditions that are affecting radio waves. The chamber, and I stress, the 'strong' sedative, are for me. If they become necessary you will need to render me unconscious and crank up the pressure as high as you can get it."

"Why?"

"Because those conditions are centred on me, and unless you can get me out of the Sargasso, they are going to get worse, maybe a lot worse, maybe enough to put your ship in danger. If that happens it is possible that by mimicking deep sea pressure and a deathlike state, we may be able to confuse whatever it is that is coming for me, long enough for you to get your ship out. Or you can get your ship out now if you can and avoid the whole situation."

"That is a wild tale Doctor Gabriel, with a massive amount of fanciful paranoia, but you are correct regarding the freaky conditions. And someone thinks you are very important, so I will treat you as though you are sane, and entitled to some respect. We need talk no further of the items you mentioned, as we are indeed heading out of the Sargasso."

"May I ask why? You mentioned combat readiness after the game."

"I guess there is no harm in enlightening you. An oil tanker has been hijacked some distance clear of these waters. We can outrun it in twelve hours."

"I knew there were pirates hereabouts but that is a bold move."

"We would not get involved if it were just pirates, Doctor. They would probably just want a ransom. No, this is a terrorist group. You may have heard of them, or their leader at least, a nut called Sadique Al-Fayed."

Eve felt the blood drain from her face, and would have jumped to her feet had Ben not placed a restraining hand on her shoulder. "You know of him?"

"He is well known in the UK. You need to be extremely careful Captain. He probably has the tanker rigged from end to end with explosives, and likely any hostages too, if he hasn't killed them already. You would be wise not to try and negotiate with him. Your best tactic would be to surprise him somehow. Kill him and his men before they know you are there. Assuming he has replaced those who were killed in London, he will have nine followers, one of them with only one arm. He will also have a very clever escape plan."

"You seem to know an awful lot, Doctor. I want you to stay on hand. You will join me in my command centre. I wasn't misleading you when I said we are stealthed. He will not know we are there until we are right on top of him."

"Don't bet on that Captain. A covert marine raid would be your best option."

"What are you going to do?" Ben asked as they walked back to their quarters.

"That's a big question Ben." Eve was rubbing up and down the sides of her nose with a closed fist and speaking through clenched teeth. "I can't go off half cocked. We're already up to our necks in shit. These Yanks are not going to let us go after we're out of here, or hand us over to Soames, or the British government, or the Vatican, or whoever the fuck it was who put in a word for us at the Pentagon. Not until they've 'debriefed' us anyhow, and I'm guessing if we can't come up with the bollocks of an amazing and convincing, slick as shit, fucking tale, house arrest and an unpleasant interrogation will quickly follow. So maybe, this is our chance. I just haven't figured out the how yet. Not only that, but I might never get another chance to nail that fucker Sadique. And Ben ..." She gripped his arm hard enough to make him gasp, her eyes like white hot thrusting spears, stabbed into his. "I really have got to get that bastard, for my sanity, for Stella, for the children, and for the fucking world. I've got about ten hours to find a way. And captain fucking Baker, wants me at his side.

"Okay Ben; this is the plan. I've been trying to second guess Sadique's strategy. The way I see it, he would have used subterfuge to get himself on board, probably a sinking boat in the path of the tanker and a distress call, something like that. I wouldn't mind betting he scuttled some seafarer's craft, and had the crew thrown into the sea. To do that he would need a powerful boat of his own, first to catch his bait, then to get clear, and to come in fast alongside the tanker, when its crew were engaged in rescue operations. He will have an escape plan, he always does. Whatever craft he has will be hitched to the tanker, or on it. It would be just his MO, to have a helicopter at his disposal. That would make things difficult but we'll worry about that, if and when. One of his followers will be manning any boat, in readiness for a quick getaway. Given the difficulty of moving from one boat to another in changeable conditions, it will likely be the one-armed guy, assuming he's still around, and that it is indeed a boat. Here's the big ask Ben, I need you to get there first."

"At last!" His shark grin was back for the first time in quite a while.

"What the fuck are you grinning about? You could end up dead, and I could end up in an orange jumpsuit in Guantanamo Bay, if this all goes tits up."

"That won't happen Eve. If need be, I will die for you, but you have a destiny to fulfil."

Eve turned up her eyes. "You had better not die you little shit, because my plan depends on you. I've been talking to some of the girls, they all seem to think you're an Adonis by the way, must be as blind as bloody bats. Anyway, they reckon the captain's as wily as a fox. That being so, I reckon I can persuade him to do a covert raid and put you in the team as an Arabic speaker, and expert on Sadique's tactics. Your job will be to slip away and secure that boat. Do what you like with the crew member, unless it does prove to be a bastard aircraft, then you'll have to try and find a way to force him to fly it. Whatever, get the fuck out of there and go to these co-ordinates." She handed him a slip of paper. "If all goes to plan, I will escape when the captain is supervising prisoner transfer and will be at those co-ordinates soon after you. Then we go hell for leather to the nearest port, and try to disappear, until we can get hold of Jackie or Freddy, or Soames, to spirit us away."

Revenge

Captain Baker had also second guessed Sadique's strategy, and his covert unit were highly trained, well led, and experienced. They had overpowered the one armed-crew member and secured the getaway boat, then located and disarmed the detonation devices. All the terrorists were subdued and captured, except for Sadique. He was cornered in the stern area. Unfortunately, he was armed with a powerful rifle, with which he was taking pot-shots at anyone foolhardy enough to show a millimetre of flesh. Captain Baker and a small team, including Eve, boarded the vessel. Zeus had somehow got out and raced on behind them. The unit commander met the captain on deck with some diffidence. Baker was on immediate alert. "What's going on Hendricks? My understanding is that only Sadique remains at large and will soon be taken or killed."

"Correct Sir."

"So what the hell are you looking so guilty about?"

Hendricks looked nervously at Eve, then at the captain. "It's the prisoners, Sir … and Doctor Gabriel's son …"

Eve felt her heart lurch into her throat.

"Spit it out man."

"Seeing as they couldn't, or wouldn't, speak English Sir, we let him question them."

"And?"

"He's disappeared Sir, and ..."

"Disappeared where?"

"He can only be in the stern, Sir. I suspect he's gone after Sadique, but ..."

"But what for Christ's sake?"

"The prisoners, Sir ..."

"What about them?"

"He castrated them all, Sir."

Eve doubled up, trying to contain a disabling surge of relief at Ben's escape, and a fit of hysterical laughter, because of what he had done. She knew Captain Baker was shouting at Hendricks, between streams of staccato orders to the rest of his team, but was unable to make out a word of what he was saying.

A female officer tugged urgently at her elbow. She was speaking into her ear in harsh whispers, and Eve started to take in what she was saying. "Listen to me. We all know who you are, and what you did in London. Someone had it archived on their phone. The video has gone viral around the lower decks. You are a hero, but you must know as well as we do, that we are not going to let you go. So whatever your plan is, now is the time to put it into action. We have arranged a distraction for you ..."

At a signal from her, a male officer put something into his mouth, hit the deck, and started to fit violently, retching and defecating himself. Seconds later, another went down. Eve quickly communicated something to Zeus, and he raced off for the stern. She could hear the rescue helicopter coming in low behind the ship. But she now knew the calibre of the captain. It would never execute its intention. Seconds later a missile obliterated it. Eve had checked her side of the tanker when boarding and had seen no boat or launch. She raced to the other side at breakneck speed and checked again. Her keen eyes saw the unconscious form of a marine, safely dangling from a line that must have previously hitched Sadique's launch to the tanker. That told her all she needed, and she dived over the side. She never came up, but a pod of Orca swiftly made away from the two ships.

The co-ordinates she had given Ben were on the outside edge of the strange atmospherics still building in the Bermuda triangle and Sargasso Sea, where Eve had divined conditions were at their most erratic. They were able to use those atmospherics to stealth themselves, and to avoid any search that Captain Baker might be initiating, whilst at the same time jumping from one erratic hot spot to another. During one such jump, Ben managed to get a message out to Soames, to see if he could clear them for landfall in the Bahamas. He responded with co-ordinates, and they were met, and transferred onto a private yacht. Their boat was stripped and scuttled and left a couple of hundred feet down. Taken ashore, and domiciled in a seafront property at a remote location, they were given a suite of rooms jutting out from a rocky outcrop, with huge panoramic windows looking out to sea.

Eve couldn't escape the notion that they were under house arrest, but was happy for now to kick back, enjoy the comforts, and wait on what Soames had in store for them. In the event, he left them alone and without contact for a week. Eve and Ben were free to roam the small private peninsula and its three beaches, but their only company was the housekeeper and her staff of five, and the gun-carrying, uncommunicative guards, who were ever watchful but never came close. The staff were pleasant and friendly, and all their needs were met, but conversation was limited to, "is there anything you need?" "I can't really discuss that just now." And, "You will know more when your father gets here." This was the first time that they had really had any time to talk since their dramatic escape from the *Ark*.

Ben was juggling with a variety of mobile phones, surfing the Internet and searching on social media. Eve came over to him, gave him a fierce hug, kissed him on the forehead, and sat opposite. "You have become a beautiful man Ben. I thought I would never get satisfaction for what those men did to me. What you did has untwisted a terrible knot of despair that has blackened my soul for so long now. I had forgotten just how debilitating it was to bear. Paradoxically, it has made me realise that the desire for vengeance is a fool's game. The present and the future are what really matter, and how we can make them better. Although I can't deny that it will take time for me not to wish that Sadique had suffered the same fate as the men you mutilated."

Ben smiled broadly. "I think I may be able to salve that wound too Eve. Freya gave me dark web contact details, and I've managed to find her sister online. He handed her a mobile phone."

She read: "From F. S tried to turn rifle on self when capture inevitable. Z leapt from nowhere, and mauled both hands beyond his ability to use them, then chewed into his genitalia before they were able to stop him. Dr says he will survive for questioning but injuries will be life changing and gender neutralizing. Z has since become docile and friendly and seems to have a particular affinity with Captain B, who has adopted him as ships mascot."

Tears were now running freely down Eve's face. Ben went to the fridge, opened some beers, and placed one in front of Eve ... When Eve awoke the next morning, she was euphoric and energetic, and for the first time in months, felt in control of herself, and ready, even eager, to confront the future.

Ben and Eve were on their way back from a picnic at one of the beaches and paused to watch the gates to the peninsula open to admit a large black limousine. Eve's shoulders dropped a little. "Soames I expect. I guess the holiday is over." The car crunched along the long drive kicking up white dust and caused them to look away and to cover their eyes. The wheels locked as it passed them, bringing the car to an abrupt and slithering stop. There was a commotion inside, but they couldn't see anything through the tinted windows. Then the door was flung open, and Jackie jumped out into the dust cloud, shielding her eyes from the sun.

In a rare show of emotion she ran up and hugged them both. "Eve! Ben! We were worried sick when we got your message to get you out. Soames called in just about every favour he could and wasn't happy about having to go to the Yanks. He thought we might never get you back. He should have known better really. He's not a great one for faith, at least not in you, but I think he's learning." She hooked an arm through each of their elbows and walked them back to the car. "I've brought someone with me."

Eve saw a sandaled foot extending backwards and out from under the partially opened car door. She pulled the door open further to assist her exit. A khaki-shorted rump met her gaze, while Helen rummaged around for the contents of a spilled bag in the foot well. Retrieving her stash, Helen grabbed a bottle of wine in one hand, and two glasses in the other. Instead of standing up, she thrust up her butt and looked through her legs. She wriggled the glasses suggestively. "Hey, I've made a discovery. You can't drink wine standing on your head." She snapped up straight and turned, smiled alluringly, and looked pointedly at Eve's groin. "Does that stir any memories for you Eve? I've got other goodies in my backpack, and I'm feeling very 'dusty' …" she lingered over the words to let the penny drop. Eve's thighs clenched involuntarily. Jackie had already ushered Ben into the car and taken off for their rooms. Helen flicked one of Eve's nipples. "You know, you could take someone's eye out with those. Let's go to your favourite private place on the beach and get … inventive. I'm sure I have a weapon of mass destruction somewhere in my pack. Couldn't let it fall into the wrong hands now, could I?"

Freddy, Matt and Janie had arrived late that evening. They were all now gathered in a large room, overlooking the crashing waves of a still restless ocean. Freddy commented on that. "The weather is still acting very strange. Flights were impossible for several days, and even now are being redirected via Miami. Know anything about that Eve?"

Eve drummed her fingers on the arm of her chair while she thought about how to answer. Eventually she responded. "Yes I do, and there is an awful lot to tell, but shouldn't we wait for Soames? I assume he will be here soon too."

Jackie answered that. "Actually no, he is staying put for a bit, sorting out the diplomatic furore, surrounding your rescue in the Sargasso, Ben's maiming of political prisoners, his stealing of a boat commandeered by, and therefore the property of the US navy, and your apparent suicide or escape."

Eve laughed at that. "God, it must be killing him to be out of the loop for once. I'm surprised he allowed you all to come without him."

Helen spoke up. "He had to really, if he didn't want a rebellion on his hands, but I still think you have the wrong idea about him. It was his suggestion that we all get here as quickly as possible. And anyway, Jackie has promised to send him a summary of our meeting here, and he will fill in the gaps as soon as he can clear up the mess at home and get here himself."

Eve turned to Jackie. "Are you working closely with Soames now Jackie?"

"For the time being yes, and so is Freddy, Matt and Janie, and Helen too. We all need to be working closely together now Eve. You too, if we are to avoid an apocalypse."

"Yes, believe me Jackie, I know. The events of the last few days have left me in no doubts about the magnitude of the danger we face. We really can't afford to have any more scruples. We have to pull together and prepare ourselves. We need answers and cannot sit on any information that any among us can throw any light on. That being so, it is time I brought you all up to date. First, Freddy, I have a question. Is the shard still safely in place in the cliff chapel?" Freddy assured her that it was and was well-guarded.

"Good, and I can confirm that another shard is at the bottom of the Sargasso. And that is exactly where it will stay. We must not, under any circumstances, interfere with it, or allow anyone else to. And the same goes for the one we have, from now on, except in the most exceptional circumstances. But we do need to locate, and more importantly, secure the others as soon as possible." She raised a hand to forestall the barrage of questions trying to burst from everyone's lips.

"Please hold fire until I have told you what happened in the Sargasso, and about discoveries I made there. I am sure Jackie must have told you all that I can influence sea creatures. I can also transform to some extent into the environment. I can breathe water, and go very deep, although the changes in my body that are required are not pleasant, and are quite frightening."

Helen shuffled her chair closer and laid her hand on Eve's.

"Jackie and I were expecting aggressive resistance from some kind of monstrous presence or foe beneath the sea, guarding the shard. We assumed it to be intelligent, as my metaphysical experiences suggested it could be bargained with. On my last dive I got about as deep as I thought I could go, about a thousand feet. It was as scary as hell, and I don't think I would ever have tried to go any deeper.

"Then, several things happened at once. First something made contact with me. It was thankfully distant and tenuous. But it was a vast presence. No ... that isn't the right word ... more ... infinite better describes it, I think. At any rate it was sufficiently fucking scary for me to want to get back to the surface damn fast. Then I discovered that my influence over sea creatures does not include all of them, certainly not eels anyway. I was mobbed by a huge shoal of them, entirely surrounded in an impenetrable sphere that started to drag me down. A clear vision entered my mind of the exact location of the shard. It seemed the presence, whatever it was, far from protecting the shard, wanted it moved, which for some reason it was unable to do itself. And it wasn't about to let go of the only creature it had ever encountered who could. At this point, I can't deny, I was crapping myself. I went into total panic and blasted out a call to any creature that could help. What the fuck it was I don't know. Ben saw it briefly, but whatever, it brought me to the surface, smashed through the sphere, and threw me onto the boat. I'm guessing you all know how that ended. The thing … the presence, whatever it was, was still trying to drag me down, with or without my boat. Thank God Soames got hold of Captain Baker. What none of you know is that I got close enough to attune myself to the shard, and I believe I can now summon a ghost of it if necessary. But, as I said, the original stays put, because I am sure it is somehow preventing that thing from entering our world." Eve looked around expecting pandemonium … There was only silence, as they all digested the fantastic enormity of what had been said.

Jackie was first to speak. "So this thing controls the eels, and you couldn't override its control? But you were able to summon help, and the 'presence' evidently couldn't override 'your' control."

Janie jumped in. "Maybe it was just caught off guard."

"Perhaps, but it brought in the eels pretty damn quick, and it had well over a thousand feet in which to wrest control from Eve."

Matt now spoke up. "Does it really matter Jackie? It doesn't need any creatures at its disposal, when it seems it can control the ocean and even the weather above it."

"Yet it was unable to prevent Eve's escape. There's a lot to think about here Matt. Its influence seems to extend only within the limitations of the Sargasso Sea and the Bermuda Triangle above it. Both of which we are currently just outside of, and therefore, apparently, relatively safe, except that is, for the eels. They travel the world, can even move across land when necessary, but always return to the Sargasso to spawn. I think their connection to this thing, may be the most important question we should be asking. And Eve, I think you should avoid swimming for the time being, and that we should conduct a regular eel watch along the beach whilst we are here, at least until we know a little more. Now, if you will all excuse me, I need to contact Soames, if the atmospherics will allow me to. And Freddy, we must talk too. Eve, when Soames gets here, all of us need to get together for a major meet, about a whole host of things, but Freddy and I need to talk to you alone first."

She grabbed her laptop and left for her rooms. The rest of them insisted Eve go through everything that happened again, but in more detail, and discussions and speculations went on until late. Finally, Freddy arranged for nightcaps and insisted they turn in. Janie came over to Eve to say good night, and clearly had tears in her eyes. She gave her a massive bear hug, which eventually Eve had to peel herself from. "Jesus honey I wish you wouldn't take so many risks. Can't you discuss with me first what you are doing, so I can arrange protection and support?"

"I don't think there is anything even you could have done to help this time Janie."

"Let me be the judge of that next time please Eve."

Helen put an arm around Eve's waist and walked her to their room. "Even demi-Gods need to rest sometimes Eve."

"Fat chance with you woman. You are insatiable."

Helen fluttered her eyelids and adopted a Southern States accent, "Why, whatever do you mean Mistress Gabriel?" Eve gave her butt a slap, and Helen turned with a wanton smile, to look directly into Eve's eyes. Dropping the accent, she grabbed Eve's hands and placed them on both of her butt cheeks. "Well now, if you want to be dominant, I think we'll just have to wrestle for it. You're not so tough. I reckon I can take you."

Eve left Helen sleeping soundly and walked to the beach in the early dawn light. Jackie caught up with her just as she was setting foot onto the wet sand. She was slightly out of breath as though she had been running. "Hi, not thinking of going for a swim, are you? Ben and I have taken first patrol, but we haven't had time yet to check for eels. Please be careful Eve. We're all fucked without you."

Eve digested that for a few moments. "Says the girl who suggested an unsupported voyage into and underneath the Sargasso Sea."

"There's a difference. I believed that risk was necessary. It was something you needed to be unhindered with, so that you could find yourself and learn to know your capabilities. And there will be more such risks you will need to take, but I think there is a real threat here, and nothing to be gained by confronting it at this time, not until we know more. And anyway you had Ben. He's a small army on his own."

Eve smiled at that. "And he has turned into quite a hunk. The girls on the ship couldn't get enough of him."

Jackie actually blushed a little. "Okay you got me on that one. I'm a girl with normal wants and needs just like anyone else. But that's not the issue at the moment. I think now may be a good time for us to get together with Freddy, while everyone else is sleeping it off. Ben can carry on here."

"Won't Freddy be sleeping it off too?"

"Freddy? You don't know him very well, do you? He's probably been up an hour at least."

They found him meditating on the veranda outside his room. The screen-saver on his laptop was still up, so it seemed he had already been doing some work. Eve hoped he hadn't been at it all night. "Ah Eve, perfect timing. I was just dwelling on all that has happened and was wondering how Jackie and I were going to drop the latest bombshell on you. Of course, it is early days, and we can't be sure of anything yet, or just how much impact it will have, but there is precedence in scripture."

"What are you talking about Freddy?"

"Oh! ... Jackie hasn't told you anything yet?"

"No, but you are frightening the hell out of me. Please tell me that it is good news. I don't think I can handle another disaster."

"Potentially, it is the best possible news. The bad news is that we just don't know for sure how far reaching it will be."

"Well, enlighten me. The suspense is tying me in knots." Freddy looked at Jackie. "I think it best if you begin Jackie, as you were first to realise what was happening, and what it could mean."

Jackie sat down next to Freddy, and Eve dropped into a cross-legged yoga pose opposite the both of them, as Jackie began her tale. "It's all to do with Ben really, and what you told me about him."

"Oh?" Eve arched her eyebrows and was rewarded with another slight blush, and an extremely rare, flustered Jackie.

"No, no, nothing like that. Or, well, yes, in a way. What I mean is. Oh God, I don't know how to say this now. It is about his testicles re-growing." She moved quickly on. "I've spoken to him about that by the way, and he says he will let Soames's medical team check him out, if you say it is something he should do. Anyway, there are no records Soames and I could find of that ever happening before, so I went to Freddy with my thoughts. It can only be you Eve; some emanation that radiates from, and osmoses into, those in close contact with you. Ben has probably spent more time with you than anyone. And if you think about it, there is a sort of precedent even in the bible. When Jesus ascended, he said the Holy Spirit would come upon his disciples, and that in his name they would be able to do miraculous things and healing. His disciples had been with him constantly for three years, and according to scripture, they were then imbued with some measure of his abilities. Of course, that in itself is pretty flimsy stuff, but it does suggest that something similar may have happened before. And there is no getting away from the fact that Ben now has testicles, working ones by all accounts." Looking awkward she sighed, puffed air up her face to blow her hair out of her eyes, and looked hopefully towards Freddy to carry on.

"Jackie is right, no actual accounts of regrown testicles that I could find, but we know you can heal the mind, and it stands to reason that you could probably do the same with the body. Ben seems to be an example of that. And the Jesus story is far from unique. Most religions have similar tales, and some of the ancient scriptures definitely suggest that through proximity and learning, there is a measure of transference." He corrected himself, "No! That is not the right term, I think it is more a question of nurturing latent abilities and potential that is already there within us. Think about Jesus for the moment. He was called teacher, and this is a familiar term in other such fables. Was he teaching just morality and ethics, or was he showing others how they could be better physically, even metaphysically, than they are? How they might emulate him perhaps? Much of what he said would certainly suggest that. Do you see where this might be leading?"

"Are you saying that people who stay near me might become like me?"

"No. I don't think so. There is no evidence of full transference, but it is possible that we can become better than we are, more than we are. Science has long been baffled by, for instance, the ageing gene. Why do we grow old when lobsters don't? Are we actually using all of our brain, and if not, why not?"

"So if, for another instance, Helen, or any of you, were to be with me for a prolonged period, might she not age so fast?" He looked sideways at Jackie before he answered. She nodded encouragement.

"This is what we have been so worried about, possible false hope, and it is why we delayed telling you. We just don't know. Ben might be a freak, or it could be a one-off healing performed by some quirky ability you have, but potentially it could mean a whole lot more than just longevity. By the time Afsoon gets here, we could have an army of fully realised human beings at your back and ready to face him, if Soames is unable to knock him out of the sky first, that is. So you see, ultimately we had to tell you, because if there is even a chance of it being true, and from my research I think there is definitely that, then we have to do all we can to bring it about. And much of that effort will have to come from you. We need a teacher."

"And what does Soames say about all this?"

"He says you are no Jesus. You are something of an entirely different order, and we should not jump to ill thought-out conclusions. But neither has he dismissed it. In fact, he has been devoting time to strategising just how it might be put to the test and researching scriptural testimony at his own disposal."

"Hmm … about Afsoon. I don't know how Soames is going to take this, but I am no longer sure that we should be thinking of knocking anything out of the sky at all. You see the shards are more important than we ever thought. We know where two of them are, and that's great, but if they are, as recent experience suggests, forming some sort of protection for our planet, should we be destroying artefacts that could conceivably house one?"

Having dropped a bombshell of her own, Eve made her way slowly back to her rooms. Her step was somewhat lighter than it had been as she contemplated a possible tenable future with Helen. But unwelcome questions started to bob to the surface. Would Helen want to cohabit indefinitely with a woman? Would she want an indefinite lifespan at all? Would we grow closer or further apart as maybe centuries passed us by? By the time Eve stood outside the bedroom door, she was in a total quandary about how to tell Helen, yet she knew she must. Helen would never forgive any more secrets or lies. Letting out an enormous breath, she entered the bedroom, wriggled in behind Helen and hugged her close.

She awoke to find Helen sitting astride her pelvis, gently shaking her shoulders and looking very concerned. "Whatever is wrong Eve? You were sobbing in your sleep."

"Oh fuck! Was I? I'm sorry Helen. There's ... well there's something I have to tell you and I don't know what it all means, and I'm scared shitless about how you might take it ..."

"Wow! That really is a sledgehammer of a revelation." Helen flopped naked into one of the chairs with a huge blast of expelled breath.

"I don't know what to say. I have to think about this. No! I can't think about this now. It is too much. Just fuck me senseless Eve, so that I can forget about everything for a couple of hours."

Soames finally arrived and asked to see Jackie, Freddy, Helen and Eve in his rooms, before he took any rest. He looked tired and was clearly under a lot of strain, but his voice was strong, and his mind as sharp as ever. Despite her reservations a wave of empathy and gratitude rose up in Eve. She walked over to him and gently kissed his forehead. "Thank you for saving Ben and me. No one else could have pulled that off. I am very grateful."

Soames gave her an appraising look. His eyes gave away nothing, but there was a slight catch in his voice when he responded. "Thank you Eve," he paused, sighed, and looked deep into the black on blue of her eyes, then added, "and you too John; that means rather more to me than you might realise."

Eve was a little startled by his use of her male name. He had been the first to use it for some time now. Was he trying to remind her of her humanity? Or was he just being considerate to that part of her whose feet were firmly planted in this world?

He looked at Helen. It was his turn now to show affection. He clasped her hand in both of his. "And how have you been my dear? Have you enjoyed spending time with your husband?"

"Yes but ..."

"Ah! There's always a butt ..." Helen exchanged a secret glance with Eve at the double meaning they had both previously shared.

She doubted Soames had missed it (nor had they missed his conspiratorial wink). "But, to business children."

Neither of them had ever seen this humorous undercurrent to his character before. Eve found some warmth in it however.

"I guess, Helen, that you have been brought up to date on Ben's current condition, and the speculations and possible ramifications of that?" Helen nodded. "It is not something we can easily put to the test. It's not practical for everyone to stick around Eve like glue, in the hope that they will gain some enhancement, but I would certainly consider it a valid test environment, if you Helen, were willing to spend more time with Eve. I think the strong bond you have, and the intimacy of your relations, might provide somewhat quicker results than has been apparent in Ben. Although what form they might take is anyone's guess. More importantly though Eve, if this is happening, then so far it has been without your conscious and active involvement. I think Freddy has already touched on this, and it is where we really need to shift our focus. Freddy, Jackie and I have spoken much about this. If they exist at all Eve, we would like you to develop your healing, or more specifically, enhancing abilities. And I want to monitor you, whenever possible when you are actively employing them."

He paused and looked at Helen again. "Helen you are by far the most likely subject to show recordable results in the shortest time, given what I have already mentioned, but the choice is yours. The ideal would be if you were to cohabit with Eve. I feel this would meet with Eve's approval, but I am not so sure about you."

Helen did a lot of huffing and puffing, and pacing, and made several false starts at a response, but in the end, asked for more time to think. Soames just nodded and carried on. "We probably need to start small Eve, as this is where we might record some early results, but let's not be coy about this, the thing that will give us the greatest advantage, and must surely be in the forefront of all of our minds, is mortality. Can you slow down, halt, or even reverse the condition of ageing? If we are wasting our time, then we need to know that as soon as possible, so that we can prioritise our efforts. But if there is even a chance that we can actually prolong life, every effort in that direction will be worthwhile. Please think on this all of you, but for now I am rather tired and need some sleep. So I will take my leave of you until morning." He rose and left the room.

On an impulse Eve followed him out and stopped him in the hall. "Soames can you give me a moment? I just wanted to say thank you again. Sleep well and awake refreshed and full of energy. I think we need you Soames." She leaned in, placed her hands on his shoulders and kissed his forehead again. Soames looked up with tired eyes, nodded, and made his way to his rooms.

Helen and Eve walked together on the beach. The last rays of the sun were colouring the underbelly of a few wispy clouds on the horizon, and a strong sea breeze was moulding Helen's dress to the seaward side of her shapely body. Eve could see the silhouettes of Matt and Janie at either end of the beach, doing their stint of eel watching, and probably, Eve and Helen watching too. "I don't know Eve … John … I know you are still in there too. In some ways it's the promise of a dream come true, to spend our lives together again, for who knows how long, and the possibility of not having to face the ills and decrepitude of age. It all sounds wonderful. And being with you now is electric. I feel like a young girl again. Perhaps the power you have has already started to enhance me, I don't know. I had expected just a normal lifetime. Yet I have sensed the weight of years out there in the not-too-distant future. Oh … nothing too morbid, just an awareness that my life will begin to wind down. And now I look again, and see a future stretching out interminably, and I don't know if that future will be good. I don't know if our relationship, or any relationship, could last for a thousand years. I want to believe it can, but I just don't know, and the thought of it withering, is perhaps more frightening than accepting my mortality. And there would never be any children." She let that hang for a bit. "But the thought of leaving you behind to face that future on your own, or even with someone else, is also unbearably painful. I'm going to take three months out Eve. I have a lovely home provided to me by Soames. I think you would love the mountains and the lakes. Will you join me there Eve, just the two of us, in three months? We can spend some time alone together. Court me Eve. Write to me. Woo me. You are still John but you are also someone else and you have grown and blended and become something new. I need to get to know who and what you are now, really get to know all of you. Please say you will. I know you have the weight of the world on your shoulders, perhaps the universe. Your responsibilities are vast. But holding onto, and developing your humanity, is just as important, I think. I'm sure Soames and Freddy will agree, and most of the others too. And, well, I'm changing too Eve, developing I hope, and expanding my own humanity.

More Revelations

Soames was up at the crack of dawn seeming fully recovered and full of energy. He called a general meeting and brought everyone up to date. He quizzed Eve heavily about her aquatic transformations, but seemed even more interested in her abilities to communicate with, and influence, sea creatures, especially the dolphins and killer whales. "Were you communicating telepathically or verbally?"

Eve explained that she would describe it as less telepathic than empathic, and she felt that the reason science had never been able to translate dolphin speak, was that the clicks and whistles didn't follow any recognised pattern. They were onomatopoeic to such an extent, that they formed images in the mind of any creature with the empathic ability to read them, sort of in the way that bats receive images from echoed sound. He asked if she was able to command or had to negotiate assistance. Eve had to think about that … "I think it depends on the intellect of the creature. The dolphins and killer whales kind of discussed and advised, but were very willing to help. With the sharks, and whatever it was that saved me from the eels, I had to occupy and override their instinctive self-control. It was something like … I don't know really, maybe a queen bee or ant. Once I established command they wanted to obey, and it was then easier."

Soames had everything recorded, and a secretary was making notes of all observations by any party present. "And last, for now anyway, what can you tell us about this presence at the bottom of the ocean? Why, and in what way do you think the shard is holding it there? And exactly how dangerous and powerful do you think it is?"

"Very fucking powerful and dangerous in equal measure. In fact, I think we should be more worried about it, than we are about Afsoon. Unless of course, Afsoon finds some way of controlling and releasing it, then we really are in the shit."

Soames finally had them all flown out. Eve and Ben had agreed to go to England, where Soames's medical team would run tests and examinations on the both of them. Eve insisted that Janie, Matt, and Ben, accompany them with a security team, but Matt cried off saying he was concerned about current intelligence operations, and wanted to be on hand to oversee them (Helen was taking a later plane to her mountain retreat). Janie attached herself like an extra limb, coordinating every aspect of the transfer. Eve felt concern for anyone who might come too close without seeking prior permission. The three of them now sat in discussion with Soames on the journey home. Eve thought about that for a moment. Yes, England was her "home" and it was good to be going back there. Weather conditions in the Sargasso had apparently quietened soon after their departure, and the hurricane that had been forecast didn't happen, baffling meteorologists around the world. Jackie had not been wrong about the eels. Large numbers had taken to the land, and this was being attributed to the freakish weather conditions. Although none had been spotted on the island they had been occupying, whether because they were outside the Sargasso or because they were somehow shielded was something to ponder.

Eve was brought back to the present by Soames speaking to her. "I need to know more about this presence Eve. What were your gut feelings about it? Did you have a sense of its location, or of the extent of its influence? Could you sense in what way it was connected with the eels, how it controlled them? Was it physical or spiritual? Did it have shape? And I also would like the exact co-ordinates of the shard, or as close as you can, if you can't be precise."

"It all happened so fast Soames. I was flooded with so many impressions and feelings, and the fact is, I have been avoiding going back there. I ... I ..." A surge of unexpected fear and emotion broke over her causing her speech to desert her for several minutes. She tried and failed twice more, before she was able to articulate again. "It was overwhelming Soames."

She was oblivious of Janie's arm around her, supporting her quaking shoulders. "The power of the thing seemed limitless, but it was contained somehow, by the opposing power of the shard. Yet even so, it presses into its containment. The shard seems to create a vortex or something, and is osmosed into the currents of the Sargasso, and into the atmospherics of the triangle. But by pushing into that vortex, the presence seems able to create a resonance with which it can influence the seas and the air, to the limit of those confines. And the eels …? I think they are its eyes, and ears, and senses in our world. They bring back information to it. They are bound to it, and would I feel, die, if they could not return to it. I don't think they are of this world, but have in some way been squeezed into it. I … I can't say any more now Soames, but I promise I will try to recall more details when I can."

Soames leaned over and gripped her wrists. "I know Eve. Just hang in there. We need you more than ever now, but we need you fit and well, so take all the time you need. I will be here when you are up to it."

Eve let Janie escort her away, and found she was comforted by her strong presence. Unconsciously, she leant her head against her shoulder.

Soames's medical team were having trouble handling Ben. In the end, Soames had to ask Eve to intervene and subdue his temper. The team leader then had a bad time coaxing his team to return to testing, several of them having received minor injuries, following some none too gentle probing. Ben became obedient though after Eve ordered him to be compliant, but glowered at anyone and everyone who failed to be gentle and show proper respect. The power of his demeanour was sufficient to ensure that they handled him with great care, caution and "respect" from then on. Apart from some scans on her pelvis, Eve's testing was more psychological. She was hooked up to brain and organ monitoring equipment, and asked to heal, influence or control various creatures and tissue cultures. Soames had been thoughtful though. He had Eve's canal boat cleaned and maintained, and moored locally, so that Eve could be in familiar surroundings, and have a degree of independence in the evenings and down times. Ben, Janie and four security staff shared the space, but two of the security officers were always outside, discretely on watch.

"Ben, Janie? I need some time alone. I'm going for a walk." They knew by now not to argue, but she knew that they would not be far behind, both were overly protective. She gave them the slip some way before her destination at the river inlet. Eve had been speaking to a fisherman earlier, and there was something she needed to check out. She found the overgrown path and followed it into the marshy river's edge. A pungent smell of fish and bog water assailed her nostrils, and sure enough, just where he had said, there were lines of writhing eels making their way overland, all along the muddy bank. She stood quietly and watched them for a while, then tried some gentle mind probing, to see if she could get a feel for communicating with, or controlling, them. At first it was like reaching into black treacle. Then, a slow bubble rose within the sticky soup, and an impression splattered sluggishly over her thoughts, finally congealing into a question.

"What are you?" She struggled to respond into the viscid, slow churning turmoil, of undulating thoughts, and it occurred to her that this question had not been from an individual, but from a collective intellect. She slowly pushed her own thought into the surface resistance of the gloop.

"I'm Eve. What are you?" During her efforts, she hadn't noticed that they had changed direction and were all now writhing over one another towards her. Her first awareness was when a huge knot of them appeared through the undergrowth, several paces from where she stood. The knot twisted and roiled, and piled until it was as high as she, and formed into a shape roughly resembling that of a grotesque man. And another thought drooled and dribbled into her mind. "Eve ... yes ... be...aut...iful ... Yes ... we ... re...mem...ber." The words were like slime squeezing into her, oozing down her body and coiling around her feet. Too late, she realised they had her, hundreds of them, pulling her down to the ground.

A hail of bullets shattered the suffocating silence that had engulfed her. Ben and Janie and two security guards burst through the undergrowth, beating at the eels with their gun butts, and shooting where necessary. Ben and Janie grabbed an arm each and hauled her away, while the security guards turned their machine pistols on the creatures, which now began to withdraw like a touched snail's feeler. Eve was still trying to disconnect her thoughts and seemed to be in a stupor. They dragged and carried her back to the boat where Janie stripped her and went in the shower with her to wash off the slime and gore. The cold shock of water brought her back to her senses, but she allowed Janie to carry her to her bed, and to bring her a hot drink, solicitously prepared by Ben, now hovering tactfully outside the door.

"What on earth were you thinking, Honey? You scared the shit out of us. Jackie warned you the eels were dangerous. I've contacted Soames and told him I want you far away from the water tonight, somewhere bloody airtight if possible, to stop those slimy little bastards from slithering in."

"You don't need to worry." She waved Ben in. "Now I've tuned into them I will know if they are coming."

"Fat lot of fucking good that did you on the riverbank. You were in some kind of trance. I'm your head of security Honey and I insist ..." Eve's frown made her modify her words. "I'm begging you, please let me do my job and make you safe."

Eve sighed and called Ben over. She grabbed both their hands. "Okay Janie. And thank you both. I know I can always rely on you. You make me feel safe when you are near." Ben just nodded. There was no need for words between them.

Janie's voice broke for a moment, but she forced a stern tone into her words when they finally came. "Then let us do our job, damn you woman."

Eve chuckled, "Of course mother dear."

Ben chuckled too. And even Janie found it hard to resist a smile.

On hearing of what had happened, Soames contacted Jackie and brought her to the testing centre. She was there waiting for them when they arrived the next morning.

"Tell me everything Eve. Leave nothing out. I want to know every slightest thought, emotion or impression you experienced, however small or insignificant, or in the background of your thoughts ... You say they spoke into your mind, and you definitely felt it was a collective rather than singular intelligence. So what? Are we talking like a gestalt do you think? Or are you thinking a collective effort, to facilitate overcoming some sort of a barrier to communication?"

"The latter, maybe, I don't know."

"And they remembered you, knew your name, and that you

were beautiful? Do you think it was you they remembered Eve, or could it have been someone else?"

"I don't know. It is so difficult. Even though my first encounter with them was very recent ... if they have such difficulty forming coherent thought, maybe it was a struggle for them to remember, but ... it felt as though they were digging very deep into a memory of long ago."

"Interesting Eve, and your impression of them forming an image of a grotesque man, can you describe it more accurately? Better, can you draw it?"

"I'll try." Soames handed her a sketch pad and pencil, and Eve started to draw, and forgot herself in the effort to reproduce a likeness. Several minutes later, she handed the pad to Jackie. Soames, Janie and Ben all peered over her shoulder.

"Wow! I only wanted a sketch Eve. This is more like a masterpiece. You've captured every detail. I feel as though I could walk into it." They all studied the picture. "It certainly is grotesque, but definitely manlike. What do you all make of it?" She handed it around to the others.

They were all silent until it got to Janie. "What do you think those short protrusions behind its shoulders are, deformity, bad modelling, or swords maybe?"

Jackie almost snatched the picture from her hands. "Shit! No ... Sorry everyone, I just had a totally off the wall thought. Janie I really am sorry, I didn't mean to be rude."

Soames interrupted. "I would really like to hear your thought Jackie." They all stared at her in silent expectation.

"It's stupid really. It was just a random thought. It's just that ..."

"Spit it out, Honey."

"Well, I suppose it is all the scriptural readings influencing my mind-set, but those protrusions look a bit like an attempt to model wings, or maybe just stunted or ruined, or incomplete, wings. Look at the way they seem to extend from where the shoulder blades might be. Perhaps images were somehow being picked up and imitated, from Eve's subconscious or something, but we should all take time to think on what our impressions are. You thought they might be swords or deformities Janie. Follow that train of thought.

"Anyway, I think there are other issues we should also be considering. The scale and speed of the super-normal events that are gravitating to Eve seem to be increasing exponentially. Is it pre-destiny? In which case we just have to roll with it and try to react to events as they arise. Or is it due to Eve's and our interference with stabilising powers, that have until now protected or confined us to our normal mode of existence. Should we exercise caution? Or reach out and grasp our futures? Do we have any choice in the matter, and can we guide events to our advantage? We have been forging forward, and it has stood us in good stead so far, but perhaps it is time to pause, evaluate and consolidate, so that we can secure and understand our position before the next onslaught and plunge into the unknown. And God knows, Eve could do with a rest, or at least a slowing down, and all of us too. We are not automatons, we have to maintain and develop our emotions, our inner selves. She looked directly at Eve … our humanity."

Apart from the obvious tensions, her brief time in England had been a welcome distraction, but it was good to be back in her desert retreat with Freddy and the black priests. If there was a place of safety anywhere on this planet, she felt it must be here. Eve sat at a table in her room looking out at the panorama of the river valley below. She bent her head, and began to pen a letter to Helen.

My dearest Helen

I don't know how to begin. Everyone is so concerned about my humanity, or lack of it, but no one has defined exactly what humanity is. Is it the ability to feel compassion, to empathise, to love? When I look around the world, I feel that much of what we call "the human race" is severely lacking in these traits, and I have to wonder – if Soames truly wants to preserve humanity by destroying any threat to it – whether he should start by directing his purgative efforts at those who would kill a man for preaching love, and at that much larger percentage who would be sufficiently influenced and manipulated into going along with it.

When I was just John, I loved you very deeply, but no matter how much I thought of myself as a free spirit I was still constrained by convention. Had you been a man we might have been friends, but we would not have been lovers, not in any sense of the word. My career too was very important to me, and at times I placed it before you. Not just because it was essential to survival and maintaining our

marriage and life style, but because at certain times, it mat-
tered more to me. My focus at those times excluded you, and
occasionally perhaps it should (obsession too is an awful
thing), but sometimes it was for overly selfish reasons. When
Anabel died particularly, I found refuge in work, and was
not always there for you when you needed me most. Later I
spent our hard earned wealth in a fruitless search for a
non-existent cancer cure, and then left you on your own
fretting – while I went off adventuring in Afghanistan –
knowing I would probably never see you again. And so I
robbed you of our last months together. Even then, whilst,
mentally at least, I was still much the man you had known,
I returned, and didn't trust your faultless love enough to tell
you the truth. Rather, I stalked you, and manipulated your
vulnerability, so that I could taste any titbit of affection I
might eke from your distress. I am so, so sorry for all of that.

But now I stand with one foot in the questionable humanity that is John, and he remains very strong within me still,
and the other in something new, someone new. And I feel
an indescribable depth of emotion. How could I know that
it was possible to love you even more? Perhaps it was getting
to know aspects of you that I never knew existed, because I
could only see you from a male perspective, but your every
breath excites me. I crave your body and your mind, and
would love you in any form, because it is the you within,
that calls to me. I think I would be content to sit or lie with
you for eternity, but even more, I want to be dynamic with
you. Whatever the future holds, and however long or short
it is, I want to go out and meet it, mould it, create a world fit
for you, and all those others I have come to love so dearly,
with you at my side – and they with us – working together to
forge a new tomorrow, and a destiny for all of life, whatever
its origins or aspects.

It is perhaps not the poetic love letter you expected, but it
is, I promise you, from the heart. Death may come to us
today or next week, Helen. Or it may take a thousand years
of hardship and toil before it finds us, but if we are together,
I will meet or avoid it happily.

I love you Helen.

Eve AKA John x

"It's great to see you again Jackie, and how is my favourite uncle Soames doing these days. Has he cut out your ovaries yet, or put you in a room and gassed you?"

"I thought we were past all that Eve. He really is extremely fond of you, you know."

"Oh ..." She sighed quietly. "I know Jackie, and truth be told, despite everything, I respect the man, and have to grudgingly admit that I am starting to trust him, even like him a little, but I have to have a whipping boy, especially right now."

"Why, what has happened?"

"Oh, it's Helen. She's gone cold again. I've written to her and sent messages, but she hasn't even responded to tell me she has received them. Do you think Soames is sending them on? Or maybe she's already decided that she wants to stay clear of any chance that I might rob her of her mortality. She must be under tremendous strain. Do you think she's ill or becoming mentally unstable?"

"You know she is stronger than that Eve. She just needs time to think. And that is what you should be doing too. How many times have you written to her, once? Twice? She needs to understand who you are now, what you have become, are becoming. One letter will not tell her what she needs to know. Are you keeping up with your journal? Send her copies of that as you write them. Refer to how you are feeling, especially concerning her, and pour your heart out to her in more of your letters. She will be waiting anxiously for them; you can be assured of that. Above all be honest. And hope Eve. Have faith. If none of that works, then you will have no choice but to move on."

Eve walked over, hugged, and held her for several moments. "Of course Jackie, as usual you are right. I'm just hyper, because for once I have time to think."

"Time is a precious thing Eve, so use it. Write and write, then write some more. Dig deep and know yourself, so that she can know you too."

"Thank you Jackie, you always bring me back to earth. So, why are you here?"

"Two reasons, to be with you, and to talk with you."

"About eels?"

"Got it in one."

"Yeah, Helen caught me before we left the island. She said she reckoned you would want to talk to me about the watchers. That confused me for a bit, until I remembered the Nephilim, so I did some research."

"Astute lady, and what do you think?"

"I don't know Jackie. If the world were normal I would say you were insane. But the world is insane so maybe your thoughts are normal. And it does kind of fit, if you can stretch your imagination that big. Have you mentioned it to Soames or Freddy?"

"Freddy, yes. Soames? No. I don't think he's quite ready to openly consider or admit to such a conjectural leap."

"Just as well I'm here then. So, you're thinking what? Some higher than terrestrial life forms, angels for want of a better word, here to keep an eye on humanity, punished, and cast down for breeding with them, and for siring the Nephilim? Can't be cast down much deeper than the bottom of the Sargasso I suppose, and it's probably fiery and volcanic in the deep trenches too, and better yet, reduced to serpent form. Almost fits too well scripturally. And the presence? Who or what would be powerful enough to control the watchers? Azazel? Lucifer? God? Mega fucking brain? What have we awakened Jackie?"

"Yes, it does seem that they either emanate from, or are controlled, by this presence; and what of Afsoon? Why do you think he feels he can bargain with it? What could he possibly offer to such a powerful entity short of release into this world? And, unless he already has some sure-fired way of binding it to his will, that doesn't seem the sort of stupid move he would make. He would likely be releasing a force he couldn't control. So, either he knew you were eavesdropping on him and his followers, and tried to sucker you into an encounter with a force that would destroy you, or he has already made his bargain, and was in effect, manoeuvring you into his parlour, where he might keep, contain or imprison you at his leisure."

"I think the latter more likely. His object has always been to degrade, torture, and impregnate me with his dynastic horde. My destruction would rob him of that pleasure and would be a defeat in his eyes. And Afsoon doesn't do defeat."

"Hmm, I'm not so sure. Maybe he's starting to see you as a powerful adversary, who might just get the upper hand, and perhaps he feels godlings born of two such powerful beings might be more than he can handle. Hybrids like the Nephilim, however, would still be demi-Gods, but not of pure blood, so probably not powerful enough to be a threat, if well managed. But that speculation is still a bit too far out there at the moment. What about our current batch of watcher eels though? If that is indeed what they are. It seems to me they have been kept in a sorry state of servility, for an immense amount of time. They likely hate their master-mistress, whatever. Perhaps it is with them that a deal might be struck. Something, possibly the shard, is preventing this presence from entering our world. This thing apparently has the power to influence conditions within the Sargasso and Bermuda triangle, but is unable to actually enter. And its influences are hit and miss at best, or you would now be in its clutches. If it needs the eels to enter and to watch, and to work beyond its confines; then they have a power it does not. Perhaps they could even close the gate so to speak. What could you offer to such creatures that would make them turn on their master; and presumably, their sustenance and compulsion to return to him-she-it? Probably freedom and a return to angelic form, but even if that could be achieved, what dangers would 'they' then represent? And what ungodly bargaining, might Afsoon already be engaged in?"

Eve was looking at Jackie aghast. "Jackie, what Moscow gym school did your mind go to, that it can back flip and somersault through dozens of wild cat theories, land on its toes and still sound like common-sense? Or am I as mad as you are for giving an ear to it? Much as I hate to admit it, I think we've got to bring in Soames, Freddy and the rest of them on this, before my mind bursts."

"I agree, but not just yet. They all have their own theories at the moment, and they need to develop them, or run them into blind corners, before they will listen to such creative leaps of imagination and conjecture. If you really need an ear to bend, talk to Helen in your letters. She is more a mistress of creative common sense than anyone I know."

"Do you really think so Jackie? She didn't believe me when I told her the truth of who I am."

"I think you are wrong. At some level, I am sure she knew before you told her. But as you pointed out earlier, it was insane to believe. The world we all knew was starting to shudder. Who wouldn't run for cover before the avalanche overtook them? She has adapted Eve, is adapting. Just as you are, talk to her. See for yourself."

Helen

Helen sat on the edge of her bed, admiring the snowy peak of a glacier through an open window, while absently lacing up her hiking boots. A sad thought rustled through the undergrowth of her mind. But as she breathed in the dewy scents of Dianthus on the fresh morning breeze, her chest expanded with a sense of hope and energy.

She had read the first of Eve's letters a week ago, with mixed feelings. It was honest, and expressed love and longing, but it was a narrow and one-sided perspective. "Not really surprising," she supposed, "she has barely had a chance to examine who she is, or what she is becoming", yet Helen had hoped for more, and had been unable to maintain her normal enthusiasm for her writing or take enjoyment from the beautiful surroundings in which Soames had located her.

This morning however, Emmaline had deposited a bundle of letters and journal entries onto her bed ... Helen lazily raised a tousled head to peer down at the serpentine script, so like, yet unalike, John's. A slow smile melted the ice of her mood, and a trickle of excitement and anticipation rippled into the extremities of her being. She quickly tied off her boots, stood, stretched, and sucked in a world of possibilities. Cramming the letters into her day sack, Helen strode into the beautiful outside, to find a right and fitting place to learn about Eve.

Soames had shown her a rock, behind which he'd hidden a coiled rope ladder, anchored at one end under the rock itself. She threw this over the precipice behind, and clambered down the overhang, to a grassy hollow beneath, from which a tiny mountain stream sploshed into a waist deep pool, before trickling over on its journey into the verdant valley below. Here she settled, in the warmth of the morning sun, with her back against a mountain, to delve into the heart of a man, and the soul of a Goddess.

Dear Helen

I feel like a schoolboy tugging at pigtails. How can someone who has known every inch of you, from both male and female perspectives, feel nervous and shy about writing to you? And yet I do, and not just because I fear rejection, which I also do. I think it is the quiver of excitement that runs down my spine at the thought of being with you, or touching you, or even of you responding to my letters. Isaac told me when I became Eve that my hormones would settle eventually, and I would not be so pre-occupied with lust, and that was true. But he said nothing about love. Why would he? I have only ever had one love, and I thought her lost to me forever. Then I saw you again, and it was an agony to know I could never more be intimate with you.

This will sound odd now from me "John,'" but I am more than John now, or maybe less, and I confess, that I cried myself to sleep for many nights, uncontrollably wept really. And then you said that time in our kitchen, that I was your type. I didn't know what to make of it. But I tell you, with not a little embarrassment, that I couldn't stop fondling myself that night, and quite a few nights after, and then weeping again, full on, shuddering, out of control, weeping. But I found a way through it, and got a job, and met Vincent. I kept busy and tried not to upset your life more than I already had. But he died, and there was only one person I could think of to run to. The only one whose comfort I could accept. And oh! Oh! Such comfort, I thought I would explode with happiness and erotic pleasure, and on it went. I am quivering now at the thought of it. Every touch, every kiss and caress, and slap, and playful domination and subjugation ... Knots ... and ... other things ...

I am sorry Helen. I am so emotional right now, and well, odd yet again, aroused too. I cannot write anymore right now, but I promise I will write again soon. For now I don't want to delay, because I want you to know what has been happening with me since I left you all, and set out to sea, and to that end please find enclosed copies of my journal entries from that time. I wish you were with me now, and that it were your hands in my shorts, and not my own.

I know I should destroy this letter and start again, but you need to know me exactly as I am now.

I love you Helen.

AKA Sea Wolfe Captain.

Ever yours

John AKA Eve x

Journal entry

We left the enclave of the black priests today, Ben and I. I am drunk on a cauldron of seething emotions. Excited to be "doing" again, and thankful for some space, but I am miserable that Helen is not with me, and sad that I am leaving my friends. Ben is here however, and that is a great comfort. Who would have thought that he would prove to be so resilient and resourceful, and devoted? Such a short while ago I would happily have ripped out his throat, as have him in my company.

My life since my death, has in many ways, been a living hell. I have longed to die on so many occasions, and I fight constantly to maintain my sanity. Perhaps I would have killed myself had not Isaac, and later, Soames, Freddy, and the rest, not tasked me with saving humanity, but when I really think hard and deep, there is only one thing that has kept me sane and alive, the knowledge that Helen continues to exist in this world. No matter my physical form and origins, my humanity is rooted in her.

Journal entry

I thought about the children today, those I saved, and those I could not, and poor Stella, another who, with all my new abilities, I had no power to save. I couldn't even prevent Sadique and his men from raping, and abusing and disfiguring me, not unless I abandoned those poor souls. I am so weak, and such a fool. How can I save a world? Madness took me back then, madness and fear like I have never known. Matt was incredible, but one abiding thought, formless and without substance, reduced to only a name, yet all the world to me, brought me back: "Helen." I wish I could have buried my head in her lap and cried and cried until it all went away. I still do.

I have to dive again today. It scares me to death. I will try to go deeper, but I think fear will overtake me and bring me blubbering back to the Ark.

If I make it, I hope Ben can cope with an hysterical woman.

There were many entries, some incomplete, some rambling. Helen read them all twice, then sorted and selected those that told her most, for re-reading later. Eyes red and sore from constant rubbing, she returned to her chalet.

Journal entry

I remember when Afsoon tried to possess me. I realise now, that he could only take control of my body, if I could be persuaded to hand it over to him. I could always have taken it back, so long as I was brave enough to do so. For better or for worse, my soul inhabits it, and is one with it. Only death and decay can release it. Something has been bugging me about that parting though. I can't quite remember, but Afsoon said something before he left, about Anabel. What could he know of her? Had he been delving into my memories?

Journal entry

It is a strange thing. I have often thought about killing myself. I take risks in the half hope that death will be the product. And yet, when I look around, despite having the world on my shoulders, and responsibilities I feel I will never be able to live up to, and the fear that Afsoon will make good on his promises, or that a fiery demon will spring from the Sargasso to devour the Earth. Despite all of this, I have blessings to count. I have friends I would die for. That is not saying so much, but I truly believe they would all die for me too, and that is saying very much. And Helen is in this world with me, and there is still a possibility that she will accept me as I am, but something about Anabel gnaws at the root of my mind. So odd, she has been gone for so long …

Helen felt drained. She placed those entries she had re-read face down on her bedside table, lay back on her pillow, and plummeted into a sleep that was like death. And a memory waited there, from when Afsoon had entered her dreams, a lifetime ago, dreams that had brought a wondrous boat journey to an end. Afsoon stood in empty space, holding the hand of a young woman, both with their backs to her. He craned his neck around to an impossible angle to look at her. "Ah Helen, if you are here, it means I didn't kill you. Bad for me, but maybe good for you, I have someone here you may wish to meet."

Maintaining the neck twist, he turned his body around to bring it into line, rotating his companion in doing so. On seeing Helen she screamed, and wept pitifully. "Mum, help me! He is a monster."

Anabel still looked like she had when Helen had last seen her, when she and John had identified her corpse in the mortuary. Afsoon was behind her now, bending and twisting her broken limbs, like a puppet with cut strings, and the song from *Pinnochio* was playing somewhere in the distance. "Do tell John that Anabel and I have become lovers, won't you? There's a good woman. Say goodbye Anabel." He snapped off her arm and waved it at Helen with a tear in his eye, and they both faded away. Helen screamed, and awoke to Emmaline crashing through the bedroom door, pistol in hand.

In the confines of the chalet's extensive kitchen, and with a cup of hot glühwein, Helen recovered quickly. Emmaline had been fully appraised about Eve, and of Helen's connection to her. She was a good listener. And that was what Helen wanted right now. "The last thing anyone needs at the moment is a panic stricken and hysterical mother. Realistically, that 'Anabel' is a construct that Afsoon has somehow garnered from John's memories. But those memories have been wrenched from a loving mind and are now in the hands of a creature that has no business having them. And who is to say, in this strange existence that is now transforming any previous conception of reality, whether some of Anabel's personality and feelings have not also been assumed by this golem, and are causing the poor thing to suffer? Of course the thing might not exist at all, probably doesn't. As I understand it Afsoon's physical body is confined, but we know his mind isn't. The real question though is why is he bothering? It must be some sort of distraction or lure, to cover a weakness or draw us into a trap. Or he is up to something, and wants to misdirect, and prevent us from interfering until it has been completed. Maybe he is pursuing his bargain with the watchers, or God forbid, the presence itself ... Emmaline, get hold of Soames please, and tell him I need to see Eve-John, whomever, as soon as possible. In fact, tell him we need a meeting of all the disciples. The bastard is up to something. I damn well know it."

Helen strode into Eve's apartments in the enclave. They were all there. As the sun disappeared from sight behind the overhanging cliff face on the opposite side of the valley, Eve stood with her back to the door looking out across the vista. Ben was one pace behind, and to her right. Soames and Freddy were huddled together debating some topic of scriptural science. Fadil stridently expounded on something profound with Janie and Matt. And Jackie sat alone, in roughly the centre of them all; chin resting on the fingers of her fisted hands, and looking directly at the space, Helen, and then Emmaline, walked into, with passive expectation.

The door whispered shut with a near silent click. Eve turned to look at Helen. Her black on blue eyes seemed to fill the entire room. A smile full of regret, twitched slowly across her beautiful features, as she walked through the becalmed air of expectation in the room. She gently kissed and hugged Helen, and guided her and Emmaline to vacant chairs, opposite those set out for Ben and herself. Helen looked around the silent room, then back at Eve, and into her sorrowful eyes. Eve blinked several times and looked down. Her long lashes were wet. She cleared her throat and started to speak, but her voice cracked. There were several moments more silence. Eve coughed and adjusted herself more upright.

Janie fidgeted and looked angry. Finally, it was she who broke the silence, in a voice brimming with bitterness. "What's this all about honey?"

Helen frowned in confusion, and looked again at Eve, who was staring determinedly down at the overlapping hands in her lap. Realisation struck ... "I'm not here to finish with you Eve." An explosive gasp of air burst from Eve's lips, and she dashed for the bathroom. Helen thought she could hear retching.

"For fuck sake! Go to her honey." Jackie rose, and suggested to them all, that they leave and re-convene in the morning.

Helen closed the door behind her and waited until Eve had chucked up the rest of her stomach, then assisted her to stand, flushed the loo, and wiped the vomit from her lips and hair with a wet flannel. Eve flopped back down onto the toilet seat, her back arched, elbows on knees, and hands and hair hanging between her legs.

"Now you see me as I really am Helen, a beauty for sure on the outside, a washed-up jellyfish within. You may not have reached your decision yet, but you are no fool. In your shoes I would cut and run too. What possible future can I hope to give you? I will carry on, and try my best for humanity, but ultimately, I see only failure. And I feel such a weight of guilt, that no matter how hard

I try, all of humanity will likely suffer eternal damnation, because I was not up to the task of saving them."

Helen put her whole weight, and every ounce of her strength, into the punch she swung into the side of Eve's jaw. The next punch was brought to a halt, between Eve's forefinger and thumb. Helen snatched back her bloodied fist, grabbed Eve's hair either side of her face. Wrenched her to her feet and kissed her full on the lips. "You're a fucking Goddess, and you can't even have faith in yourself, let alone in me. Whether you like it or not, I'm here for the long haul, and if you haven't got the wherewithal to take on the universe, I will drag you by your perfect roots through the fires of hell, and throw you into the face of Satan himself, if I have to."

All the disciples and Emmaline met the next morning. Tentatively, they entered the broken bed chamber of Eve. A table and two chairs were intact, at which Eve and Helen calmly sat in dressing gowns, both apparently glowing with health. Helen reached for the jug of milk with a perfectly unscathed punching hand and invited everyone to join them for breakfast. "I think you'll find something to sit on amongst the wreckage. If not, Freddy would you mind, and arrange something for everyone? I think we all need to start the day with full bellies, and then I can explain why I really came here …

Janie leaned forward. "So you think Afsoon is creating a distraction, to give him time to deal with whatever is lurking under the Sargasso? I don't get it. Why would he need a distraction? Sounds more like a trap to me. It would be right in there with his MO. Way I see it, he's trying to get Eve to lose her shit again, and go raging off down the dream road, straight into whatever psycho metaphysical crap he's got waiting for her. Best course of action, ignore it, and stay safe in the physical world, where we can take the time before he gets here, to consolidate our plans and secure our position."

Freddy interjected. "You make a good point Janie, and I agree he is likely setting a trap, but only because he would leave no avenue unprotected. It is even possible, that Eve might form part of the price of any bargain, or be the unintentional medium, through which it is made. So we do have to be careful. But it is equally possible that he is worried about Eve's successes and growing power and seeks to forestall her. She has one shard and believes she can ghost another. She escaped three attempts by this powerful presence, to bring her into its clutches, not to mention closing down Afsoon's own attacks, with the help of some 'very powerful' friends." He gestured with wide-spread hands to include all those present. "And almost daily, she is gaining and learning to use, new abilities."

Soames joined the discussion. "The truth is, we can't sit on our backsides waiting for Afsoon's next move. Our best chance is to hit him in any way we can before ever he gets here. But this time, we slow down and plan. I know him well, and I can tell you we will never second guess him. So we need to be equally unreadable and original, in everything we do. It is time to be creative with our strategies."

Helen sat back, and listened to all the arguments, until a natural silence occurred, while everyone considered what they had learned. "I've had time to think about this, and I think I have some ideas. Perhaps, if you all agree, we can get our heads together and make some of those 'creative' strategies."

Everyone turned to look at her, some indulgent, others cautious, Eve with amused pride, and Jackie, as always, with intense interest, and open-minded expectation. Helen looked around a little contritely, and began, with a slight blush, at her own choice of words. "After reacquainting ourselves, Eve and I talked, long and hard, last night. We know there are five shards depicted, and that another has been suggested. It is unseen, maybe because it is only visible in the metaphysical realm. We know the whereabouts of two. Eve successfully ghosted them both last night." This caused some worried looks around the room. She looked at Eve, who gave a nod of encouragement. "Eve feels that a third may possibly be housed in Afsoon's pod, it being the only artefact left from the habitat. If that is so, it is unlikely that Afsoon is unaware of it. It may even be that it has facilitated his interference here on Earth, and may also be how he is communicating with the thing under the sea, assuming that is his intent. Freddy? Soames? Do you think it possible we might be able to triangulate the location of the other shards, and therefore, possibly the pod too, using the two we have, much like tracking a mobile phone?"

Everyone's interest was now apparent. Soames was already jotting down notes, and showing some to Freddy, who nodded but frowned ambiguously, and said something in low tones, that got an equally ambiguous response from Soames.

Jackie spoke now, and everyone stopped to listen. "Welcome to the fold Helen. We need every original thinker we can muster. And Emmaline, Helen has obviously spoken with you, and you have heard what everyone else here has had to say. Have you got anything to add?"

Emmaline was clearly taken off guard, and her usual remote professionalism, was momentarily shattered. Looking guiltily at Soames, who nodded, she responded. "Possibly one thing."

She looked at Soames again. "Go ahead Emmaline. If Jackie wants to hear you, so do I."

"Okay then. Helen has mentioned the healing and regeneration Eve may be capable of." She cast a look at Ben, who fidgeted restlessly. "It seems important, urgent even, to find out how powerful this ability is. Enhanced, long lived humans would make fearsome soldiers and, sorry Mr Soames, but if Eve can't enhance you soon, you will probably be dead well before this Afsoon gets here, and the rest of you will be feeling the effects of age. If all that can be reversed reasonably soon, then, well ...?" She shrugged and left it there.

Happy to let Helen do the talking for once, Eve reflected on last night. She didn't know why she had reacted so demonstrably. It was something John would never have done. She supposed it was a combination of the stresses she had been under since her metamorphic change, and of what had seemed to be the final nail in the coffin of her fears, that she was going to lose Helen forever. But it was more than that. She had made a raft of friends to support her in her new life, and in all the responsibilities that went with it. But they were Eve's friends. They knew only the "her" that she was now. Helen, however, was the link to her past, and to the whole of her being, the strengths, frailties and "humanity" of John, and the genesis and mixed bag, of God knows what, of Eve. And, if Eve was finally going to take the plunge, and seize the dragon's tail of fate in her left hand, she wanted to be damned sure she had a firm grip on Helen, and the rest of humanity, in her right. For the first time, Eve could discern a glimmer of something worthwhile in the future. It may or may not be possible, to regenerate or rejuvenate Helen and the others, but no one really knew whether even Eve herself, was going to have anything other than a normal life span. And the value of longevity was questionable anyhow. There was every chance that all of their lives would be cut short, given the forces amassing in the shadows against them. But events had taken a new turn. Everything important to Eve was gravitating towards her. With Helen agreeing to re-commit to their relationship, and the firming up of support of all the disciples, hope had taken root. Protecting it was something worth fighting for. If fate decreed that Eve was to be the shepherdess and protector of human evolution, then … "Fuck it!" She was not going to cringe anymore. "But anyone in my flock, had damn well better be ready to show their teeth too, when I fly at the throats of their enemies!"

Eve Rising

Eve stood and looked at Soames. "Soames! Our on/off feud must end for good. We have a common cause, and we need to commit to it, and to each other. So I'll live with and forgive your butchery of my organs, but you have to accept me for what I am now, someone with the means to help humanity survive and evolve, not a monster that is a threat to it. Be doubting Thomas if you must, but 'commit' you also must. Physically, you are the frailest of us. You are no use to us, or to humanity, if you are dead. I am starting to gain control of my healing abilities Soames. You have helped me with these in the past. You know my potential. Helen's hand was damaged last night, now it is healed. But the human body doesn't heal itself well. Why that should be is unknowable. Bodies build themselves from scratch in the womb and continue through-out life to make small scale repairs. The triggers that make that possible must still be in our DNA. With yours and Freddy's help, I intend to find those triggers, and reactivate regenerative capabili-ty. You need fixing Soames. Your heart is weak, and several others of your organs are functioning well below capacity. We absolutely cannot afford to lose you.

"I want you to be a guinea pig for my early attempts. There are risks of course, but Emmaline was not wrong about you. Frankly, your waking up each day is a risk. I'm sure it is only your willpower that keeps you upright. You know this is true. It is still a revelation to me to know that you have one, but I think we need to start trials with your heart very soon." She forestalled any reaction with a raised palm. "Before you start with any objections, think about it. You have been complaining that you do not have enough time with me to plan and to strategize, and to study me. This way you get a whole lot more of me. And if I am successful, we get a whole lot more of you. I could tell by your reaction earlier that you think there is merit in Helen's plan. And I also know, that if we can locate the pod, by whatever means, that you will want to destroy it, shard and all. If another shard does indeed reside within it, which it must if we can locate it by Helen's method, we will need some of our time together to discuss that course of action in depth. Because I think maybe we will need the combined force of all the shards to maintain for earth a shield from predatory forces of unknown power and origins."

The room was quiet. And so was Soames for some considerable time, during which he studied Eve intently. They all knew he was trying to read facial features, body language, voice tones and eye responses. Eventually he nodded slowly. "Agreed, but understand this. This will not be you telling me what to do. This will be a partnership. Also, it will not all take place here in your enclave. I know you thought you had good reason to escape my clutches on my home ground, but we need state of the art laboratories, and research equipment that can only be found in one place. We will share time, here, and in my facility in England, where you too will continue to be a guinea pig, for my team's observations and tests, which will be far more vigorous, even invasive, than any previous."

Freddy, Matt, Janie and Ben all started to protest, but Eve silenced them with a gesture. "That will be subject to agreement, as to the format, and what kind of tests, and, as before, Ben, Janie, and any who Matt deem necessary, will be present at all times, in equal number to your own personnel. I intend to trust you Soames, but these are early days, and my other friends here, I think, will need further convincing of your motives before they too will lower their guard. Helen of course, will be wherever she wants to be, but

I would prefer her here," Eve glanced at Helen, "as my proxy when I am in England."

"Agreed."

Soames stood to leave, but Eve placed herself between him and the door, put her hands on his shoulders and bent to kiss him, then hugged him to her chest. "Thank you Soames, I think we are friends now, aren't we?"

He harrumphed. "Just don't call me one of your damned disciples." Then he was out of the door.

Eve smiled and muttered absently to herself. "Time will tell Soames." Then louder to them all, "While Soames organises our schedule, as I know he will, there is no excuse for us sitting on our backsides. Freddy, I want you to set up a ritual at the altar. I intend to ghost the second shard. I did so briefly last night, but that was just to see if I could. I now want to feel the two together, extend myself into the combined power of their vortices, and see what I can learn. Physically they are separated, so triangulation may be possible, but if the two ghost shards are in the same place, maybe not. Also, I think from now on, the actual shards should, where possible, stay in their original locations. I am concerned that any unnecessary disruption from where they have been located all these millennia, may disturb whatever force-net the things are generating, and I don't like to think what might be on the other side of that net, baying to come in. Hopefully we can get something to convince Soames that 'not destroying a shard' is a good idea, even if it does mean that Afsoon gets a stay of execution. He's a scary son of a bitch who needs to be destroyed, but not at any cost."

Freddy officiated at the head of the altar, and priests in robes, with candles and incense, lined the walls, all rhythmically chanting. It was like something from a Gothic nightmare, but Freddy was right, the atmosphere and ritual had a force of its own, and somehow, it generated a greater force, drawing it into the cavern like a tamed wind. Eve had requested her disciples to stand around the altar. She felt strong when they were close. It was like basking in the vortex of a warm current of air that dispersed the chill fears of the night. At Freddy's signal she shuffled her rump across the cold stone and wriggled into place, until she filled the man shaped depressions on the altar, or was it woman shaped she mused, noting just how perfectly she moulded into them.

She waited whilst the rhythmic chant started to take on a life of its own, surging like waves through her feet to crash into, and against, the hard bone of her skull. The incense smoke weaved back and forth like the head of a snake, undulating a serpentine path toward her face. A silver nimbus swelled into the human opening in the cliff face, increasing in luminosity as the moon rose. The two horns of a crescent moon pushed up from the feet, rising until they pierced the empty abdomen. Eve felt her stomach contract, and she summoned the ghost shards, feeling them solidify in her hands as the horned moon pushed further up towards the head. When the area where the nose would have ended and the forehead began was cupped in the crescent, the smoky serpent struck deep into Eve's nostrils, writhing down her throat, and threading throughout her vascular and nervous systems.

She went rigid and felt herself explode. Her arms encircled the world. Her feet disappeared into infinity, and her essence encompassed solar space. She reached out a ghostly hand and cupped the Sargasso Sea in her palm. She held it between forefinger and thumb and brought it to her eye like a spy glass. In the murky depths a star shone, but beyond it was an ink black slick, surging, ridged and cracked. Leathery, like the face of a mummified corpse, its sluggish swells heaved. A hugely magnified eyelid opened. Eve dropped the spy glass and quickly withdrew.

She looked outward into the stars, and the shards in each of her hands bucked, and fired piercing bolts of light left and right, one directly into the shard above her head, the other into the Sargasso. They then zig-zagged, and formed into a pentagram, each of those points, both remote and within this chamber, emitted a rod of laser light, directing her to the locations of all the shards. A pinnacle of darkness formed in the centre of the image. The shock of what these locations revealed, and the draw of the dark, caused her to contract like a snatched fist into a foetal position. Gasping and hyperventilating, she was back. Quickly she dispelled the ghost shards, and shaking violently, slithered, sweat slicked, off the slab and into Helen's arms. "Shit! Shit! Shit! Hold me tight Helen, and get me the fuck out of here!"

Several shots of a medicinal rum preparation, organised by Freddy, and Eve felt ready to talk. She looked around at the expectant faces. "Freddy have you managed to get hold of Soames?"

He shook his head. "No, already taken off in his helicopter, unreachable at the moment I'm afraid."

"God, I don't know how I'm going to tell him ... I know where all the shards are." Everyone started talking at once.

Helen's voice cut through the hubbub. "But Eve, that's great news. Soames will be over the Moon."

Jackie then spoke, and as usual, everyone listened. "He's not going to be though, is he Eve? What did you see that he won't like? Are any of us going to like it?"

Eve hesitated, flexed her fingers, and started to rub her nose. "I don't like it, and I don't think any of you will either." She hesitated again.

Janie placed a hand on Eve's shoulder, and bent to look into her eyes ... "You can't put lipstick on a pig honey. Just say it as it is."

Eve sighed deeply. "Okay, the third shard is on the moon, the sixth is something I can't explain. Helen was right though, it is metaphysical. All I could see was a dark double pinnacle extruding, both ways, through the centre of the pentagram, more like an axle really, impossible to look outwards from the apexes, the darkness just seemed to swallow sight."

Matt spoke, and Eve realised that he rarely did these days, when they were all together. She also knew that he would go straight to the heart of the matter. "That is a great concern Eve, and something that Freddy and Soames will no doubt apply their expertise to, but that is not your immediate concern is it? What is it about the other two shards that is troubling you?"

Eve pinched the bridge of her nose hard, and squeezed her eyes tight shut. "I found the pod! And I was right; there is a shard on it. The trouble is, Afsoon ... He is the fucking shard!"

Freddy had finally got Soames up on the computer. Everyone crowded around the screen. He sounded tired. "What is it Eve, that is so urgent, so soon?"

"A multi-dimensional load of crap is what it is. Please don't hate me again Soames. I can locate the damn pod for you, but, but you won't like what I have to say."

Soames leaned forward, a frown creasing his forehead. "You went back on the dream road? It seems you are still prone to haste

Eve, but we anticipated the possible value of the pod, and you suggested there was plenty of time for debate, so, what is different than expected?"

"Afsoon is what is different. He is the bloody shard!"

Soames took a long time to reply. "Bugger! ... And you, I take it, are the other?"

Eve couldn't look at him. She responded in almost a whisper, wringing her hands between her legs, and nervously opening and closing her knees, with her head down. "Why was she letting him get to her like this?"

"There is something else ..." She wriggled uncomfortably on the foot-stool she had inadvertently grabbed to sit on, and which was triggering a host of unwanted memories, all clamouring to discharge past poisons into her floundering self-assurance. She cast a quick glance around the room, but failed to find the support she needed. Eve looked as though she would bolt for the door as soon as she had blurted out whatever it was she had to say. "I haven't told the others yet, because I didn't want you to be the last to know again. I was in space Soames, and ... I was a ... a darkness; a darkness in which the stars and our sun shone. I could feel the planets move, and comets come and go, and the pod, I could see and feel, and locate it, within the fabric of my being. I could feel Afsoon, as himself, and as a shining shard. And I knew the energy of his thoughts, seeping from the shard. I remembered what you said though Soames, what you all said."

Eve was becoming increasingly agitated by the seeming indifference of her friends. "I knew I daren't go close again, for fear of being trapped, or of alerting Afsoon as before. Instead I ... well ... I ... I kind of allowed his escaping thoughts to disturb the dark water that was my mind, I absorbed them, and I watched where they went; how they formed. It was so difficult though. It was like trying to see a fish in a sun-sparkled sea. I, I hope you don't think I was wrong in not following his reflections to their fully formed destination, but I needed to get out, and back to you with what they revealed, before anything went wrong ... He plans to destroy technology Soames. We will be back in the fucking dark ages. You ... We ... All of us ..."

Again, she looked around at the others. Finding only an air of contained and indefinable expectancy, she carried on. "We need to get our computers backed up, and off the net, and in a totally closed and protected condition … as soon as possible; before he lets out a plague of …" the words wouldn't come, and she started to gabble, waving her hands in frustration, "super-buggy, mmm … monster, virus thingies." She didn't know why she was talking like a two-year-old. The stress just seemed to be suffocating coherent thought, and she was so in need of everyone's approval – and they were all being so fucking neutral – as though they were holding back some explosive emotion, rage or something at the new disaster she had once again come begging for their help with.

"And Soames … they are already so very sophisticated. Some will penetrate a system with coded speech alone, others with visual patterns, and still others through music. Some are instant, and some are holding viruses that can trigger to just a sound, or a beam of light, or a key press. And …" She hesitated, not wanting to say more, but her fears and emotions would not be held, and took domination of her words. "And, I don't know if we should hurt him Soames. I know what you might think, all of you, but I promise Soames, I am not trying to protect him. I hate him, I really do. Please say you believe me. My only fear is what will be unleashed if there is any damage to the pentagram. I don't know what might happen to me if part of it is destroyed, but it seems we – Afsoon and I – are inextricably linked, and I don't know what that means for me, or for all of you. Although …" Her voice became very small and quavering. "I promise you Soames, please, please believe me," she looked around sheepishly, "and every one of you here, if my death can save or benefit you, or the rest of the planet, I will accept it willingly. Just please … I know I am a horrible monster, but don't hate me again, not so soon after we have all finally become a family. Everyone … Please …"

Eve was looking around baffled, confused and unsettled by the note of amused indulgence in Soames's voice. "It's not like you to panic so Eve. We knew something like this was going to happen. You are not bringing home a poor school report. You don't have to impress me. Pleasant as the prospect might be, I am not your father and I won't be angry if you haven't done your homework."

Eve was jolted into the present and realised that she had been prattling on like an errant schoolgirl caught with her hand down her knickers. She was flustered and began to bluster. "Well no …!"

She looked around guiltily, and in a high flush (were they all enjoying her discomfort, were they … laughing at her?) She tried to subdue her rising anger, at the mocking cruelty of them all. "Thank God! … I don't think of you like that! God no!" She looked around again … I don't … really … I don't…! Oh shut up the lot of you! I guess … I guess … Well I guess I just wanted your fucking approval damn it! Advise me, or tell me I am an evil bitch, and that I need to be destroyed. Give me your opinion, you drooling fucking idiot." Soames couldn't contain himself any longer. He lurched forward, clutching at his chest.

Eve panicked. "Soames! Soames! What's wrong? Don't die on me you old bastard, not now when I need you most! Someone help him, for God's sake!" She looked around bewilderedly at the others, who all seemed to be trying and failing, to contain their mirth, then back at the screen, when she heard a guffaw emit from it.

Soames had straightened up and was dabbing tears from his eyes. Between gasping, head bobbing, and shoulder shaking silences, he managed to get out a few words. "Well, if ever I doubted your … your, childlike, innocence Eve. I think … I think you have just shown me the error of my ways. I promise you Eve. The worst pun … punishment I will ever want to … to … inflict on you, will be to send you to the … the naughty stair." He dissolved into another fit of silent laughter, which found voluble release in the spluttering cackles of her companions, in what now seemed to be a very small and embarrassingly uncomfortable space.

Eve blushed. She tried to regain her composure, but every attempt just seemed to set them off again. "Okay, Okay, you've had your fucking joke. I get it, I panicked, but it's nothing to laugh about. This is serious stuff. We're not a bunch of giggling schoolgirls. Our bloody existence is at stake here! Now shut the fuck up, will you? We've got work to do."

The months of coiled tension had finally thrown the super charged jack out of the box, straight into Eve's face. And Soames's red face, and gasping thigh slapping, just seemed to pour rocket fuel onto the firestorm of hilarity directed at Eve. Helen managed to squeeze a spray of words out between spluttering giggles, "Or what? You'll … You'll thscream and thscream until you are … until you are thsick." Everyone dissolved into paroxysms of uncontainable hysteria.

Eve looked around in exasperation. She was barely able to prevent herself from stamping her foot. "Oh grow the fuck up, the lot of you!" By now everyone had lost it. When she saw Helen mimicking her, she realised both of her fists were on her hips, and quickly dropped them. "Oh piss off! You're like a bunch of mentally disturbed fucking hyenas!"

She turned her back on them, and tried not to storm out of the room or slam the door, but the peals of laughter burst out into the hall before her, providing a gauntlet of embarrassment, that forced her to turn back, and finally (with her alter ego John, also looking down on her distress with apparent great amusement) to slump, and to see the funny side. And with that adjustment of perspective, a cathartic deluge broke over Eve, and all of the companions, and washed through them like a river of good wine, plenty of which Freddy ensured was manifested into reality. Matt produced his guitar from somewhere, Ben and Jackie danced, and Fadil proved himself a talented comic, with a never-ending barrage of bawdy stories and irreverent jokes, mostly at Eve's expense. Even Janie and Emmaline got stuck into some embarrassing and ridiculous charades, with ingenuity and gusto. All of them generously made fools of themselves, to share in and to ease Eve's discomfort. Freddy, always one to surprise, happened to have a saxophone handy, or at least within summoning distance, and proved to be a talented player and accompanist. As for Helen: Helen was on fire, and with superlative grace and wit even stole the limelight from the indefatigable Fadil.

"You sang beautifully Eve. But of course you did, you do everything beautifully."

"Made a total fool of myself earlier though, didn't I?"

Helen swivelled into a cross legged position, facing Eve on the bed, with a serious expression on her face. "Nonsense! You showed us the child in you, the child your new persona's responsibilities never gave you a chance to be. You demonstrated that you are just one of us, struggling like everyone else to find your way and your place in this world. It is why you are so loved Eve ... John was a cynic, except with me and Anabel. He would never have acted so innocently and naturally. You really impressed Soames, and all of us. We saw who you really are, with your guard entirely down."

"None of you seemed that impressed."

Helen laughed and slapped Eve's rump, then pulled her over, sat astride her hips, and tweaked her nipples. "You were sooo sweeet. I could have gobbled you up then and there." She bent forward and kissed Eve hard.

"But it is deadly serious Helen."

"I know. Shut up! It's time for you to be chastised, you adorable little pixie." Eve gave up and complied, with rather more enthusiasm than she felt was appropriate, given that the fate of the universe hung in the balance. But she wasn't going to be anyone's pixie bitch for too long and, having drained Helen's enthusiasm for domination to the point of exhaustion, took the opportunity to finish on top with an unexpected crescendo of inventive love making, that took them both by surprise.

Helen lay gasping. "If I'd known fucking a deity was so mind blowing, I would have spent much more time in church praying vigorously for holy intervention. You've wrung out every drop of me Eve, and yet I'm still gurgling down there for more."

"You don't do so badly for a frail human. Why do you think I'm still in bed? My legs are like rubber. I can't stand up."

"Mmm, yes, well I think we'll keep that bit a secret. Your athleticism was amazing though, even for you. We can blame the wreckage on your somnolent early morning fitness regime. Hey! Guess what? I think I'm ready again; get over here! You don't have to stand up, just open those, oh so bendy, rubber limbs … mmm."

Healing Soames's heart hadn't been going so well, and Eve had brought in Freddy and a few monks, to add some ritual to the proceedings. "The problem Soames isn't promoting recovery though, God knows, that is proving difficult enough, it's that the heart is an internal organ. When I healed Helen's hand, I only had to get attuned, and that wasn't all that difficult, being as we were virtually in each other's skin, and minds too, at the time. I just kind of encouraged the healing process to full speed and potential. All infection and waste exited the wound, and dropped away, or was absorbed into the blood stream and filtered out. But you have a big piece of dead heart in there, and nowhere for the waste to go. I can't do anything with dead tissue, and I certainly don't want to disturb it in any way. Toxins and clots might kill off the rest of your heart, and you in the process. I've thought about trying to bypass the dead area, and regrow a new bit, but I don't like the idea of a dead piece of organ sitting inside you, still attached by ruined blood vessels. It could work, but I want better. There is something spiritual about the heart, and I can't think having a dead lump of it in your chest is going to help you to be the best you can be."

Soames sighed in exasperation. "We're only trying to prolong my life Eve, not make me into superman."

"Not good enough I'm afraid. You are my friend now, and I am damn well going to do the best I can for you. I have an idea. It is risky but so is everything. I want to use the shards. My main worry is that Afsoon will become aware of what I am doing and may try to interfere. I want to summon up the complete image again. I don't think that will necessarily alert Afsoon, it didn't before. But using it probably will. I may have a way around that however. It is bone freezingly scary, but what isn't these days? And I don't know what will happen, but it is going to have to be tried sooner or later, and sooner is better if we want to stay ahead of the game. I've discussed this with Freddy, and while he isn't entirely happy," she looked across at Freddy "he is giving it his support."

Freddy gave Soames a nod but couldn't disguise his worried frown. "This will be dangerous for Eve, Soames, but also for you. Maybe you should think carefully before you agree."

He sounded hopeful, but Soames had picked up on all the nuances. "No. I trust Eve on this and your judgement too. If she is willing to risk herself, then I will accept her guidance. Caution hasn't always been my friend."

"Okay Soames, I've told you about the sixth shard, which projects each way from the centre of the pentagram image, so more of a dilating axle really. I think I mentioned that it seems to swallow sight. Perhaps I should have said second sight. And that is the point. If I am close enough to it, I don't think Afsoon will be able to divine what I am up to. Unfortunately, that is also the crunch, I have a creepy feeling in my gut, that it isn't only sight it will swallow, so I am going to have to be extremely careful how close I get. It has to be close enough to hide me from Afsoon, but not so close that I can't get out. Freddy has suggested that I take Helen in with me, not too far, but enough that I know of her presence there, close to normal space, to act as a sort of beacon to help me find my way back. I'm not entirely happy about that, but Helen was never going to sit on the side lines. She is part of this now, and I have to accept she is going to take risks like the rest of us. The truth is I wouldn't have it any other way. It is one of the many reasons I love her. When death catches up with us this time around, we will know we faced it together, on all sides, as partners. I think we could both accept, even the death of the other, knowing that we went out fighting, and covering each other's back to the end, rather than the in-looking fear of parting, and of trying to survive what I experienced as John. We know how strong each of us is, and that we can both fall back on that strength. And I think Soames, that I am beginning to understand that I can say that about all of my friends here too, of which you are now one."

Eve was nervous. The dark shard had been calling to her ever since she had seen it, and she hoped that was not her true motivation for dragging Soames into the unknown, and putting Helen at risk. She thought not, but the forces she kept encountering were both awesome and subtle, she couldn't be sure. Either way she knew she had to keep probing them. Even with all that she had learned so far, and the abilities she had acquired, and was learning to use, she could not escape the feeling that Afsoon knew more, and could take her out, if he weren't trapped a billion miles away. She had to be ready when he came. The slab in the cavern seemed colder than usual. She laid blankets for Soames and Helen on either side of her, but shuffled herself naked into the body shaped depression, with nothing separating her from the obsidian rock. Ben, touchingly, placed her shorts and top over her torso and pelvis. His presence bolstered her spirits. And it was comforting to see that Emmaline seemed equally protective of Helen. Eve grasped the hand of Soames on her left and Helen on her right, and gave a convulsive shiver. And then, to her surprise, the rest of her disciples filed in, and her heart leapt, "Bless you Freddy."

She lay back and waited to absorb the incense and the moonlight. At the appropriate time she summoned the shards. Her mind became one with the chanting. A single torpid thought meandered through the cadence, trying to rise through the clamour. Then, as the incense struck, it exploded, and she with it, and she was back in solar space.

Helen looked around in awestruck wonder. "Oh Eve, it is beyond imagination ..."

"I must leave you now. You have Emmaline's hand?"

"Yes."

"Don't let go of it. Can you see the pentagram?"

"Yes but you never said how beautiful it was, how beautiful you are."

"Can you see the dark shard?"

"No. Just a hole in the middle, stars on the other side, and right in the centre, the Earth."

"Really? Okay. Imagine a black bar passing through that hole, stretching and dilating into infinity on both sides. Then you will understand my movements as I try to circle it and go closer. I may disappear from sight or fade. If I do holler, I might hear you."

As Eve drifted away with an unconscious Soames in tow, Helen felt the space around her grow bone chillingly cold. An exclamation was involuntarily forced from her lungs, and the frozen "oh!" of her breath hung in the space before her; she began to shiver with increasing violence. Eve seemed to glide over the imaginary bar, and then drop over the far side, and to jump down through space to a point, just below where the bottom of the bar might be. She then came up normally on what would be this side. She repeated this manoeuvre several times, inching closer on each circuit. She moved away a little, and left Soames floating. She then went close again and started to fade.

Helen screamed a warning but there was no sound. Eve became amorphous, and was barely discernible, and then was gone. An age seemed to pass. Then a hand reached out and pulled Soames closer. He faded too, and Helen was truly alone, and so cold. Sometime later, Soames reappeared with Eve pushing him out and looking around. Eve's upper torso emerged, and took on more form, but her lower body remained cloudlike. She seemed to be struggling. Helen screamed again, soundlessly. But Eve seemed to hear and launched Soames towards her. Movement was so difficult in the numbing cold, but Helen managed to grab his arm and hold on. Then suddenly Eve broke free, and was swimming toward her, but on a trajectory that would have missed her completely. Helen screamed again. Still nothing came out. Eve was now on a level with Helen, about to pass her, but thousands of feet away. Then her head tilted left, as though she strained to hear something beyond hearing, the trace of an echo of Helen's scream perhaps. She stopped, and scanned the space around her, then peering, as though through fog, she came to a decision, and headed straight for them. Frantically, she grabbed at, and clasped, both Helen's and Soames's hands, and sent them spinning, but with her touch, all the warmth returned. "Get us out of here Helen. I haven't the strength."

"I don't know how."

"Just pull on Emmaline's hand."

Emmaline was looking down on Helen, with deep concern etched into the lines of her pale face. A sudden powerful yank almost tore her off her feet. Snatched from her body, she glimpsed the entirety of a universe, and thought she would fall forever. But Janie had a firm grip of her, and pulled her back, Matt pulling on Janie. Helen gasped, and instantly rolled over to check on Eve, who to all intents, seemed to be sound asleep and lightly snoring. Matt checked Soames over. He seemed fine, but also sleeping.

Eve rolled over in bed, stretched, looked out at the panorama of the valley, and gave a contented sigh. Ben came into view. "Hi Mum."

Eve smiled. "I'll go and fetch Helen."

The door clicked quietly shut, and then open again shortly after. Helen entered with two steaming mugs of tea and sticky buns. She placed the items on the bedside table, kicked off her shoes, and ushered Eve over so she could slip in beside her.

"Ahh sticky buns. Where on earth did you conjure them up from? I've missed them so much."

"You're not the only one with magical powers. Give me a kitchen and, abracadabra, I can rustle up almost anything if I've a mind to, especially with a troop of kitchen staff to do my bidding. Do you know you've been asleep for two days?"

"Mmmm, wonderful." She bounced up onto her rump, and then crawled over Helen for the goodies. Realising she was ravenous, she crammed the first bun in her mouth. Sloshed a mouthful of tea and reached for the second.

"Get off me you oaf. You're dripping tea and crumbs all over me. Here let me … You've got icing all over your face." She licked a napkin and started to wipe off the icing. Eve let her hand drop and smeared the bun across her naked breast. Then she raised her fingers to her lips and said breathily. "Oh dear. Look what I've done now ..."

Helen stretched, arched her back, rotated her feet and wriggled her toes ecstatically. She turned to Eve with a look of consternation. "John? You're a slut!"

Eve walked out of the shower. "How is Soames getting on?"

"Still asleep far as I know."

"Good, best thing for him. Who else is in the enclave at the moment?"

Helen frowned in thought. "Freddy of course, Ben, Matt, Janie and Emmaline. Fadil and Jackie both left last night."

"That'll do. How do you fancy a picnic?"

"Wonderful. There's a lovely spot near a waterfall, where the river drops down in pooled steps, deep enough for a swim."

Eve sat on a log lost in thought. Matt came and sat next to her. "It's great to see you looking so relaxed Eve."

"It's great to feel so relaxed Matt. No matter what happens in the future. I will count myself lucky to have had this time among all the people I love." She placed a hand over his. "You know I could never have come this far without you Matt, thank you for being there ... and for staying here with me."

"Always Eve, I think I can safely say that for all of those here, and for those absent." There was a short silence, and then Matt heaved a breath and spoke again. "I'm not sure whether I should raise this just now, but we have guests, somewhat reluctant guests, but guests all the same. Janie's people picked them up at the escarpment that gives access to the plateau leading here. Probably as well she got to them before they entered the black priest territory. Your priests can be aggressively protective."

"Oh? Tell me more."

"CIA operatives, I've had my eye on them for some time. They got interested in your activities in the Sargasso. And, even though you were reported missing presumed dead, they decided to continue investigations. I think it was Soames's involvement that made them suspicious. Fortunately it was not given a high priority, so they were given autonomy and a limited budget, to see what they could come up with. I don't think anything has been reported back to date that will generate further involvement. But that is only because we have intercepted their latest reports, and now have them under house arrest. If we keep them too long though, some-one will come looking."

"Where are they now?"

"Back at the enclave, they have been allocated a suite of rooms, under the watchful eye of some of Janie's best."

"That can't be too pleasant for them. Send word and invite them here. Let's see if we can't get to know them. Maybe we can be friends. Have you brought your guitar? That was a skill you kept quiet from me. You play wonderfully ..."

Helen and Eve were lounging near the water's edge listening to Matt play. Freddy, Janie, Emmaline and Ben, were knocking about a shuttlecock, and a couple of priests in shorts and t-shirts, were tending the barbecue when four horses reined in at the edge of the clearing, and a male and female dismounted, followed by two of Janie's guards.

Eve stood and approached them. She offered her hand. "Please? We would love you to join us. We have beer or rum punch, and you can help yourselves to any food. I think you already know Matt, Freddy and Janie." She pointed to each of the others in turn and introduced them. Sit with us for a while and tell us all about yourselves and your mission here."

Looking bemused, they came and sat on the grass with the others, but gave Janie a suspicious look when she joined them. "You know you can't keep us here, don't you?"

"I'm sorry. Alan isn't it? We could, but that would not be nice. You are free to go whenever you wish, but we would like you to spend some time with us. You have come a long way, and I'm sure you would like to know more about us too."

"Will you let us report back to our superiors?"

"Not while you remain with us Carla, but when you choose to go, we will drop you at a destination of your choice with any equipment you brought with you, and it is then up to you what you do. But we would prefer you didn't involve your organisation any further and hope you will decide not to. That is your call though, not ours."

"And you expect us to believe that?"

"I expect nothing, but please forgive me if I hope for much. I have a lot to say to my friends here just now, and you are welcome to listen in if you wish, although you may well think it is the ramblings of a mad woman. If you stay long enough maybe we can convince you otherwise, but, like I said, that's your call."

Matt played some more, and Helen put her head in Eve's lap. Eve watched Carla wander over to the water. Her right arm was in a sling. She was cradling it in her left and appeared to be in some pain.

"Excuse me Helen." She gently raised Helen's head, and wriggled out. "I need to speak to our guest." Wiping her hands on her shorts, she wandered over, and stood next to Carla, looking into the pool. "Beautiful isn't it? I wish I had more time to come here and just think."

"You're very young ..." Eve waited until she spoke again. "To be the leader of such a ... what exactly is it, an army, a business empire, a terrorist cult?"

"My friends would call it a church. I don't really like that title much, but as we have taken to calling them disciples, and as we have also set up places of worship around the globe, I can't really avoid the description, but it is really about protecting the planet, and helping everyone to achieve their potential."

"A cult then."

"If you like, but definitely not a terrorist one, and our intentions are good, stay and listen to what I have to say. You will probably see it as confirmation of your suspicions, but I hope you will be open minded enough to stay and explore further what we have to offer. What happened to your arm? Not anything our guys did I hope?"

"Well yes, it was actually, compound fractures. I suppose it was my fault. I was fool enough to pull a gun on your head of security, that Janie bitch! I've never seen anyone move so fast, broke my arm in two places, radius and ulna. Your guys did a great job of putting it back together and plastering it. But they are worried I will never have full use of it again, so am I."

"Painful?"

"What do you think?"

"Let me see."

She managed to raise the arm a little towards Eve.

"What are you going to do, kiss it better? Hey! What the fuck!" Carla never saw her hands move, before Eve had ripped the plaster in two.

"You don't need this!" Eve gripped the wound in her two hands, squeezed and let go. "Go on make a fist. Strike me if you like." Carla was thunderstruck but did as she was told and made a fist, then flexed her fingers, and looked wide-eyed over at Alan. Alan had been watching their conversation closely and still hadn't managed to close his mouth. The rest of the group were also looking, and although surprised, seemed to just take it in their stride.

The sun had set, and the guys had raked back the shingle to create a fire pit, and placed logs around to sit on, and to shield it from the evening breeze. The glow of the full moon did little to diminish the starlit sky. And the cicadas, and mixed scents of exotic flora, made the coming of night a magical experience. If a centaur had come to lay down among them, it is likely that everyone would have just shuffled up to give it room. Eve got up from her place by the fire and went to sit on a log. Matt put his guitar to one side, and everyone stopped talking to listen. Eve looked at her feet for an uncomfortably long moment, then took a deep breath, raised her head, and began to speak in a low, but eerily bewitching, contralto. "You all know I have been trying to heal Soames's heart." Both Alan and Carla leaned forward at the mention of Soames. "And you were all present at the ritual when I entered into that other place. Soames will remember nothing of this, but Helen came part way with me, and I think Emmaline got a glimpse when she pulled us out." Emmaline nodded, but kept her lips tight shut and said nothing. Eve looked at Freddy. "How long was I gone?"

"Two hours, or as near as …"

"It felt like weeks, or maybe years, to me. Helen could not see what I saw. She saw a hole in the centre of the pentagram filled with stars, and the Earth at its centre. I saw a dark core filling that hole and stretching out to infinity on both sides. I believe that core to be the Earth in its metaphysical form. Science would have us believe that the Earth is an insignificant dot on the outer arm of our galaxy. I believe it is the densest thing in the whole of multi-dimensional space. They talk of super black holes at the centre of galaxies that could swallow everything, and yet the Earth is being thrown away from that centre in the continuing explosion of the big bang. Why? Because it is not an explosion, these things are keeping their distance for fear of being sucked into the vortex of the dimensional density that is our planet.

"Earth is insignificant of itself. It is tiny. But it is the fulcrum of existence. If the forces that impinge on it do not stay in balance, everything collapses. If any one of those forces accrues too much gravity, too much power, or too much energy, the balance is lost, and we all cease to exist. To all intents, our planet is God, and all those forces and powers want a piece of it, want to control it, want to feel the sheer power of being fully cognizant. No longer nebulous entities, with thoughts flowing and ebbing in the sea of infinity, but solid beings with coherent minds, able to act in a solid environment. The closer they get, the more they are able to act and influence existence. And they are constantly trying to force open a back door, to come in and seize control. What stops them is a shield, the pentagram, the turbulence around the eye of the storm. It is, I suppose, like the consciousness of a subconscious earth, acting for, and protecting its core being, so that life and creation can flourish.

"There are other existences along the axle of that core. Ours is the densest, and so I think it can be called reality, but those in close proximity are lesser realities, almost as dense as ours. They are possible alternatives. The further from the core centre you go, the more chaotic, unstable, and magical these realities become. I found a teacher to show me how to heal in one such, and I brought in Soames to receive the benefit of his knowledge and ability. But these existences are some of the doors I spoke of. They draw you in. They want your reality, because it gives force to theirs. Stay too long, or get too close, and the balance shifts. First it is hard to remember the way out, or to take that route if you find it. Leave it too long, or get too close to the core, and all is lost. You are swallowed up, and reality has shifted. Balance is disturbed. These are things of a magnitude beyond imagining, and we are so small, yet we are so significant because we sit at the centre of everything. Even our efforts, miniscule as they are, can shift the balance enough to crack a door, or to push it to, if we can but see where it is, and how to push it, which brings us back to our old friend Afsoon ..."

Gathering Disciples

"How are you feeling Soames?"

"Good Eve. I don't look any younger, but I feel vibrant and more alive than I have for years. I was thinking of attempting the cliff face across the valley. I haven't been able to climb for so long. Care to join me?"

"Another time perhaps, I take it Freddy has brought you up to date on everything. How are you getting on with protecting all your computers and technology? I really think he intends to force us back into the Iron Age. If he is able to maintain his own technology whilst destroying ours, we are lost. And he is devising so many ways to attack us."

"I've been giving this a lot of thought. I confess I went to Jackie for some ideas, and as usual, she came up with what should have been obvious to us all. The fact is, we may not be able to keep our technology safe. So as you inferred, we need to mount a similar attack on his, as soon as possible. That said, if both sides are successful, we need to prepare for a world devoid of technology. Freddy, Matt and I have been in talks with Janie. She is looking at teaching ancient battle skills to her strike forces, swordsmanship, catapults, ballistas, Greek fire, battering rams and the like. Matt and Emmaline are studying ancient war craft and strategy. Jackie is looking at farming and food preserving methods, and is arranging food storage facilities. Helen is researching methods of health, medicine and surgical skills delivery; but really she needs to be at your side, in any venture you are considering, or rather 'you need her' at your side. You are always stronger when she is near. Ben, surprisingly, is assisting us in looking into energy sources, and is making an equally surprisingly good job of it. Both mine and Freddy's research teams and resources are at their disposal. Fadil continues to promote your church with Jackie's helpful PR initiatives, incredibly subtle little lady that one."

"This is all good Soames, but I know you have been tracking the projected course of Afsoon's pod. Do you still intend to try and destroy it?"

"Given your discoveries, I am putting that on hold for now, but I can't escape the feeling that letting him set foot on this planet is a mistake."

"I have been agonising about that myself. What if we try to direct his landing location to a place of our choosing? Or at least predict where it will land."

Soames thought on that for a few moments. "If we can prepare adequately, it might give us an edge. But he will know we are going to try and trap him. He will be prepared and may spring a counter trap. And what are we going to do with him if we do succeed? If he really is a necessary part of the shield, he would not be an easy prisoner to keep, and we don't know how long that would need to be for, forever for all we know."

"Bear with me on that, I have sort of an idea of what to do with him, if we can bring him under our control. There's also a very long shot possibility on how that might be achieved too. Both are near suicidal, so I need to think long and hard on how to approach it, but I can't see any other options at the moment. As soon as I have the bones of a plan, I will let you and the 'other disciples' know."

Soames didn't bite at that, and Eve smiled inwardly. "How are our two guests working out?"

"Still here at any rate. With Matt's permission I let them send a placating report to their mission manager. Couldn't detect any coded messages, and as no one has come looking, I am hopeful. I think you impressed them with your healing abilities, but mainly, I suspect they want to observe you and your followers, and find out all your secrets before they bring in the big guns."

"What do you know about them?"

"Misfits as far as the CIA are concerned. Loose cannons, tend to do their own thing, but very creative, and they get results."

"Hmm, they sound perfect. Maybe I should talk to them again. Do you think you might find them a job to do? Perhaps Matt or Janie could put them to good use."

"Questionable strategy, but I will see what I can do."

"Do they know you well Soames?"

"As well as CIA case files have me documented, and I suppose that depends on their clearance levels. It would have to be quite high to get anything worthwhile."

"But they would probably know your medical history."

"I see where you are going with this. I'll invite them both to accompany me on that climb. It will be a good chance to discuss with them if they are interested in working with us. As it would put them on the inside, I expect they will agree." He made to leave, but Eve again forestalled him with a hug, and enjoyed his embarrassed "harrumph" as he disengaged himself.

Eve debated over the best approach, but in the event decided to invoke her John persona, and invited them to an evening of pool, darts and drinking games with the disciples and a few of the priests. The women challenged the men, and reckoned they won everything, but so did the men, and by that time everyone was too drunk to care. They took a few crates and went outside to get a bonfire going and carried on. Someone suggested a midnight swim and a race across the pond. Unfortunately, there was so much cheating and ducking, no one could tell who won that either. But the exercise and cold water relaxed their spirits, and they settled more quietly around the fire, sipping their drinks. Matt played, and several of them sang. Something powerful stirred in Eve. She stepped into the circle and sang a haunting folk melody in a forgotten language from another time. It was bewitching and trance inducing. Everyone was spellbound. As the melody started to take on more strident tones, she looked up at the stars, and swung her arms in a wide arc. Ghostly shards appeared in each of her hands, and a false, rich, golden daylight descended on the area around them for as far as they could see. Lush woodland, abounding with shimmering streams and heavy scented flora, surrounded the standing stones which now circled them, and creatures from legend walked from the forest to join them by the fire. Carla was startled to be nudged by a unicorn settling down beside her. Pipes played discordant and hypnotic harmonies, and some of the half human creatures started to dance. A young elfin girl stepped forward and held out a hand to Alan. Just at that moment, the ground split open with a thunderous roar. A giant horned horseman clambered out, swept the poor little screeching thing onto its saddle with a clawed grip, and disappeared back into the fiery pit from whence it came. The woodland creatures scattered in all directions. The spell was broken, and the pre-dawn dark descended to refill their little meadow. Absent now, of any but themselves, it, and the world, seemed colourless and threadbare, and a lonely and desolate place to be.

Eve asked Carla and Alan to accompany her on the walk back. "You have been with us a little while now. What conclusions have you drawn? Are we terrorists bent on world domination, or a dangerous cult of religious fanatics, also bent on 'world domination' or even, annihilation? Or is it possible that you think (she drew a circle in the air in front of Alan's forehead and plunged her finger into it), somewhere deep down in your psyche, that we are trying to save the world, and help humanity to survive and evolve, and may even have the capability of developing the means to do it?"

Carla puffed out her cheeks. "You don't believe in chit chat, do you?"

"I am afraid the threat is too big and the time too short for that."

"Some show you put on back there, lady. I reckon casting illusions like that could be a dangerous weapon in the hands of the wrong people."

"That's an interesting idea Alan. I take it Soames has spoken to you? Perhaps it would interest you to work with Janie on developing that."

"Oh yeah, the FBI bitch. Seems like you want to poach operatives from all our organisations."

"Yes I do, especially guys with the sort of initiative you two have shown. We need every dynamic and original thinker we can get. And you should get to know Janie. She can be a bit of a bully, but I can assure you she is no bitch. If you can make a friend of her, you will be a lucky man indeed, but you could equally well work with Matt or Soames. If you have an open mind and enough imagination, you might even find working with Freddy would suit you. What I would also like, is to not have to deal with your government breathing down our necks. We have enough obstacles to overcome as it is. I would like you to help me with that but ..." she shrugged, "I guess that is up to you."

"How do you do that healing thing? All our records indicate that Soames is on death's doorstep, yet he climbed the cliff over the valley like an athlete, and my arm ..." She raised it, twisting it this way and that and flexing her fingers.

"And there's the problem that separates us. I'm not sure I can overcome it. I'm afraid it is down to faith in what you see and choose to believe. You've witnessed my healing abilities, and my summoning of another reality. You have doubtless noted how fast I am, and I would bet that you have a thousand, probably unsubstantiated theories about my past and where I come from. If seeing really is believing, then perhaps in time, I can win you over, but not everyone has the ability to see what is right in front of them. If it helps, I can tell you I am not superwoman. Soames, ill as he then was, bested me, and he is not the only one. I desperately needed him though, and still need people like you, to help us to save the future."

"Are you the policewoman in London who had her nose cut from her face?" This unexpected comment dropped like a mortar shell behind Eve's defences. For a moment the history of those events swept over her like a tidal wave, and she was back there, enduring the pleasure of Sadique and his men. Her knees gave out, and she staggered, grasping at Carla for support. Alan was instantly behind her to stop her falling.

"I guess that answers that question, and frankly, if you are her, then whatever Alan decides, I will come on board, for now at least."

Alan grunted. "I guess I can come on too, provisionally anyway. It's going to be a rough ride though, creating a credible story to keep our current masters off your back."

Eve was now sat on a rock shaking, and for the moment couldn't speak. She managed to squeak out "I'm sorry" but her voice cracked, and she had to gather herself for a full minute before she could talk again, and still could not stop the tears welling from her eyes. "I … I really am sorry. That has never happened before. I guess whenever I have had to revisit those memories, I have done it guardedly, and at my own pace. I've never had it thrown in my face like that before."

"No apology needed. You plainly don't realise what a hero you are to half the women on the planet. We were all devastated when we heard of your death. If they knew you were alive and where to sign up, you would probably have millions queuing at the foot of your plateau, to swear their allegiance to your cause."

"Yeah, I reckon a fair number of men would probably be in that queue."

Alan squatted in front of Eve, and quite tenderly, dabbed at her tears with his shirt tail. "Thank you Alan, I ... I think I will be okay now. Thank you both. It is awful knowing how vulnerable I can still be, that I can be disabled with just a few words."

"I think it shows humanity, and the kind of strength that makes people want to follow. Don't ever lose that."

Eve smiled. "You have done me an immense service Carla, and you too Alan. I am so afraid of losing my humanity. Soames among others has often caused me to doubt it."

During the rest of the walk back, Eve showed them some of the secret places she had found to go to when she wanted to think, and explained the different types of flora, and the fauna that frequented the area, and also explained a little of the folklore and traditions of the black priests.

Eve lay with her head in Helen's lap. "I have to go back in there Helen. I can't see any other option. We need metaphysical defences and weapons to withstand the dark forces gathering against us. The trouble is I am terrified of what I must do. I seem to blunder from one nightmare into another, and I'm not sure how much more I can take. I just want to slither into the nearest dark hole where I can sob out my shame and shit myself, until I dissolve in my own excrement."

"Stop feeling sorry for yourself Eve! You are not the only one in this you know. If you have to go back in there, I'm coming with you."

"No you can't! Definitely not! It's impossible. You wouldn't survive."

"Why not! You took Soames in and he came out better than before."

"He was comatose and had no experience of the weird and mind twisting forces prevalent there. Even so, it took all of my strength to get him and myself out. I nearly died in there Helen. Lost souls clung to me like limpets. Demons sunk talons into my feet. They know Helen. They sense the power of the reality in us, and they want it for themselves. It was only knowing you were there waiting that drove me on."

Helen's voice softened. "Then how much more will you be

driven when I am there with you?"

Eve sat up and gripped Helen's shoulders. "Helen, you don't understand. It is your very soul that will be at risk."

Helen pushed her hands away. "Will? You see, you have already accepted it. You know I would have it no other way. I will not have you risk your very existence, while I lie easy in my bed. And besides, if you don't come back, we are all lost anyway. Wherever you go I will be with you. Into oblivion if I have to."

Eve heaved a massive sigh. "It may well come to that Helen."

Helen placed her hands on Eve's shoulders, and pressed her back onto the bed, then rolled on top and straddled her neck. She looked down on her, "Now shut up! If you must go slithering into holes, I happen to have one or two handy ..."

When Eve and Helen presented their intentions, Janie threw a fit: she was having none of it. In the face of their determination she eventually agreed, but insisted, "If they must go on this insane mission into the unknown, then they must have combat training first, both ancient and modern, and preferably be accompanied by herself, and one or two others at least." Eve mastered the new skills with ease. Helen, whose vigour had seemed to grow with each passing day since cohabiting with Eve, was a good student, showing particular skill as a swordswoman with light to medium blades, and not so bad with a bow. Ben was like a dynamo, and never stopped training. He was soon a master of any blade or shield, and had a good working knowledge of unarmed combat, which was wonderfully enhanced by his own street skills. No one even considered denying his place beside Eve. They decided on two more. To her great disappointment, Janie was rejected as being too important in her current role. Freddy put himself forward. He was already skilled in martial arts and weaponry, but more important, he had more mystical knowledge than anyone else. Soames was up to speed on most of their current research and projects, and could hold the fort until their return, which it was hoped, would be soon coming. Having glimpsed the universe already, Emmaline was reluctant, but also insistent, that she go wherever Helen went. This did not please Janie, but she had to admit she was the perfect choice.

Freddy brought together a powerful conclave of priests, who were skilled artisans in the mystic arts, and had them working night and day to create a powerful beacon and link into the access and egress points of the alternative realms. Eve drew the companions together, and tried to describe what they might encounter, which was literally anything, but her own experiences, however difficult to relate, would, she hoped, give a flavour of what to expect. Having listened to Eve for a while, Ben came forward with what proved to be a brilliant and innovative suggestion. His idea was to use hallucinatory drugs to induce experiences of altered reality. Freddy suggested that Eve might even be able to influence some of the visions, to reflect her own experiences, if she could still recall how she had summoned the vision in the valley glade. He supplied LSD, Mescaline, Jimson Weed, Peyote, and various other cocktails of drugs, plus a skilled expert in their use and dosages. One or two bad trips were experienced, but these were managed well, and were likely the best learning curve possible for those involved.

Other Worlds

The temple was painstakingly prepared and sanctified by Freddy and a cohort of skilled priests. As the trance-inducing chants began an ill wind gusted into the chamber. Candle flames were disturbed or extinguished. Fine hairs at the base of necks were lifted. Sweat dripped chests and clammy hands were frozen with frost. The five sat cross legged on the altar, and resolutely linked hands. Eve was becoming adept at these transitions now. She summoned the ghost shards, and Freddy lent force and direction to her efforts to open the way. They quickly plunged into solar space, and were descending on what, to Eve, was a black dilating core at the centre of a vast silver bright pentagram. The others saw the pentagram, but only the earth occupied the hole at its centre and star filled space beyond, except Freddy who thought he could make out a faint and shadowy aura. The priests had constructed a small sun in the ethereal space where the five entered and were ready to run shifts to maintain it. This tiny star sang with a high pitched and continuous note, that set teeth on edge, and followed the companions' right up to the darkness of the core. Eve moved them away from the earth, through the orbit of Mars, and descended slowly through the orbital path of Jupiter, into the void of the sixth shard.

There was a sudden uprush of warm air as they fell through a scarlet sky filled with smoke and the sounds of cannon fire, then a bone juddering impact as they hit the hard surface of a dark and choppy sea. Splintered wood flew from the side of a ship as a cannon ball ripped through its timbers, just above the waterline. The force of the fall when they hit had split them apart and sent them deep into the murky depths. They were all gagging on salt water, as they made for the surface. Helen didn't know which way was up, but a steel grip closed on her wrist, and she was ripped upwards to the surface, and thrown through the hole in the ship, into the stinking hold below decks. Ben was already clinging to the edge of the hole, with Emmaline's collar fast in the grip of his other hand. Eve boosted him in after Helen, and he hauled Emmaline in, whilst Eve raced off to assist Freddy, swimming hard towards them. Boarding planks had been dropped to the gun rails, and an army of cut throats, wielding strange blades and clubs, were swarming aboard. Emmaline had thrown up a gut full of water, but was already being assisted to her feet by Helen, and seemed to be recovering quickly. A hard-fought battle was raging above.

Eve looked at the companions, turned up her hands, and shrugged. "Ideas anyone?"

Ben drew a vicious looking scimitar from the scabbard at his back. "I say we join the fight and repel the boarders. We might make some allies, or at worst, have only a weakened crew to face, if they turn on us."

"I see five pirate ships, or at least that's what I assume they are, and only three flying the colours of our would-be allies. One of the other two is putting up a good fight, but I think the third is nearly done for. Could be we're throwing in with the wrong crowd."

"Yeah but the one still fighting is the flag ship. This hole is well enough above the water line. I reckon if we repel, and cut and run, they'll leave us, and concentrate on the bigger prize. I don't know about you, but this lot look a bit more civilised to me."

Eve looked at the others, and they all nodded consent. They raced for the ladders and made their way aloft. The deck was a sorry sight. Three quarters of the, roughly eighty strong, crew were lying on the deck, dead or seriously injured amongst a slightly lesser number of the pirates. The remaining crew were fighting amidships on two fronts. Eve hit the pirates from behind, in a whirl of double blades, slicing a path toward the nearest boarding plank. Ben was on her heels guarding her back. Emmaline, Freddy and Helen, fought their way forward towards the beleaguered crew. By the time the pirates realised they were being attacked from behind, Eve had tipped three planks, and those still on them, into the sea, and was making her way to the last. The crew seeing that reinforcements had arrived fought with more vigour, and half joined with the three, clearing the decks of the pirates on that flank, then turned their attention to the remaining flank that Ben and Eve had just reached with devastating shock effect, and were now carving a path to the ship's wheel. Ben took the wheel and adjusted their course to catch the cross wind. Eve guarded his back, maintaining a clear arc within slash and thrust reach of both sword hands.

By the time they had lost sight of the death throes of the flag ship, the five or so remaining boarders were fought into a corner where they were killed or injuriously disabled. Dead pirates were thrown into the sea, and the crew were now seeing to the wounded. One blue uniformed and bloodied sailor with insignia on his shoulders approached the five now clustered around the wheel. He fixed his gaze on Ben. "Who and what are you, that you come to the aid of strangers and separate us from our comrades at arms in the midst of deadly battle? Where did you come from, and how did you get here? One of my men says he saw you fall from the sky. Are you from Olympus in answer to our prayers, or from Hades to ferry our souls into the underworld? In truth the course you have set seems to favour the latter."

Eve and the others remained silent and formed in two pairs, facing the officer with Ben at their centre. Ben thought he knew Eve's mind and acted on initiative. "Neither! We were prisoners and jumped ship when you were engaged. We figured enemies of our captors were friends of ours. We could see you were outnumbered and overrun. Your other ships were lost already. We apologise if you wished to die in a futile rescue attempt. We took what we felt was the most expedient action to save you and ourselves. If we did you wrong, you have our deepest apologies. Should we turn the ship and re-engage? We apologise too if our course is ill chosen. We are not sailors, and do not know these seas."

"You show remarkable skill for someone with no knowledge of sailing, but we are grateful for your intervention and we are in your debt. May I request however, that you alter our course by at least 35 degrees? You are currently set fair to take us through the ill-fated seas that separate us from the edge of the world. When that is done, and with your permission, my man will take over. I would be honoured if you and your warriors would join me in the captain's cabin. He having taken a fatal injury in the battle, the dubious distinction of running this ship falls to me, until a replacement can be found."

"You have a large hole amidships that will need attending to."

"Fortunately, our carpenter survived the battle and is already assessing repairs, but thank you for your concern. My immediate disquiet, however, relates to our reduced crew and the wounded. Most are dead, but we have one of our own still living. Alas we are not the flag ship and have no skilled healer on board. Our surgeon is preparing to amputate. I think he is wasting his time, but we must try. There are two Gargans also near death. We are trying to question them, but they are incoherent. As that seems to be their normal state of cognizance, it is unlikely we will get anything from them before they die, but you need not worry yourself on that front."

Eve leaned toward Ben and whispered in his ear.

"My companion has some skill with healing, and requests she be allowed to assist with the wounded."

"Why not? She can do no harm and may do some good. She can join us later."

Eve managed to forestall the surgeon's first cut, just as he was breaking skin. She pinched his brachial, deadened his arm, and bumped him to the side before he knew what had happened. The wounded man's shattered femur protruded four inches from a gaping wound, just below the cut. His strong thigh muscle had shortened the leg to half its natural length. Eve pointed at the men who had been pinning him to the deck. "You two! Grasp his shoulders and resist my pull." She palm-thrusted the heel of her hand to the back of the screaming man's jaw, rendering him unconscious. Ripping a dead man's belt from his trousers, she formed a figure of eight knot around feet and ankles, and yanked his legs taught until they were evenly stretched, then looped the belt over a dagger she had plunged into the deck, to maintain traction. She fed the bones back into the wound and manipulated the shards to a semblance of their former shape. Calling for good splints, a needle and twine, and strips of material for binding, she spat into the wound, and carefully worked congealed blood and spit around the shattered thigh bone.

The surgeon, somewhat recovered, handed her a vial of medical alcohol. She poured it into the wound, deftly cocooned the bones in the damaged sinew of the tattered flesh, and sewed the wound shut. Then she splinted the leg, and had men nail the splints to the deck, ordering that he should be made comfortable where he was, and not moved until she gave the word. The crew had already dispatched one of the dying Gargans. The other still had a sword buried in his chest. Eve sensed that no vital organs had been pierced, and could feel through the substrates of the spiritual realm exactly how to remove the weapon without further compromising his injuries. She was also able to promote and encourage the healing processes of each damaged cell the blade left in its wake, while she painstakingly withdrew it. She had him strapped to a board and ordered him taken to a secure place of safety, and to be watched but not disturbed, until she had examined him further.

The surgeon was looking at her with awe. He dropped to one knee and placed his forehead on her foot. "Fear not Mistress Magus, I will ensure your wishes are closely adhered to."

Eve sighed heavily and went to join the others. "I will be in the captain's cabin if you need me."

The door was open. She went in, but the cabin was empty, apart from a swinging lamp and a mess of charts cascading from the desk. Eve ran outside. From her high vantage she could see most of the deck, but could see no sign of the others. A sailor with a spy glass stood at the rail of the poop deck over the cabin. She called up. "You up there, where is your captain and my companions?"

The sailor snapped to attention. "Our captain is dead. Are you not our captain now ma'am? Your companions left near an hour past. Your horned leader instructed that you would stay and command."

Eve was up the steps beside him in an instant. "What are you talking about man? Your officer, the one who took over as captain, where is he? And what has he done with my friends?"

The man was looking nervous and confused. "I don't understand ma'am. Our surgeon was preparing to amputate the leg of our only remaining officer when you intervened. The horned one, who came aboard with you, said you would stay in charge. Then he took the rest of your companions on our landing skiff and set off toward the fabled isle."

Eve felt a cold plunge of panic crash into her bladder and bowels. Barely able to stay continent she bellowed at the man. "What! Assemble your crew here ... now! What the fuck are you waiting for? GO!"

The sailor nearly broke his neck leaping down the steps to do her bidding. She stopped him, teetering on the spot, with another bellow. "Wait! Give me your spy glass. What direction did they go? He threw up the spy glass and pointed. "What's your name?" "Aergris, Ma'am."

"Don't stand there like a fucking moron. Go and get the others."

A minute later, the whole of the remaining walking crew, some eighteen or so, stood below Eve. "Right! Who saw the officer who approached us at the wheel?"

A couple raised their hands, Eve pointed. "You! Who was he?"

"I don't know ma'am; we thought he came with you. It was strange that you were led by a horned one, and we weren't happy about it, but you all seemed to obey him."

"Horns! What fucking horns? There were my four companions and your officer, in a blue uniform with insignia on his shoulders."

"Our uniforms are red Ma'am, and the horns curl behind the ears. If you were facing him, you perhaps could not see them."

"There's no time for this! Aergris get up here, I've scanned the horizon and I can't see shit. You mentioned the fabled isle. Where is it? Get your pilot to set a course immediately under full sail. How far is it? They have only a rowing skiff. If they are no more than a couple of hours gone, we should catch them easily."

"I don't know where it is ma'am. It is fabled."

"Are you taking the piss? You said they went in the direction of it, so you must know where the fuck it is."

"No ma'am, I only heard the horned one say that he was taking them there."

"But you saw which direction they went?"

"Yes."

"Then follow, you fucking idiot! The rest of you, get us under full sail, and finish repairing that hole, and any other maintenance that needs doing."

"Begging your pardon ma'am."

"What now Aergris?"

"Even if our direction is good we may not catch them."

Eve answered with exasperated sarcasm, "Why Aergris? Enlighten me."

"The horned one summoned sea serpents to tow them."

The air around Eve was now crackling with static, and Aergris found it difficult not to flinch and cringe. "Jesus Christ. I'm surrounded by fucking idiots." She wracked her brains for some plan of action, anything. "What flying creatures are there in these parts?"

"None would venture this close to the ill-fated seas, except ..."

"Except what? Spit it out man!"

"Well ... fabled creatures ma'am."

"What kind of fabled creatures?"

He hesitated, and Eve forced herself to wait. "Flying serpents ma'am ... dragons."

Eve looked incredulous and aghast. She started pacing the deck, pounding up and down, and mumbling to herself. "Dragons! What is this, a fucking fairy tale?" She paused, speaking to herself. "Well yes ... I suppose it is. It is only a possible reality. None of it is real. It is just dreams. But if dreams are what reality is made on, then perhaps the reverse can be true, Shakespeare thought so didn't he? Especially when five real entities enter into it ... We need to get the fuck out of here and fast. Shit! Shit! Shit!"

She closed her eyes and summoned the ghost shards, then screamed an unearthly call into the night sky that echoed like high pitched thunder, over and over. The sky darkened, and Aergris and the crew scanned the skies in fear. The world seemed to pause, and a giant wave crashed against the side of the ship from the wash of a grizzled head, shoulders, and leathery wings, as they split the surface of the sea nearby. The rest of its serpentine form slithered from the ocean, and its wings beat slowly and rhythmically, as its horse-sized muzzle rested on the gunwale, inches from Eve's coldly calm face. Its irises were golden orbs, containing bottomless black slits that dilated round and hypnotic. Eve withstood the glare, and the creature spoke into the echoing cavern of her mind.

"Who are you that calls the worm from his duties, and stands so fearless in my presence? The heavens and the deeps are my domain, and I can spare no time from them for the insignificant foibles of this unformed world."

Eve didn't know what prompted her to respond in the way that she did, but it seemed right and fitting. "I am Eve, and I am reborn. I am here in this half reality with four others of solid form. I cannot command you, but we share common cause. They must be found and we all must return. The quantum void at the centre of all things is creaking in its readiness to turn. If we do not soon return to shore up and seal its density, reality will tilt, and balance will be lost. All thought and cohesion will be subject to chaos."

"You are almost nothing. I could rip your substance into an infinite number of sub-atomic particles. You have no idea of the vastness and complexity of existence, or of the powers that rage through the universe, yet, in your pathetic arrogance, you speak true. You are indeed the centre on which all things hang. I will take you to your friends, but do not think to ride my magisterial flesh. Summon your own wings. Take on your spiritual aspect."

"I don't know how."

The worm snorted a globule of black pitch onto the deck in disgust. Eve watched as it smouldered. A slim forked tongue flicked out between rows of razor-sharp teeth and split to adhere to each of her temples. It felt to Eve as though a snake slithered down through the darkest reaches of her unconscious mind, jostling every secret thought she had ever had. Never had she felt so invaded. The snake paused, seemed to study a shadow in the dark, and struck, tearing a hole that let in a blinding light of knowledge. Her whole body flexed like an opening fist. Wings sprouted from her back, and her hands and feet became talons. A glowing nimbus emanated from her. Without volition she sprang from the deck and hovered fifteen feet above it.

She called to the cringing crew below. "Aergris you are in command. Go where you will. I will find you if I need you. Don't fail your crew, or me. The surgeon is a good man. Make him your second."

"Come!"

Eve followed the worm. They flew high and fast, and Eve spotted a small boat. "I think that's them."

"They are not your first concern. If you would save them, there is something you must do first. Follow."

Eve was reluctant, but somehow knew the worm was right. "Why can't I save them now?"

"They don't want to be saved now. You must lift the enchantment."

"Where are we going?"

"To the fabled isle, look below."

Eve peered through a hole in the clouds, at an up-thrusting fist of rock, crowned by a castle with a tall and prominent keep. Worm led them down, and they perched on some turrets. "The central keep is the horned one's domain. It is his seat of power. There are deep vaults below, at the centre of a labyrinth. His power is stolen from those imprisoned there. They were masters here once, Magi healers. This world has been denied their presence too long. Free and restore them, and perhaps your friends will be free too, of this puppet of the sleeper."

Eve was lost in her thoughts as to how she could achieve this. That last word jolted her from her reverie. "Sleeper! You mean Afsoon?" But the worm was already just a dot in the sky.

Eve was alone and helpless, and once again, afraid. The world was a churning mass of grey. Sea raked shingle grated in a constant and deafening roar that poured vagueness and confusion into her mind. The wind tugged and nipped, and pressed on her eyes, squeezing bitter tears onto stinging cheeks. There was no sign of the boat. Had she been tricked? What was this place of dreams and part formed reality? Was she real? Was anything real? She held that thought ... Was anything real? ... Part formed reality ... Why, at mention of dragons, did one appear? Perhaps she was the realest thing here. She, and Helen, and the others, were from the centre of all things. The possibilities in this world clung to them for substance, confused and trapped, and held them, and more importantly, separated her from those in whom she found sustenance and support. The damned dragon had nearly succeeded too. Even Helen had faded in her mind. But not anymore: That same worm that had been coiled around the hidden knowledge in her mind, had been torn from its slumber, and made incarnate, to release some of its captured hoard of knowledge. And it had shown her how to manipulate and reform the possibilities of this realm. The static began to crackle around her again. She dismissed the wings and talons but flew anyway, high and straight up like a bullet, then turned and dove straight down through the stone in the towered keep, down and down to the vaults beneath. She recognised the symbols on the cell doors, as parts of the writings from the tunnels mined beneath the temple in the priest's enclave, and they spoke to her in a language that only she, and perhaps Afsoon, understood. She completed each phrase begun in those symbols, and the doors shattered. The physically broken, but still mentally acute occupants, spilled out.

Seeing her stood there, windblown, in the arch of the labyrinth, with static crackling around her, they knelt. All bar one prostrated themselves. Eve spoke to her. "The horned one has misused your power, and he has enchanted some friends of mine. If I set you free, can you lift the spell?"

"If you release us, we can undo him and all the harm he has done. But you are stronger than he. Why do you not destroy him?"

"My use of power reveals me to a creature I would rather keep in ignorance, especially when it concerns those close to me, and I would not give direction to his venom, nor do I know well the workings of this realm."

"Any entity that you fear must be terrible indeed, and we would not want to attract its attention. We will do as you ask and will bring your friends here. It is as safe a place as any, and you and they may stay as long as you wish. We owe you a great debt, and you may always come here for rest or sanctuary. But we must be about our business, before the horned one does more harm."

They had been given rooms at the top of the tower. The servants were jubilant to have their true masters returned, and the companions had all their needs attended to. Eve and Helen occupied the sumptuous apartments hitherto inhabited by the horned one, who had been forced to reveal his name "Valak" by Eve, and which she had shared with the Magi. This distressed him profoundly, as it apparently left him enslaved to them. The Magi understood Eve's companions to be otherworldly, and to themselves, a possible source of self-realisation and completion, but they felt Eve to be of another order again, a deity of sorts, and would at her command, assist them all to leave, even though this meant the loss of something fundamental to their sense of self and being. Eve talked long and hard with them, especially Glitonea, who knew much magical lore, and showed Eve scriptural texts that she had searched for and been unable to find in her own reality. These she understood more fluently than Glitonea herself and committed them to her remarkable memory. Glitonea revealed that their fabled isle, had in earlier times been known as the island of Apples, and took Eve's translation of "Avalon" as seer sight.

"Indeed, that is a holy and secret name, a name of power, known only to the prime Magi who have ruled this isle for millennia."

"In my realm it is said to be surrounded by the waters of other worlds."

"This would fit well in our folklore, for the edge of our world sits just beyond the western horizon. All beyond is mist, but it is said that sometimes the mist clears, and those few souls fool enough to venture there, and the even fewer who have returned say that other worlds or futures can be glimpsed there, among a sea of stars."

"Then I believe that is the place I and my companions must go to leave this world and return to our own realm."

"I, and my brothers and sisters, will do all in our power to help you in your venture. Praise be to you Eve. You will be our Goddess, our lady of the isle."

"When can we go Eve? This place is like treacle. It sticks to you, and I get the feeling that if we stay too long it will set and keep us here forever."

"That is exactly what could happen, but I understand this place better than I did before. It is reality, or creation if you prefer, in the making. Some of what happens here is fully realised in our world. This is the halfway point between heaven and Earth, God's melting pot if you like, and I am able to influence it. Here I can be a magician, a small-time creator. Using that power is fraught with danger I won't deny, but if handled carefully, the possibilities are endless. You are right though, we must leave soon. Glitonea is making preparations for our departure, but I must question Valak some more before we leave. I will do so tomorrow. Freddy and I also need to consult further with Glitonea. There is so much we can learn here." Her tone softened. "And ... I need time to be with

you Helen, time to be in this magical place and to recharge my
batteries, before I face what I know will be the trauma of achieving
an exit from here ... and there is something else ..."

"What? What is it?"

Eve hesitated then blurted it out. "Here ..." She spread her arms
to indicate the entirety of this world. "I can make myself a man
again Helen." Seeing Helen's stony-faced reaction made her want
to snatch back her words, but it was too late, and she blundered on.
"Not for long Helen, but for a night or two ... I could be John
again." She held her breath, waiting for Helen to speak. Eve could
see nothing of the whiplash of emotions twisting and untwisting
behind Helen's fixed stare, but she could see the rigidity of her
muscles, and the sweat forming on her brow, and was already
condemning herself for her own stupidity, in thinking Helen would
want to see again the man who had lied to her, and cheated on her.

Finally Helen managed to regain her self-control, and allowed
her muscles to slump, and dispel the toxins that had backed up,
and were desperately seeking release. Her teeth unclenched and
she spoke calmly. "John is dead! No! That isn't right, John is in
you Eve, and I love him still. I always will. But you are more than
John now. You have developed into something greater. I have
developed too. My love has grown, and it is you that I want, the
whole of you, of which John is a part, but you are so very much
more, and I do not want to see you diminished by resurrecting
your own ghost, and pushing the wonder of Eve into the background, however temporary that might be. No Eve! Never suggest
such a thing ever again."

The companions sat on the terrace of Eve's and Helen's apartments, and drank the excellent wine and ciders provided to them
by the Magi. It was a mellow occasion infused with the relief of
once more being in each other's company. Eve sympathised with
Emmaline who, as a newcomer, had had such a traumatic initia-
tion into their cause.

Emmaline shrugged. "Apart from nearly drowning on our arrival here, and the adrenalin rush of the battle on the ship, I have been
in a numbing fog of unawareness, until your Magi rescued us, and
the time since has really been quite pleasant."

They all nodded their agreement. "But I can't say that I am not
eager to leave."

And the company leaned in to clink glasses to that.

Helen and Eve lay together in bed looking out of the open terrace doors at the starlit sky and listened to the waves crashing below. The night was hot, but a lively and temperamental breeze brought welcome respite and the crisp salt smell of the sea into the shadowed ghost-light of their room. Helen turned towards Eve, and Eve could see the sheen of the moon reflecting off the curve of her raised hip and shoulder. She needed no sight to see the wistful smile that accompanied Helen's low toned words. "Eve …?"

"Yes."

"What you said earlier?"

"Yes."

"Could you just grow a penis?"

Eve was taken aback, but was able to respond. "Well yes, I suppose I could."

"How big?"

"Any size I suppose."

"How long would it take?"

"Pretty much instant I think, maybe a few minutes."

"Mmmm."

"Would you like me to grow a penis?"

"Yes, I think so."

"How big?"

"Do you remember our weapon of mass destruction?"

"That big?"

"Mmmm?"

"Bigger?"

"Maybe a little."

"Do you really think you could handle that much?"

"Mmmm … Not me. You!"

Eve sat up shocked. "You want me to grow a cock on you?"

"Why not? It would only be for a night or two. You said so yourself. What's it like? I've always wondered."

"Helen I … I don't know. I said I would never let a man touch me again."

"But it wouldn't be a man. It would be me, and I would still have all my bits. And after, it would all be back as it was. We may never have the opportunity again …"

"Helen, I'm not sure."

"You're tough Eve, and I promise to be gentle. I've been getting excited all day thinking about it."

"Well … Perhaps we could just see what it looks like … You might not like it when you see it …"

"Hmmm. I like it Eve, but it's a bit floppy. How do you make it go up?"

"Oh for fuck sake! Don't do anything! Promise you'll just watch, okay?"

Eve dropped onto all fours arched her back and aimed everything at Helen.

"Oh … Oh … Oh Ohhhhh! Fucking hell! It's enormous."

Eve looked over her shoulder. "Shit! I miscalculated." She tucked one leg under her and began to turn on her butt. "Here, let me make some adjustments."

Helen put a restraining hand on her shoulder. "No! It's okay … I think we'll work with what we have."

Eve was suddenly confronted with the whole length of it at close range. "Helen I'm not sure. I … I don't think I can."

"It's okay Eve … I'll stop."

"No you fucking won't! Oh shit!"

They sat eating breakfast. Eve put down her spoon. "I don't know Helen. I'm not sure it was right."

"Oh come on Eve, you literally exploded with pleasure. I thought you were going to drown me. We could die tomorrow, in which case we would have missed out on a unique opportunity. Or, we might live forever. I don't know about you, but if that's how it's going to be, we need to be able to adapt, and enjoy anything new that comes our way, or what's the point? Life has to be an adventure. We try to save the world, and we take what pleasures we encounter on the way." She put her finger to her mouth and whispered breathily. "You can be the Mr tonight if you like."

Eve threw a napkin at her. "God you are insatiable woman …" She went quiet for a moment and continued haltingly. "Thing is Helen, I get scared when I lose control. I damn near lost consciousness last night. I didn't know where I was."

"Yes, I guess I am that good. You were in heaven, Eve. So was I. And you would not be human if you were always in total control. Sometimes you have to relinquish to others, or you may be in danger of becoming a tyrant, and that would not be you. Just lie back occasionally and enjoy. Truth is I've never seen you looking so calmly exposed and relaxed, and that's got to be good."

Eve puffed out a long sighing breath. "I guess you are right."

"Damn right I am."

"Okay, okay I get it, but I'm taking you up on your offer. I'm riding you tonight!"

"Mmmm, can't wait."

"Since when did you become a nymphomaniac?"

"Always was where you were concerned, you were just too busy enjoying yourself to notice."

"Mmmm, really ... Now you'll have to excuse me. I have to go and talk with Valak, see what, if anything, he knows about Afsoon."

Eve started to leave, but stopped at the door, and after a long pause turned, with a grave frown shadowing her features. "By the way, you were not gentle."

"I was as rough as you wanted me to be."

"Yes ... but what does that say about me. Was Afsoon right? Is it my lot to be dominated?"

"It says that you don't have rigid boundaries thank God, and that we are totally in tune with each other. I knew exactly how far you were willing to go. You can't be lovingly dominant if you don't know what it is like to be submissive, so just allow yourself to know the full extent of enjoying both. I will, you can count on that."

Even Eve was unable to persuade any creature to tow their skiff to the edge of the world, and she didn't think it right to command them. But Glitonea assured them it was only a few hours steady rowing before they caught the current that would take them the rest of the way, although she warned them to be ready for rough water at the last. And then to look out for the calm water beyond, for this was where the world dropped away. She provided them with provisions and wished them luck. She asked Eve to bless them and their island before she left. And awkwardly, with a little prompting from Freddy, Eve complied. Ben and Emmaline took first shift on the oars. Eve looked back at the sixty or so Magi and household servants, amassed on the shingle beach, until they disappeared into the thin mist that hung over the grey sea. She trailed a hand in the water, and thought she felt slim fingers pass over her palm. When Eve withdrew her hand, she held a dagger with a black stone set into the hilt. The blade was also black and of a strange metal that reflected no light except at its razor edge, which conversely seemed to gleam with a light of its own. She cut a piece off the hem of her cloak, feeling no resistance as the blade cleanly parted the material. Carefully, she wrapped it in the cloth, and pushed it into her belt.

Everyone had had enough of rowing by the time the current finally started to tug at the bow. It wasn't long, however, before they were into the heaving waves of the rough water described by Glitonea. Despite the ferocity of their churning passage, and the frantic baling, the current eventually took them through the squall, until at last, and abruptly, the waters calmed, and they found themselves on the watery rim of a star filled abyss. Eve dipped the oars and guided them slowly to the edge. The gentle plop of her stroke was all that could be heard. There was an odour of sanctity to the silence that nobody was eager to break. As they neared the edge, it seemed to bow out and away from them, until it became a small lagoon, with a narrow opening. Eve stopped rowing, and the boat stopped dead in the water. She shipped the oars and spoke quietly. "I think I am being offered a gateway to another place. But it is not one that any of you can pass through. Wait for me. I will be back soon."

Before any of them could object, she slipped silently into the water without a splash, and swam with long powerful strokes across the lake. She walked over a gravel beach into a cave. A small cavern within contained a pool of glass smooth water. Eve cupped her hands and drank from the sweet liquid. Then, following some inner dialogue, she removed the blade from her cloak, and sliced across her palm. Squeezing blood onto the blade, she observed it. Her blood, instead of igniting as it usually did, just boiled over the surface, and seeped into the metal, leaving it smooth and unblemished.

Eve placed the dagger on a stone ledge, then removed her clothes and bathed in the icy water. A golden glow emanated from the ripples, as she gently splashed and rubbed water over her face, hair and arms. Her mind wandered, and she dreamed of leaf flecked sunlight and grassy meadows, babbling streams and woodland creatures. A clatter of hooves disturbed her reverie. She reluctantly opened her eyes, and observed a cloven-hoofed man entering the cavern. There was a scraping of horns, as he manoeuvred his antlered head through the low hanging rock, and stood at the edge of the pool, observing Eve through slitted golden eyes.

Eve addressed him. "Do you want to speak with me?"

He opened his mouth, but no sound emerged. He looked around searchingly. His eyes alighted on the dagger. He retrieved it, slashed his palm, and dripped blood as Eve had done. She watched it boil and seep. He leaned forward over the pool, and plunged the knife into the water, and on into the rock beneath, between Eve's parted ankles. Now he spoke, and a deep and rich voice, reverberated around the cavern. "I must talk with you. Find this place in your world." There was a blinding flash, and his arm and fist exploded.

When her eyes adjusted, he was gone. Eve left the dagger embedded where it was and swam back to the boat. She climbed in naked. Nobody remarked on this, as she unshipped the oars and rowed them into the abyss. The boat floated out, then disintegrated and faded away, leaving them hanging in space. Eve swam around them, pushing and prodding them together, and made them link hands. The ear-piercing sound of the priest's sun alerted them to the direction they must look, and there they saw the small super bright star that was their way out. Freddy pulled, and Eve pushed at them until they were in motion, and headed in the right direction. As they neared the sun, there seemed to be darkness at its centre, in which shadows moved. And then they were in the cavern, cross legged on the altar again.

Freddy asked a question. "How long?"

One of the priests responded. "Four hours."

Eve leapt from the altar. "I need to piss." And she was gone.

Lucifer's Child

The rest caught up with her in her apartments, showered and dressed, and tucking into a meal and several bottles of beer. She indicated that they should join her, but they all cried off to attend to their own refreshments, except for Helen, who made straight for the shower, calling over her shoulder. "Leave me one or two of those would you. And I'll have whatever you're eating too."

She emerged from the shower several minutes later, drying her hair. "By the way, I meant to ask. Have you been enhancing my appearance?" Eve stopped with the last spoonful halfway to her mouth, looking very guilty, and replied hesitantly. "I may have firmed up your tits and buttocks a little bit. You said we should take our opportunities whenever we could. Anything else is incidental to you being so much in my company, I promise."

"Hmmm, you sure you didn't make my tits a bit bigger and the nipples protrude more."

Eve reddened and blustered. "Well, not intentionally, but while I was making adjustments, I suppose it's possible, I could have slipped."

"Slipped?" Helen threw the towel at her head. "You are full of shit Eve. But hey, I like my new tits, and after what I coerced you into in that other place, I guess I can accept you being a little creative. But next time, ask before you go ahead with your little fantasies. One more thing; do you think I'm looking younger?"

Jackie had arrived back in the enclave, and Ben had gone to greet her. Helen was on their terrace with her head close to Emmaline's, gossiping about something or other, which was causing them much amusement. Eve and Freddy were inside discussing the events in the other world.

"Half reality Eve. Not an alternative reality? It's an interesting concept. So what is reality then? Are we it? There's nothing else?"

"Yes, and no. For a start, I think there is at least one other half reality and I will need to visit it soon. Another way of putting it is to say there are two realities, but only one fixed point. The big reality (she spread her hands and turned up her eyes) is out there in space, across the dimensions and into infinity. But it shifts like the tide. Nothing is stable. You could be a God one moment, then nothing (she clapped her hands then turned them up). Then you might re-emerge, or you might not, or you might reform into another entity entirely. There is limitless power out there, Freddy. Power that can be incredibly focussed, realities form, but in the very act of forming, they disintegrate and reform, or don't.

"I think Freddy, our God condensed and stayed put. He, she or it, was the only one to achieve sufficient stabilised sentience, for long enough to know that density and cohesion were the way to sustain existence.

"With a dense, fixed, and cognitive centre, everything else could hang on it. Nothing would have to be swallowed up again. I suspect creation draws on oblivion like the moon does on the tides. The void is disturbed by this relentless pull, and heaves into violent motion, becoming a cauldron of chaotic possibilities. And chaos it seems, from what I feel, when I am out there in the ether, is the birthplace of existence. As long as the centre is stable, and develops and evolves, then the counter force of chaos and entropy are kept at bay. But a balance has to be maintained, or one day the moon might crash into and destroy us or, worse, become detached from us, leaving our seas, and those of chaos, to separately stagnate into their own hellish voids." She reached for Freddy's hand. "So dear friend, insignificant little dot that we are, I think that perhaps, we are also, quite possibly, the kingpin of creation. And every transient and often powerful entropic entity, across the multiverse, wants to usurp our stability and have control of us. And if any of them gets it, reality will topple, and all will fall. We are teetering Freddy. We have to find some way to restore balance."

"But we don't have the greatest gravity in the universe Eve. Even a tiny black hole would swallow us, without so much as a burp. So how can we be the centre, when there is a vast hole in the middle of our galaxy, and probably every other galaxy out there?"

"You've been spending too much time with Soames Freddy. If balance were lost, it is us, our earth that would do the swallowing. We may not be the densest in this universe but that is just a tiny piece of us. Our gravity is in the multiverse, and we are the densest thing in it, and in the whole of existence. Our universe spills away from us for fear of being consumed. The sixth shard, and the seventh, that being the other side of the axle, are I think, each the tip of a shard of other, though in size, vastly greater pentagrams. I think these patterns link infinitely to form the sphere of the multiverse. The multiverse must, I think, be fluid. A stagnant centre would not hold infinity. We must develop and evolve Freddy, at just the right rate. Too fast, we enter chaos. Too slow, and we fold in on ourselves, and take eternity with us. We have moved too slow for too long, and not only slow, we are misshapen. There are dents and weak spots, where destructive forces congregate and build pressure, even pierce on occasion. Lateral collapse is also imminent."

During their conversation Freddy had become aware of a nimbus, of what he could only describe as black light, seeping into Eve, as though she were physically drawing on the dark knowledge of infinity. He kept this to himself. "So what do we do?"

A long silence occupied the space between them before Eve spoke again. "That is what we have to figure out Freddy. We need Soames and Jackie, but all the disciples have a part to play in this."

"About that, have you noted that you have twelve now. Mystic number, same as Jesus, twelve zodiacal signs etc. Possibly it is a good omen."

"My count is eleven."

"Depends on whether you count John."

"That's an odd way of looking at it."

"Perhaps ..."

The disciples congregated in the meeting hall below Eve's apartments, the original disciples (minus Soames) and the four more recent additions, being Helen, Emmaline, Carla and Alan. They all looked out over the growing shadows, as daylight chased the sun out of the valley and into the night. All were lost in their own thoughts. The first star winked into existence, and Soames entered the room.

Eve immediately went and hugged him, then took his arm and walked with him to a chair. "I may still look old but I'm not a frail man anymore Eve, as you well know."

"Yes I do, but I like to think of you as my favourite uncle, so you will have to indulge me. Also, I still take a perverse pleasure in your awkward discomfort. Old habits die hard. Please sit and enlighten us with your conclusions, now you've had several days to digest all of our information."

He did as he was bid and sat. But, not one to lose the initiative, he launched straight into his narrative. "I've consulted closely with Jackie and Freddy on this, and if your conclusions are accurate, we have to widen our focus, to include how to remove barriers to the developmental progress of this world. But in order to do that, we must first neutralise the forces that are poised to attack it. And the one that is already fully in this reality, and bent on destroying us before we can ever start, is still Afsoon. We must not get side tracked with our plans regarding him, or he will be behind us before we know it. Unfortunately we can't destroy him, not yet, not until we understand what his being one of the shards actually means, and whether we can kill the entity that is Afsoon, whilst still maintaining the shard that he embodies."

Eve looked uncomfortable with this line of thought but said nothing. "And the fact is even his prison is not proving all that effective. He is still able to act indirectly here, and on the dream road, and if what Eve found out from Vakal is anything to go by, in the half reality too. Eve you have hinted that you may have an idea of how to contain him. Have you had any more thoughts on that?"

The question was rhetorical for this meeting, but clearly he expected an answer later. He ploughed on. "Eve, Freddy has explained to me your thoughts on the human condition, and how we are somehow dragging our heels in fulfilling God's plan. I can see too that there are scriptural precedents that give validation to your concerns for our future, in original sin, the flood, and Sodom and Gomorrah, to quote the more obvious. Our world is in a sorry condition, and I must agree that we have to find a way to kick start, and evolve the conscience of our collective mind, before we become unacceptable in the eyes of God, and risk his disfavour and retribution. I can only hope that we have the time to address that problem, and to remove any barriers to redemption that the evil in this world has put before us." He cast his gaze around the group before continuing. "Unfortunately, for now we must prioritise and make the world a safe place, so that we have fertile ground for nurturing spiritual growth. When we have achieved that I will do all I can to assist you, in your efforts to save our world, and to guide us to fulfilment."

Eve gave Freddy a look of grateful admiration. He had converted all the concerns she had presented to him into Soames speak, and neutralised her fears that Soames would see them as blasphemous. It was always a mistake to forget that the coldly clinical and scientific mind of Soames, also harboured deeply spiritual and conventional Christian values. "Thank you Soames, as ever, you have brought clarity to all our thoughts and concerns, and your support for our long term goals and our souls, is something on which I know we can all depend. As for saving the world, it's time I was about that." She looked at Freddy. "I mentioned before that I needed to visit somewhere. Back soon." There was a clap, as the air rushed into the space that Eve had just vacated.

She was back out in space and looking down on the black double dilating bar that protruded from the pentagram. Only this time she was on the other side of the axle. Again, she was out in the orbital path of Jupiter, and was descending onto the area at the edge of the world, the mirror image of that she had so recently escaped. As she neared the calm waters along the rim to the abyss, the rim bowed out as before. But there was no lake this time. Instead a broken floor of black and white tiles presented itself. From which a spiral staircase led to a small chapel. She touched gently down onto the foot of the stair and began the climb up. It did not look far, but it seemed to take an age to get to the top. Eve was becoming inured, however, and took time to admire the magnificent scene that surrounded her. As she entered the last circuit to the chapel, she felt resistance to her progress, and had to force each step, as though through viscid oil. The surface of each step was also slick and difficult to maintain balance on, but with much effort, she finally arrived breathless at the top, and made for a stone block before the chapel door to sit on. Weariness descended on her. She lay down to rest her head and was enveloped in a shroud of black sleep.

After a while, she could not say how long, she became aware of her own light snoring, and someone talking. With the fog of sleep fast dissipating, she began to understand the imperious words, and realised that she was being addressed. "Who are you? What is your business here?"

Eve opened her eyes and swung her legs off the slab of rock. An angelic being confronted her. Whether male or female she was unable to decipher. "Perhaps I should ask what you are?"

"I'm Eve. Who and what are you?"

"You should not be so free with your name, but because you have given it to me, I will give you mine also. I am Serathiel. Do you come here to do penance?"

"I don't think so, but maybe, yes, perhaps. I know I need to enter this place."

"The penance may be severe. Are your sins great?"

"I don't know. I suppose I am the result of original sin, and if the scriptures are anything to go by, I don't think anyone in my world is free of that curse."

"You speak strange. I ask again, what are you?"

"I am the second of my kind."

Seraphiel looked thoughtful. "There was an Eve before, also a sinner, who was second of her kind. Are you she?"

"No."

"Then let me touch you and look into your eyes."

Eve held out her hands and let him/her raise her. She looked into silver eyes that looked into hers and dilated black. With shocking suddenness Serathiel threw her hands back at her and stepped back hissing, "Lucifer's Child!"

The creature convulsed bringing wings around its body as though to protect itself. When the wings opened, two further angels appeared within their arc. "Be gone! This place is not for you. You will never enter here."

"Yet enter I must, and if you need to summon support. It says a whole lot about your confidence in being able to stop me. Look, I intend no harm to this place. It is just that I have an overwhelming feeling there is an entity here that wishes to meet with me, and that for the good of creation, that meeting should take place."

Serathiel turned its back, but the others drew fiery swords. Clearly Serathiel was either thinking or communing with something. Eve sat down again. She was tempted to lie down, but she thought that would be rude. After an indeterminate time, Serathiel turned to face her again. "You may enter, but you must leave something dear to you with us. You will leave Helen. She will be unharmed if you cause no harm." Eve was not especially surprised that Serathiel knew of Helen, nor that this creature demanded her as a hostage, but she was not at all happy about it.

"Very well, but there are three of you. If she agrees, I will bring Helen to you, but also three others, to ensure her well-being while she waits with you."

Serathiel closed its eyes for a moment. "Agreed."

There was a tiny gust of air displacement as Eve leaned her torso back into the meeting room, where they were all still registering their surprise at her disappearance a few moments before. "Helen, I need your assistance, you too Ben, and Janie and Emmaline please. Link hands and I'll take you through."

Nonplussed, they all did as she asked, and stepped onto the plaza before the chapel, where Serathiel and its companions awaited them. Eve did the introductions and explained to them what was going to take place. "Are you okay with this Helen, and the rest of you?"

Helen gave Eve a kiss, and the others just nodded.

"Let me pass."

Serathiel stepped back and allowed her to walk through. A low Gothic arch led into a square altar room, where the black and white floor tiles persisted. The altar was a granite coffin-sized cube, into which a thin runnel had been cut, leading to a small spout at one end. Halfway down, on what Eve divined to be the head end, was a niche containing a sacrificial knife. She picked it up and inspected it. The blade glowed with a light of its own, but the black razor edge absorbed light. Set into the hilt was a large misty diamond. Resignedly she breathed out a light breath, and sliced across her palm, then dripped blood onto the blade. Eve watched it crystallise, before it seeped into the surface, then replaced the knife. She washed in the font and sat on the altar. Eventually tired of waiting, she took off her top for a pillow, then lay back and studied the black and white mosaics on the ceiling. They were mesmerising, and her thoughts wandered ... She looked up at angels from a river of sulphur smelling magma at the bottom of a steep sided chasm. The world and all the planets floated there like stepping stones that began to slowly sink as she placed her weight on them, so as to make her keep moving or burn in the hell fires below. The sulphur smell became incense, and she heard the scrape of steel across stone. She opened her eyes, and levered herself onto an elbow, in time to see a knight removing gold armour and placing it in front of the altar. When done, he prostrated himself in preparation for his vigil. He seemed unaware of her presence. She addressed him, but he seemed not to hear.

Remembering a previous occasion, she reached down to retrieve the knife, and threw it to clatter before him. He finished his prayer then raised himself to sit back on his heels, and she got her first real look at him. He was not handsome, as she had expected. He looked the right side of forty, but his face was weather-worn, scarred, and craggy, and his nose looked as if it had been broken more than once. His hair was golden blond, but being close cropped to his head it did not soften his harsh looks, this said, none of it detracted from the charisma of the man. He seemed to glow with it. He picked up the blade and examined it, looked along its edge, and hefted it from one hand to the other.

Finally he spoke. His voice was neither loud nor deep but it carried resonance. "You should not throw a weapon at your enemy unless you intend to kill him with it. Nor should you lie on a sacrificial altar in the presence of someone with a knife, especially a blade that has already tasted your blood." He walked to the altar and swept her feet over the side with a swipe of his huge hand, so that she was sitting, then sat down next to her. He handed the blade back to her. "Keep this. It is yours now. You will need it shortly." He gripped her chin between the thumb and fingers of one hand and examined her face closely. Then he looked down at the entirety of her body, pulling her head this way and that, so that he could see all of her. "Lucifer's brat!" He discarded her head with a light shove. "How the fuck did you not only get out from your entombment, but also manage to steal a soul on the way? Souls are mine to give. I'm sure I did not give one to you. And I thought I'd dealt with your sorry carcass aeons ago."

Eve felt like a little girl, swinging her legs over the side of the altar stone while his were planted firmly on the floor of the chapel. "Are you trying to tell me you are God?"

"I'm trying nothing. I'm telling you how it is. Of course, some people do refer to me as the demiurge, might be something in that. Why shouldn't I have a God too? An unknowable God makes a certain amount of sense when you think about it, and your presence here has to make one ponder. I certainly did not plan it, but then Lucifer always was a tricky bastard. Anyway, forget that for now, your faith is your own business. Why are you going under the name of Eve? When she was named, she was a pure and unsullied creature, whereas you are the embodiment of sin."

"Yet she fell into sin. Can I not fall out of it?"

"That's an interesting thought. I will think on it. But all the same, you should not be going under a false name."

"Afsoon gave it to me."

"Oh yes him, more about him in a moment. I should tell you that he was made after you. You were the first. That may have some significance, but that is for you to discover. Your right name is Sophia. There is power in a name, and you should use it."

"Vakal seemed to think that knowing your name gave others power over you."

"Only if you are too weak to use it yourself, as your shield and your weapon, discard it and others may pick it up and use it against you. I have another thing to tell you, and then we will part company, for now at least. I need none to guard my chapel Sophia. Sarathiel is an imposter. You should have recognised him. Cut off his wings. You have the means now. It will not kill him, but he will have the devil of a job returning to his solitary lair among the stars, and return he must. It takes enormous spiritual energy to assume a body here. Stay too long and return is not certain."

Eve was already off and running, with the knife tightly clutched in her hand. She gazed at the scene on the plaza with horror.

Afsoon in the guise of Sarathiel, hovered twenty feet above the ground with a taloned hand clutching the arm of a violently struggling Helen. He was lashing about with his fiery sword at Janie who clung like a limpet to his thigh, and fended off his blows with an extended asp, and Emmaline, who had a double handed grip on one of his feet. Ben was standing over the corpse of one of the other angels and trading blows, with his machete, with the other. Eve observed him feint to one side, and as the angel lunged, grab its hair, and pull it through to expose its neck. A final slashing cut and the head went rolling off the edge of the plaza. Wasting not a moment, he leapt and grabbed Emmaline's waist, to add his weight to the two already weighing down the escaping Afsoon. Eve was on the back of Afsoon in an instant and was already using the fearsome blade to slash through his wings, where they protruded from behind his shoulder blades. Realising his peril, Afsoon dropped Helen, and shook free of the others, and then clawed at his back to try and dislodge Eve, but it was too late. She ripped away his wings and threw them into the abyss. He turned to face her and they floated in space. He was becoming increasingly insubstantial and ethereal. He gave her a sardonic smile. "You are becoming a severe pain in the arse Eve, but think on this. Right now, I am just a ghost loafing around in the dream world and taking the odd pop at you to relieve my boredom. Yet time and again, I have all but beaten you. However, are you going to stand against me when I am free to walk the earth, and can assume the full mantle of my power?

"But you do bring me light relief. It is so funny to watch such an insignificant little flea posturing and preening herself, in the belief that she can challenge her almighty God."

"I'm the little flea that imprisoned you, you psycho arsehole, and I think you'll find the throne you covet so much is already occupied."

He faded away completely but his last words trailed a short distance behind. "Prison?" he managed to make his yawn fade into a slumberous light snore. "I'm just catching forty winks Eve." He sighed and seemed to speak from sleep. "Heaven help you when I awake little flea."

Eve spoke to herself, as much as into the abyss he had just vacated. "Enjoy finding your way back to your vampire's crypt Afsoon. I understand it is going to be a long and difficult journey for you without your wings, and meanwhile, I shall be preparing a warm welcome for you back home. Now fuck off you insane bastard, and dwell on the agonising eternity that will be the only result of all your efforts and machinations." She dropped to the plaza and scooped Helen into her arms. Instructing the others to hang on, she stepped back into the meeting room at the enclave, and was already calling for Freddy.

Helen disengaged herself. "It's okay Eve. I'm alright. Damn near broke my fucking arm, but apart from some claw marks and bruising, I'm fine."

Seeing everyone safe in the enclave was the trigger for a delayed reaction, Eve was overcome by a surge of nausea, and had to cling on to Matt for support before her legs gave out. He assisted her to a chair, where she retched and vomited over the side. Wiping her mouth on her sleeve, she managed to calm herself. "Thank fuck for that. I'm so sorry Helen. I was incredibly stupid and neglectful of your safety, and to you three too, sorry and thank you, I don't know how I can ever repay you. Thank God I at least had the sense to have you there with her." With a violent shudder, she lurched and vomited again.

Helen took her to their apartments and got the kitchen to send up some tea and sticky buns.

Helen spoke around a mouthful of bun. "Are you sure you won't have one Eve, they're delicious? Still feeling a bit icky, huh? I don't know what we are going to do about you Eve, these reactions are starting to become commonplace."

"It's just that I am so damn connected with you. All of you, I want you as an equal partner Helen, fighting, and risking all alongside me, and being an integral part of this vast undertaking, and I need my friends doing their bit as well. The fact is, it is just too much for any one person to handle, but when I find I have put you in danger like that, and worse, that it was not even necessary, and – to cover my mistakes – that my friends also had to risk their lives. It just hits me like an earthquake, and the aftershocks follow."

Helen put her hand over Eve's. "And we all love you for it Eve. It's why we are so fanatically loyal to you. We have to take major risks Eve, or we will never stand a chance of achieving our goals, and mistakes will inevitably be made, but look what we have found out about the extent of Afsoon's abilities by this, so called, mistake. And I am sure your sojourn in the chapel was not fruitless either."

"Nevertheless, I have to up my game and not jump into things so rashly. If you feel I am going overboard, just punch me in the gob again. It should get my attention … Oy! Give me one of those, you greedy cow, you've nearly scoffed the lot!" Eve sighed. "I guess we'd better get the others up here for an update. By the way, I think I may be changing my name to Sophia. Don't ask! I will tell all when the others are here."

Helen repeated the name slowly, rolling it around her mouth several times. "Hmmm, I think I like it. Never was all that fond of Eve. Bit too mainstream biblical. Whereas Sophia … much more mystical, enigmatic, and … well, interesting."

"Hmmm, bad girl you mean?"

Matt was first to arrive, and stood on the terrace next to Eve, with a bottle of beer. "What do you reckon on this character you met in the chapel Eve? Do you think you might have conjured him from the half realty that seems to respond to you so much?"

"If I did, you had better shoot me now, before I unleash a hoard of grisly demons, from the sick nightmares that lurk in the back of my mind."

"Yeah that would be a worry, especially as the creatures you encounter seem to be getting stronger. And this time, you brought back something physical. He turned the knife over in his hand. The look of this thing would strike fear into the heart of any opponent."

He tapped the neck of his beer bottle with the edge of the blade, to see what kind of ring it had, then quickly handed it back to Eve when it sliced clean through the neck without shattering the glass. "You had better get a scabbard for that thing, before you accidentally cut off a limb." He paused for a moment, and when he spoke, his voice was full of concern. "Listen, before Soames arrives, be careful how you present your tale to him. I think he is your man now, but he gets spooked when he has to cope with anything too far outside the dogma of his lifetime of religious indoctrination. He is already far removed from his comfort zone, coping with your newfound ability to pop in and out of existence at will. Also, he is under pressure. The Vatican is not happy with the rapid expansion of your church, and its unorthodox teachings, nor of the reports of the mysticism surrounding you and it. I don't know how Soames has kept them at bay for this long. I think they are watching the growing tension between your church, and that of the sleeping God, in the hopes you will destroy each other, and leave them a new source of ready-to-be-converted lost souls."

Eve remained quiet for several minutes, while they both explored their own thoughts, then responded in a wistful tone. "You are such a wonderful friend Matt. Sometimes I miss those times when you used to turn up at my safe flat with a bag of sticky buns, and just have tea with me. Can we do it again soon?" She gripped his arm with both hands and laid her head on his shoulder, content for a short time just to bask in the reassuring comfort of his strong and calm presence.

Sophia

Soames had a deep frown creasing his forehead and enunciated his words with clipped deliberation. "What does this mean Eve? Sophia appears everywhere, in one form or another, in every ancient culture's sacred writings. She is the first created entity, or the personification of wisdom, or the mother of the Demiurge, or any number of other things. Some even say she was Adam's first wife, and later, the consort of Lucifer. Should we then name you Lilith? Might this creature, this figment, you believe you have met, be disassembling your power rather than enhancing it by confusing who and what you are? Your name has been a constant Eve. Through all the changes you have undergone, yet still you have been Eve. Your church has risen on that name. Your followers follow that name. I think it would be a rash decision to change it to the insubstantiality of a confusing and nebulous other."

"As always, you make some good points Soames. I just don't know. I don't know what I met in that chapel either, but I do know he was damned powerful, and I feel he named me right. And let's not forget, that it was Afsoon who named me Eve, and that hardly inspires confidence. Also, I still have another meeting to attend, with an entity who seems to be the chapel dweller's opposite number.

"For some reason, this one can only speak with me here, in this reality. I have to find the place I met him, but on this side of the veil that separates us from the half world. I want you to come with me Soames. Maybe he will let you speak, maybe not, but you can listen, and advise. Help me to decide what to do next, with all the information that is being pressure fed into me. Be my conscience. Regarding my name, we will leave that open to debate for now."

Eve withdrew the blade from its marvellously worked scabbard. The third that Freddy had made, before discovering that a way had to be devised to prevent the knife edge from touching any part of the scabbard, or suffer it to be sliced apart on every sheathing and unsheathing. A clever arrangement of tiny ball bearings eventually solved the problem. The blade sang in the pre-dawn light, as she waded with Soames into the shallows of the lake that had lifted from the marsh mist, and although they had only walked a few steps, they were already on the opposite shore and crunching through the gravel that led to a familiar cave entrance. Eve led Soames to the pool chamber and told him to sit on an overhanging rock at the back of the cave.

"Now would be a good time to avert your eyes Soames." She undressed and placed the scabbarded blade onto the pool edge, then stepped into the icy water, taking great care to avoid that other blade, plunged into the stone at the bottom of the pool. She bathed, and as before, slipped into a reverie. Dreamily she unsheathed "her" blade and dipped it beneath the surface. There she reached for the handle of that "other blade" and without thought, slid the tip of hers effortlessly down through the centre of the handle. With shocking violence, the handle extended clawed fingers that snatched at her wrist, yanking her arm into the blade and up to the shoulder, where it clenched and punched her bodily backwards. A grinding roar and flash of white light exploded into the cave, and she wrenched a new-forged blade from resisting bedrock. A worm of scalding energy writhed through her vascular and nervous systems. Every heartbeat pumped up her system with electric vigour. She had never felt so alive. Her throbbing hand now held a beautifully wrought sword that hummed with any movement. Her arm felt a desperate need to wield it, but another urge, that seemed to veil a warning, tugged at her, and with great reluctance she sheathed it into the knife scabbard, which eerily accommodated its larger proportions.

A few moments later she heard rustling, and the metallic scrape, slide, and grunt of someone, or something, losing its footing. A thrown pair of blood red stilettos, clattered off the wall above Soames's head. "Stupid fucking shoes!" A barefoot and red-haired beauty, stepped from the shadows, shedding a satin cloak, before stepping naked into the pool opposite Eve. "Brrrr! that's fucking cold." She lowered herself beneath the surface, then came up spitting water, and flicking her hair over the back of her head, "exhilarating though." She smiled beautifully, and said nothing for minutes, bathing sensuously and absently, while looking around the chamber, and then at Eve. "This is nice isn't it? Although not just the two of us as I had imagined. Your little old man is not going to join us, is he? Couldn't he at least wait outside? Dirty old bastard has seen far more than he needs to."

"Far too much of your deceitful hide demon! I will leave." He turned to Eve. "But I will stay in calling distance should I be needed?"

"Be about it then, there's a good little man."

Soames stood his ground and raised his eyebrows at Eve. "Don't go far Soames." He nodded and left.

"Good man that one, loyal. But he has harmed you."

"You might say our relationship was forged in fire."

"Perhaps all the best ones are, although water can be good too." She shuffled forward sliding her feet under Eve's knees and encircling her waist with them, at the same time pushing her hands under Eve's arm pits and pulling her opened legged torso tight towards her, until their foreheads touched, "and … far more sensuous," she whispered. "This way we can talk without being overheard."

Eve was breathless and panting. "Why do you come as a woman? What spell are you trying to weave, I … I love someone else." Eve could feel her hot breath, as the creature nibbled at, and whispered, into her ear. "I won't tell … promise. So, if you don't … who's to know?" She flicked a forked tongue over Eve's rebellious nipples.

Eve gasped wiltingly, but managed to include a name and a request, in her unbidden exhalation. "Soames here, now, quickly please!"

He was there in an instant, aiming a pistol at the entity's forehead. The creature stood up in a cascade of dripping water and threw her arms in the air in exasperation. "Him! You thought to call him! You might at least have drawn the fucking sword. I could have dealt with that." She huffed. "Well, you've ruined the moment now." She stepped out of the pool. Scooped up and donned her cloak, then sat back on the side, dangling her legs in the water.

"Put that toy away old man. Your unwanted arrival has achieved its purpose. I only wanted to seduce her, not harm her. I thought it might add a bit of spice to the occasion. Giving guidance is so mind numbingly boring." She stifled a yawn. "You might as well make yourself comfortable old man. This concerns you too, and all of your kind. As to your question Eve: 'why a woman?' Men are not really your bag these days, are they? At least not mentally, you can't always control that monster libido of yours though, can you? I suppose I should commend you on your restraint. Although I really must point out that you have missed out on an incredible opportunity, I would have blown both your mind and your body. Let's try to think of it as a test though, shall we? On this occasion, you passed. Give the girl a prize."

She looked witheringly at Soames, then back at Eve. "Used correctly, sex can be an extremely powerful tool or weapon. Of course misused, it can also be extremely dangerous and destructive to the user, and anyone else fool enough to get in the way." She cast another piercing stare at Soames, before continuing. "You already have some experience of that I think." The demon opened her legs, placed her hands on her knees and stood. "Excuse me for a moment while I change. I think you and your old man will be more comfortable if I adopt a shape more in keeping with your expectations of a devil."

The antlered man-beast of her former encounter now stood at the pool edge. He turned to look over his shoulder at Eve and placed a hand on his fur covered butt. "Do you think my bum looks big in this?" He turned back. "Please excuse the generous genitalia, but if you can ... Well ... who wouldn't?" He was smiling lecherously and gave a palms-up gesture. "And in this form, I'm not exactly a man. Maybe I could tempt you with a little inter-species diversion?" His oversized manhood started to engorge. He glanced again at Soames. "Mmm, Perhaps not," and it disappeared altogether, leaving only a smooth groin covered in coarse hair.

"Now, where were we? Oh yes, 'sex!' Sex is power. I think you've met my brother ... father ... twin? If I'm honest, I'm not really sure what he is. We used to be one, but he was self-aware before I was, then for a while I was kind of like his conscience, and then I was me, weird huh? My birth if you like, was the outcome of immaculate spiritual sex, some might say self-abuse. That is to say, metaphysically speaking, sex is the point at which spirit begins to condense and prepares to embody matter.

"And that is where the power is. The spirit world is chaos, unformed energy and possibility. It ebbs and flows. Worlds and universes form and crumble, or fade away, except that sometimes a patch of awareness senses the proximity of creation, and stubbornly holds onto its crumbling form, for long enough to know that it doesn't want to die.

"Such an entity will promise servitude to anyone who can maintain its existence or give it purpose. Whether through conception, possession, or diversion of its primal energy, it really doesn't matter which. Beggars can't be choosers after all. A strong hand can hold and direct such primal energy. Lesser magicians often imprison it inside a stable object until required, a cave or a jewel, or even a lamp, but that is a dangerous misplacement of raw spirit,

Places can be entered, and things can be stolen. And the entity within will readily barter for release, often with dire consequences for the intruder or thief, and for the world they are released into. Properly subdued chaos matter, however, is a reservoir of immense potency. It can be used to make or to unmake, to build or to destroy. But the true adept knows that the points of conception and death are the truly sharp edges of sorceress potential. For these are where God has given passage for a soul to enter or leave created space. And it is here that some of God's own power can be borrowed and used. If you are strong enough Eve, you can hold God's lightening, and throw the thunderbolts of Zeus at your enemies."

He looked at Soames, as one might at a wounded animal. "Mortality is a terrible thing Eve. And your little old man here, looks just about ready to shuffle off his mortal coil. What say you Soames? Shall we experiment with your violent release into the ether?" He drew sharp fingernails down his own torso. Eve and Soames watched the blood boil over their black sheen and curdle in the coarse hair of his chest. "Your mistress will not often have the chance to be coached by a master of the sorceress and necromantic arts." His voice became a mesmerising, crooning whisper. "You would be doing her and the world a great service, and perhaps you will find peace." He suddenly clapped his hands and released Soames from his somnolent trance.

"Okay Eve, I know that look, I was only joking ... I promise. I should probably tell you that chaos, that seething, infinite and disorderly mess out there." He threw his palms up above his head, and exhibited an image of the cosmos, on and between them. "The cosmic all, that has so accommodatingly shuffled aside to allow time and space for the genesis of existence, does have a cognizance of its own, but it is like someone suffering from dementia. Moments of clarity, then all reason and cognitive thought flows away like sand through open fingers. I think you have already figured a lot of this out, but for the sake of clarity and the enlightenment of your decrepit companion, I will continue. Once, in all of infinity, the density of one intellect held, and fully and completely stabilised, and all of creation emanated from it, and that is good. But now think of a lump of coal. At a certain point of density something happens and it is transformed from a dark, porous, and incredibly dull lump of black rubble into a shining, super hard, impervious diamond. And 'impervious' is something you don't want. Nothing gets in, nothing gets out. No magic, no new possibilities, just stagnation on the inside, and on the outside, no disturbance, no half realities, nothing to hang existence on, just more endless, chaotic, making and unmaking. And, with nothing to cause it irritation, even chaos may become lethargic and sluggish.

"My twin or whatever he is, the guy you met in the chapel, believes himself to be that one entity, or 'God' as you might say, and he is quite possibly right. He is the first known stabilised being, and all else in creation has emanated from him. He takes and forms chaos into matter, possibilities into reality, and he constantly battles the opposing forces of entropy, to perpetually maintain and reform his created universe. Between creation and absolute chaos are all the partly formed realities. The closer they get to earth, the more solid and real they become. He takes forming chaotic possibilities, manipulates them, and makes them real, but there must always be that balance between order and disorder. That is where I come in. I am his opposite, the bridge if you like, to the counterforce of chaos. Not evil as scripture would have it, just opposite. I should be his equal, and in a way I am.

"At first I was his conscience and reminded him to stand at the cross-point of the two opposing forces, observing, and playing with the magic of chaos, then choosing viable possibilities and making them into reality. But 'He' became fixated with his created works, and started to close off possibility in favour of a fixed, and therefore stagnant, cosmos, so it became necessary for me to emerge as a separate entity. I left with one third of his power. He retained one third, but here's the catch, he also controlled a third." He turned to Soames. "And that third old man, is you and your kind. As I have indicated, he has the power to condense a stable spirit into a soul for habitation in an independent body. And that is fine. It, in effect, divides power three ways, and why shouldn't he have the controlling share? He is after all the creator. In theory it works. He creates a stable, free-thinking being, and we both vie for that being to embrace, either what is, or what might be, resulting in stable progress. A race of beings where some are chaotic creators and others are creative maintainers, both moving away from, and at the same time embracing chaos and disorder, but you old man, shouldn't be an old man. You were meant to be immortal.

"That's where it gets messy. 'He' argued that if someone became powerful enough to gain control of your race; as an immortal, he could if he chose make eternity a living hell, for all of your very dense and therefore, entrapped souls. Think Hitler, Stalin, Afsoon. So he proposed death, and a return to spirit, as certain escape from everlasting misery. All well and good, but what do you do with a stabilised, free-thinking and disembodied spirit? You can't return it to chaos; that would be as bad as the alternative. So when death dispatches them, he absorbs them. Ostensibly to be re-sanctified in his perfect godliness, whilst awaiting rebirth and a new start, until eventually, it was hoped, a natural and balanced order would emerge. To simplify, where Lucifer, that's me," he waved jazz hands in the air, "is chaos power, Lucifer = one third. Where God, my father … twin, is creative power, God = one third, plus X, X being the number of currently absorbed, stabilised spirits. Are you keeping up with this?

"This equation does not balance. Embodied souls minus X = a diminished third, which you must have figured out for yourselves by now, is equal to a lack of sufficient dynamic power to maintain and improve. A slippery spiral of stagnation, decay and bureaucratic infighting beckons. Meanwhile," he clawed quotation marks in the air, "God, plus X has a surplus of power, and starts to harden, to shine, and to become impervious, reflecting back all possibilities, and thus containing, crystallising, and stagnating; (imprisoning if you like) creation. Result: the third part of the trinity, 'humanity,' collapses, releasing all souls to absorption.

"They can't get back out to chaos through God's hard and impervious shell, and they get really pissed and destructive. Creation is turned inside out, and you old man, and the rest of existence, become unbalanced and under threat, very bad. My argument was that without immortality man would have little interest in building a sustainable future anyway, beyond maybe third generation descendants. This Eve is where you come into the equation."

Soames had been fidgeting restlessly throughout this entire dialogue and could contain himself no longer. He jumped to his feet, clutching his cross, and thrust the barrel of a gun into the creature's chest. "Still your lying and deceitful tongue Satan! Your twisted arguments confuse the soul. I will not let you slander our Lord, or obscure the mind of our Saviour."

Lucifer gave a slow hand clap. "Oh bravo old man," he cocked his head, and looked up to heaven, "Saviour? Mmm ... I like that. What do you think about it Eve? Does that title do it for you? Does it ..." He licked his lips and raised his eyebrows suggestively, "turn you on? I prefer Lucifer by the way, old man."

"Satan! You said yourself you vied for souls! Where are yours? What happens to the ones you take, and what hell do you put them in?"

"I do indeed take souls. I would certainly be taking an interest in yours. You have had it far too long. And yes, they usually do go to one of many hells, but it is none of my doing. I try to prevent it. I get the corrupted souls, those that are unable to maintain stability, and are crumbling back into chaos, the opposite of creation and order, and therefore evil by definition in the eyes of the faithful. Unfortunately they are un-absorbable. I try to hold them, but they always drain off to one of the ebbing chaos creations, most of which are indeed hell. So, 'He,' your God, gets fatter, and 'I' cannot maintain any extra weight at all for very long. The seesaw is nearly down at his end I'm afraid, and I will soon slide towards him, and be re-absorbed with the rest of you. Or I can make the jump into one of those decaying hells, where doubtless you think I rightfully belong. And if nothing changes, you and the rest of your kind will either join me there, or remain in your current hell for eternity. That sounds like the arse end of a deal to me. And it gets worse. As creation becomes increasingly impervious, the chaotic souls will increasingly be unable to escape, and chaos, or evil, will stay and multiply in the world."

"And what, 'Satan,' is the alternative? What would you have done about it?"

"Ah good, we can finally come back to Eve, and the random factor in the equation. I made you Eve, your body anyway. I saw the way things were going, and I made a perfect human body to seed your race with immortality. Your purpose was to pull back and to re-shape their dwindling power to its original third, thus reforming the trinity, and re-establishing equilibrium. So you see Soames, she is what your kind were supposed to be. All your concerns were groundless. She is more 'human' than you are. I was sure my brother would come around once he saw your perfection. And how you could perpetuate existence, and put creation onto its intended path, but I needed a fait accompli. Trouble was I couldn't animate you Eve. I tried to hold onto and manipulate the dying and dissipating souls that were mine. I even tried to ply several together, to place into my beautiful creation. They just crumbled and faded away, drawn like iron filings to the magnetic pull of their chaotic beginnings. I then moved you consecutively out into the near and denser partial realities. But I could neither create, nor hold onto, anything resembling a soul. Unfortunately I am more fitted to disassemble, than to assemble as my brother does. Lastly, I took you out much, much further, into primal chaos itself. As far as I dared to go, before I was myself disassembled. I wandered there in the wildness and wildernesses, with you in my arms. Keeping my stride barely ahead of the fading and all-consuming nothingness, that was busily un-creating all that was made. And there, at the edge of oblivion, you were grazed by Sophia, and you were briefly animated. Of course, the nothingness soon took her, as it always does. But in that brief time, you were wondrous Eve. I have loved you ever since."

"So who, or what, is Sophia?"

"There you have me. No one truly knows who Sophia is. I can only speculate ..."

"Then speculate."

"Sophia is ... the intellect of chaos. She is possibility, vast, unknowable, and unfathomable, yet she is the one constant in the tempestuous void. She disassembles like everything else, but she randomly re-appears. If there is a God before and beyond my brother, then she is it. When she slid through you, you should have been unmade. But she left you bodily complete, just void of her. Oh Eve, if you could see yourself as you were then, before she left you. Aside from my brother, I am probably the most vain and arrogant creature in creation, but I tell you. I just wanted to kiss your feet, suckle at your breast, and make endless love to you." A forlorn note entered his voice. "Then ... she was gone. So I brought you back and gave you to 'Him.' I didn't know what else to do. I had some insane hope that he could pull her back.

"He was as mad as hell I can tell you. He took you to that chapel where you met him, laid you on the altar, and thrust his hands into you. They were like burning suns writhing under your skin. He was searching, and seemed to be sweating, such were his exertions. I was worried sick. What God sweats for Christ sake? Finally, with a gasp, he pulled that wondrous blade from you. He had somehow collected Sophia's afterglow and residue, and forged it into that blade that ripples with light and darkness. But he had not finished. As though it were still molten, he pulled it apart, and formed it into the two blades you have recently re-forged. He left one in the chapel. No one has since been able to remove it, until you Eve. The other he gave to me and instructed me to throw it into the lake, in the opposing half-reality to the chapel, in another solar system, in another void, and another polarity ... Something of Sophia, something indefinable and out of reach, remains in you yet Eve, so he named you correct, but through John you have dual heritage, and may rightly lay claim to the name you have grown into. Unlike 'His' Eve however, you are the first of your kind. Make the name fit Eve. Be the Eve of a new humanity.

"I thought never to see you again, but when I returned from my task, you remained complete on the altar as I had left you. I think you were in some way protected from him, and that is why he sought to empty you instead. Elohim had been busy in my absence. The habitat I had prepared for you was in his possession. He was inside inspecting its functions, and had activated the bio forces that would finish the task I was still working on, that of a consort for you. He had placed the knife within the space your consort was to occupy, so it would be absorbed into it. I think I got the nearest thing to a compliment he had ever given at that time ... 'The work is good Lucifer. Although I could have done better, a shame it will have to be destroyed, along with that other poor creature you so haplessly forced into and out of existence. You are a fool Lucifer, and a blasphemous one at that. I really can't have you interfering with my work anymore.'

"When your consort's body was whole, he took the blade from it in similar fashion as he had with you and replaced it in the altar niche. He threw you down onto the bio bed next to your intended consort. Then he grasped the whole habitat in his fist, stepped without, and punched it and you into the molten core of the earth, the densest place in creation, from which nothing could escape, and all would be consumed. But either I had built better than he or

I thought, or whatever was protecting you, protected it also. I was banished and thrown into a hell at the furthest reaches of the universe. I was disassembled and dispersed, and corruption seeped into my parts. It took a while, but somehow I was spat out and was able to reform. I came back, not quite the creature I was, but still in essence, the 'Me' that had been cast into the fire. The trouble was, by then the earth was guarded by a wormlike force, that kept me from passing closer than the half realities of Jupiter's orbits, nor could I commune with any within its sphere, so I needed to have you summon me here.

"I think your blades were the force used to create the creature. They hold the vestige of Sophia. He couldn't destroy that vestige, so he made it inanimate. He divided it into male and female blades, and he employed me to help separate them across the multi verse, non-sentient entities that he thought could never be reunited. He made a male counterpart to complete, and give power to, the ritual sacrifice of your genetic body, and cruelly allowed my brief return, so I could watch when he thrust you both into the unmaking furnace forever, or so he and I believed. None could have expected the bodies would survive, or that two souls would transmigrate without God's active participation or say so. And fate too must have lent a hand at that time. For it was in the twisted mind of Afsoon that the power of choice was given of where to place your souls.

"By consigning them to sexually opposite bodies, a paradox was created in your psyches. You were an anomaly of disorder in an ordered universe. And only such an anomaly could have bridged two realities, to re-forge the anomalous sword of Sophia. The power you felt when you did so was Sophia's residual essence. Keep it close always. It will guide and support you in what is to come. It can summon me into this realm, and I suspect you could walk unharmed through primal chaos with it in your hand. But beware, another may also be able to wield it ..." He heaved a vast breath that nearly knocked Soames off his feet. "And there ends the lesson, thank God! What a depressing thing it is to teach. I can't imagine why Jesus chose it as a career. Decent guy like that should have been out having fun. I really must look him up. He does like good wine, and he apparently has an endless supply ... I expect we will meet again Eve/Sophia, hopefully minus the little old man." And then – as though he had never been there – he was gone. The cave seemed an empty and desolate place without him.

The snow outside was thick. Eve sat with Soames in his Georgian mansion, in front of a huge log fire, sipping mulled wine. "Well, what do you think?"

"I'm not sure what you want me to say Eve."

"Come on Soames. Be my conscience. Tell me what I must do. Was he the real article or just some bull-shitting demon, or a conjuring from my own sick mind? Where the fuck do we go from here?"

"Listen to me Eve ..." He looked at her with tired eyes. "I have always believed in God ... I have felt his presence within me, and his hand directing my life. But it was on faith alone. I had nothing other than the scriptures, and my own conclusions, to base it on. Now ... Now I have met, and spoken with, an entity claiming to be Lucifer, and have seen proofs that he is at least a powerful spirit ... and you, you have seemingly communed with God himself. What's more, if Lucifer, bogus or otherwise, is to be believed, you are in some way outside, and beyond control of God's almighty self. So then, is my God not all powerful? Not omnipotent! I am on the edge Eve. I don't know what to believe anymore. I feel like one of Lucifer's chaos creations, about to disassemble and crumble into oblivion, and I am not sure that I don't want to."

"Don't say that Soames! I need you. We all do."

"I just do not know what to have faith in anymore."

"Have faith in us Soames, in humanity, in me for fuck sake. I can't go on if I don't have people like you around me, supporting me, believing in me."

"Believing in you? Are you a god then Eve that you must be worshipped?"

"Not a god Soames. A template maybe, for what we can all become." She knelt before him and gripped his hands. "I am nothing without you, and Helen, and the others. You brought me back from insanity and possession Soames, and you all ... are the reason I want to stay. It is I who will crumble without the support of every one of you. You eleven are not my disciples, I am yours. If you crumble, you will only be the first. Then I think we will all eventually slip and slide back into stagnation, or into the infinity of chaos. I find it so hard to stay sane Soames." She rested her head on his knee, wet from the tears she had dripped onto it.

"So, what's the deal with you and Soames then? There has been a sea change since you returned from your meeting with … well, with whatever it was. Of course he's still the devil's advocate, if you take my meaning, nothing new there, but now it is in a positive way, finding the cracks in every plan or suggestion yes, but then exploring how to fix them and see if they are workable. He remains cautious, but is also a driving force behind any viable strategy. Don't get me wrong. It's fantastic to have him fully on board, no doubt about that, but it is a little un-nerving."

"I think he … No! We have come to realise that in order to fulfil God's plans for mankind, humanity must step up and take responsibility for our destiny. Rise to meet him as equals, in status, if not in power. In the same way that children are equal with their parents, under guidance yes, but reaching for independence, and not always in the wrong when we disagree with our father. We have to make it known what we want as part of the whole deal, and work to bring it about. It is a shed load of responsibility, and an awesome task. It will take all of us, the whole of humankind, to find a way to work together towards a common goal, resolving our differences, and achieving communion with God. I just wish we could do it peacefully, but there isn't enough time for that. Chaos and oblivion are closing their grip on us. God … and the Devil, help us all."

She barely breathed out this last, but Helen heard and responded in kind, "Amen to that."

Dark Age Descending

"Hi Janie, how are things with you? You look more vibrant every time I see you."

"Thanks for coming Eve. Emmaline and I wanted to show you what we've been up to with your army."

"Yes, I've been meaning to ask. How's it going with Emmaline? Are you ready yet for a fake messiah to bless the union? I am sure

I could pencil you in. Or perhaps you would prefer a full-blown wedding. We could do with something joyous to lighten the mood around here."

Janie gave her a sour look. "You are no fake Eve, and I think we will put any wedding plans on hold until we have secured the future. For now, just inspect the troops." She led Eve out onto a low ledge some forty feet above the valley floor.

Eve sighed and strode purposefully out to the edge. "Okay let's get this formality over with. I know how important it is to our young warriors to see their deity. I'll go down and have a chat with them afterwards, and then perhaps the three of us can catch up." As she neared the edge and peeped over she took a step back. "Jesus Christ Janie! You didn't have to bring the whole fucking army. There must be ten thousand down there."

"Twenty, but of course that is only a proportion of them."

Eve's eyes went wide. "How many Janie? In total, how many?"

"That's a difficult one to answer honey. Do you mean here in this country, or worldwide? And do you mean the whole army or just the crack troops?"

"Worldwide?" she managed to squeak out.

"That depends on how you look at it. What do you think we've all been doing these past years, Eve honey? If you take the field troops, the shock troops, Matt's intelligence operatives, and Carla and Alan's special operatives, we're probably talking around four and a half million. Here, should the need arise … at short notice, we could muster maybe … ninety to a hundred thousand."

"Bloody hell, you don't do things by halves do you? Okay you can fill me in with the details later. Let's go and inspect our war force, shall we? I think we had better do it all from the ledge. We can't favour just a few with personal niceties. We must try to maintain equality." She stepped into view and they all snapped neatly to attention and saluted with fists on hearts. It was like looking at a malformed timeline in a history book. Adaptations of Roman armour design with Kevlar under-suits. Modern upgraded combat gear, light-weight Kevlar Roman shields, exoskeleton, impact hardening plastics, long bows, crossbows, spears and swords. Right up to modern day weaponry; rifles, machine guns and artillery, and many unrecognisable armaments.

"Of course these are just the foot soldiers. We have a very broad base of cutting edge modern and historical weaponry, anything really that requires no computerised or electric parts, although we have a carefully protected reserve of those too. As you can see, the various regiments are colour coded in their uniforms and insignia, but they are also skilled in every type of weapon outside of their various specialties. Our aircraft too are mechanical and pilot driven. But we have recourse to hi tech versions and drones just in case, all currently in stasis and protected. We haven't forgotten your concerns about cyber-attacks, and can't rule out virus induced hi tech mutiny. It is certainly something we are trying to perfect as a weapon against our enemies. Everything has a kill or destruct fail-safe. As for our small navy, you would need to speak to Ben about that."

Eve stepped forward. There were no microphones; technology was a dirty word here. But Eve could project louder and clearer than any ordinary person, and the acoustics in this part of the valley were exceptional. She walked forward, drew her sword and knelt, plunging it into the bare rock where it quivered, shedding black vapours from which molten white and gold sparks dripped, until it settled rigid. Jackie had had an inspired solution to the Eve/Sophia conundrum regarding Eve's names. The ever-present sword that had become the symbol of Eve's church, was named Sophia, while Eve retained her own simple syllable.

"My brothers and sisters, you are our hope for the future of humanity. Together we will prove to our God that we are worthy of the paradise, that in unity and compassion, we will re-forge from this struggling world." Eve placed both hands on the pommel of the sword. "And this is our banner, under which we will fight to create and protect all that is good and great." Standing, and with a flourish, she withdrew the blade, shedding shards of rock as she arced it out in a shower of sparks. It sang when she raised it high above her head for all to see. Without intended volition, or any order to do so, the whole force sank to one knee, and a hissing chant began. "Sssophia, Ssophia, Sophia, accompanied by a steady shield beat and thump of weaponry. Eve re-sheathed her sword, saluted the troops, and backed out of view.

Janie and Emmaline clapped her on the shoulders and back, and ushered her inside. "Wow Eve, talk about less is more, where the hell did that come from?"

"I don't know Janie, probably from 'hell.' I'm a regular visitor there these days, in my dreams at least, and sometimes for real."

"Well it seems we have a new battle cry, and an eerie one at that. It should strike fear into the hearts of any enemy. Come inside, let's talk."

"So, who is looking after the troops while we chat?"

"Oh don't worry, they are already being deployed."

"Deployed where?"

"Emmaline, will you bring Eve up to date?"

Emmaline took a deep breath. "Matt decided to keep security light on this mustering and has set Carla and Alan to have their operatives watch for any hostile activity, pretty easy in a desert. Fadil too has been keeping us informed through his connections with the locals. It seems Afsoon has accepted the bait, and his forces are moving to surround us. They've got some pretty heavy-duty weaponry. We could have taken them out already, but we don't want any unnecessary deaths. Freddy is directing our forces through hidden trails and passages, to positions surrounding and amongst them. If all goes well, we should have a fair haul of captives for questioning."

"Okaaay ... It sounds a bit dangerous though, to let them so close with all that weaponry."

"Always a risk, but worse-case scenario, we obliterate them. There is so much hardware pointed at them we could take out a city, but no populace to worry about, only dunes and bedrock."

"Nothing is ever a sure thing Janie."

"True but some risks need to be taken."

"But so close to home?"

"Better to expose any of our weaknesses now than later, when things have escalated, and our attentions may have to be focussed elsewhere, or on a number of fronts."

"Are you sure that isn't already the case? Afsoon's a clever bastard. What if he suspects a trap, or perhaps has even deliberately manoeuvred us into such actions, and is testing our defences? Is it possible he has another attack plan in operation? What forces remain with us here in the enclave?"

"No large numbers of hostiles could get anywhere near this place without our knowing about it."

"Who said anything about large numbers? What about a hi tech attack? It's all still usable at the moment."

Janie looked concerned. "No ... Not unless they have developed something far in advance of anything we have suspected. Our surveillance would have spotted any such activity, and if necessary would have destroyed anything, or anyone, sent against us, way before they could think about entering our territories, but ..."

"But what Janie?"

Janie's face was a study in deep concentration. It was long seconds before she finally articulated through clenched teeth, punching out quiet words with agonising and slow precision, as though speaking from another and faraway world. "Chemical or bio attack!" She rubbed her chin nervously, speaking to herself. "Water or air borne maybe ... Water would take too long ..." Suddenly she was back!

"Shit! Emmaline scramble the drones and get air support, probably looking for one or two guys with a rucksack – somewhere upwind of the enclave, likely at the valley apex, high level stuff – surveillance only. Inform the priests and tell them of any sightings. They're all skilled fighters and can move around this place like wraiths. Hopefully, if anyone is out there, they'll have them neutralised before they know what's hit them. I'll inform the troops, in case there are any similar nasties carried with the main troop of hostiles." Eve was already off and running towards the valley apex.

"Eve, don't go alone. Fucking shit!" She radioed her captains on the command wavelength, whilst running a very poor second in pursuit of Eve. By the time Eve arrived, the priests had the two of them staked out on the ground with rifles pointed at their stomachs. A rucksack was placed some distance away, with the contents displayed on the gritty sand between two heavily armed priests. Eve wasn't sure what she intended, but she drew Sophia and walked towards the two captives.

The nearest priest addressed her in a German accent. "They are tight lipped for now Lady Eve."

"Thank you Dieter. Let's see if we can't loosen their tongues. She held the point of Sophia above the throat of the nearer captive. A thin trail of black and gold vapour oozed from the tip. On touching his Adam's apple that part of his throat crumbled into the dust, yet he remained alive. He was speechless and terrified. "Oh dear, didn't know it would do that. I suppose we had better question your friend instead. She waved the sword in his direction, trailing vapour. "Tell me about the contents of the rucksack."

He was clearly terrified and was struggling violently, but he spat out his words defiantly. "Biologically time triggered! We will all be dead in a few minutes."

Janie arrived breathlessly, just in time to hear. "Quick, get Eve out of here," she ordered the priests.

"Wait!" Eve walked over to the rucksack and looked down on the contents. "If this was meant to take out the whole valley, we will probably be unable to escape in time, unless ..." She dripped vapour onto the two containers and watched them crumble into nothingness. "Interesting."

She walked back to the second captive. "Any more surprises for us, here, or in your forces approaching us?" She dribbled more vapour onto his little finger and he started gabbling ... "Nothing more of concern it seems," she said to the others. "Be vigilant none the less."

She spoke to the second captive again. "In what way would you show your gratitude if I were to grant you mercy?" She passed the tip of Sophia over his face, moving it away just in time, so that the blackened light dripped into, and oozed through, the sand and rock beneath his head, making it into a deep well, into which he began to slide, until Eve leaned forward to grab his hair and pull him out. Dropping him at the pit's edge, she turned about and left him with the priests. "Think about it."

"I don't know how they got past our metaphysical traps Eve. Until now no one has been able to find this place without our allowing it. It seems they must have some adepts amongst their number. We suspected it of course, but proof positive is no less shocking."

"As you say Freddy, we knew it was likely, especially with Afsoon's arrival being so imminent. How the hell he managed to speed the progress of the habitat's pod is baffling, and extremely bloody worrying. God knows what forces he has access to. The pod just seemed to jump instantaneously through space and may do so again. It's impossible to keep track of him. We have no idea anymore of when and where he will appear. We anticipated just about everything except that. He is so fucking dangerous Freddy.

You think you have him in a corner and he reappears somewhere else, usually right at our Achilles' heel. I sometimes think he has just been playing with us all this time, so that he can better savour his victory when he does arrive."

"Yet every time, you have foiled him."

"Just so long as he isn't letting us Freddy, as part of his sick game. It would be just like him to play with his trapped mouse until he is ready to eat it."

Matt spoke up at this. "Who's playing with who Eve? Every time he fails, we learn more about him and the way he thinks, and each time you have come out stronger. Look at that thing you wear on your belt. Whatever forces he is messing with, I'm betting Sophia is stronger."

"But I still don't know its full capabilities, and now there's no time."

"I'm not sure you need to Eve. The thing has a sentient quality, and it seems to want to protect you, and do your bidding whenever it is needed."

"Don't you find that worrying Matt? What if it has its own agenda? And what if somehow Afsoon wrests it from us? Remember Lucifer's warning that 'one other can wield it.' That has to be Afsoon, doesn't it?"

"We'll prevent that eventuality somehow Eve. A more pressing problem right now is the way our drones just dropped out of the sky, and our communications systems went down. It seems your fears of cyberattack have been well founded. I've got our scientists and Freddy's adepts working on them to establish the means of their failure. Hopefully we'll have some results soon and can begin to formulate protective or counter measures against similar threats. If you'll excuse us for now Eve, I need to go with Freddy and check on progress."

"Don't worry Eve, I don't think anyone is going to have an easy time wresting Sophia from your grasp. I think you are attuned to it. It sticks to you like a magnet. If it were a woman, or a man for that matter, I would probably scratch its eyes out."

"Never knew you for the jealous type Helen, but you are right. I have tried to leave it in different places, but whenever I look for it, it is always already there within reach of my hand. And thing is, it is so bloody reassuring. I constantly fight the urge to draw it. It is like a jolt of pure energy, shot through with abject but delicious fear. I can't really explain it."

"Now I am worried. Just don't tell me it is orgasmic, or you really will see how jealous I can be."

Eve knocked and walked politely into the bare rock chamber where the speaking prisoner was domiciled. Not that he had said anything since his transfer to this room. "Hi. We haven't been formally introduced so I will correct that oversight now. I'm Eve Gabriel." She offered her hand but the gesture was ignored. She withdrew it. "And you are?" Again she was ignored, but his eyes followed her every movement, although they kept straying to the weapon at her side with little darting glances. "No matter, have you given any thought to my question?" Receiving no reply, she persisted. "Is it that you don't want mercy or that you don't want to offer gratitude? It really isn't an option to treat them separately. Are you more afraid of Afsoon than you are of me? Or are you just loyal to him to death and beyond? I'll tell you what I am going to do." She unsheathed Sophia and ignored his involuntary flinch. "First I am going to protect you, or rather Sophia will. Then I am going to give you a choice." She described a circle in the air with the tip of the blade, and blew the resultant black and gold, white shadowed ring, towards him, with a gentle puff from her lips. It distorted for a moment then moved towards his cringing form and dropped over him like fairground hoopla.

"There, nothing can harm you now, except me that is, or my blade. Okay, now your choice. Show me how grateful you are by offering me something I can use against your master, or have your body slowly unmade, and your soul drunk by my sword. I don't know about you, but I suspect any soul devoured by Sophia will know eternal agony and despair. Would you like to find out?"

He began to blubber. She reached into the ring and gently stroked his hair. "Don't be afraid. You are the master of your own destiny. If you can abandon your loyalty to your master and offer it to me, all will be well for you. I will give you some time to think. Don't take too long. I have to concentrate hard to prevent that ring from fulfilling the wishes of my blade, and I am afraid I will soon weary of the task. Don't touch the ring or let it touch you. If it wobbles or moves, stay right in the centre of the circle and you should be safe. If you want anything while I am gone just call, someone will see to you." She turned to leave and opened the door.

His cry was pitiful. "Don't leave me with this, this demon ring!" He screamed. "Please! It is shrinking!" He had dropped to a foetal ball. She turned back and watched him crab carefully towards her, stopping after every inch, to ensure the ring moved with him. Finally she stood inside the ring with him as he tried to kiss her feet and babble his undying loyalty. "Mistress, my Goddess. I will cut out my own heart if ever I fail you." He was crying pathetically.

She reached down and grabbed his upper arms. He maintained his foetal ball, but she lifted him bodily off the floor to a level with her face, gave him a rough shake, and commanded him to stand tall like a man. With slow and sobbing reluctance he complied and uncurled, but could not look at her, and kept his head down and his eyes averted. "No good man need ever be humbled in my presence. Follow me and tell me what you know of your master's plans." She waved her hand and dissipated the ring, then continued her withdrawal from the room. "Don't just stand there. If you are true to your word you have nothing to fear. Follow!"

On route, she stopped at another chamber, where the man with half a throat was silently weeping in a corner. She went through a similar process, touching the blade to his throat, despite his panicked efforts to resist, and restored that which was taken to enable him to respond. She walked with her two new converts to where Matt had set up office, and passed them into his care. "This is Matt. He will interview you both. This need not be unpleasant. Just answer him honestly and tell him anything and everything you think will be useful. Then I will consider how else you may serve our cause." Matt did not show surprise, but waved in several armed personnel, to ensure the new recruits behaved when Eve left.

"How did it go with our converts Matt?"

"Seemingly very well, they are now terrified of, and worship you. I watched the footage of your interviews with them. It seems you are getting to grips with the capabilities of Sophia very well after all. How did you know it could do that?"

"That's just it, Matt. I didn't. It kind of lets me know what I need to do and how to do it. It seems to be becoming a symbiotic relationship."

"Your tone tells me you are not sure that is a good thing."

"I don't know Matt. It is just so powerful, and the thing feels like it has a personality of its own. I'm not sure that I am in charge anymore. I wish we hadn't named it."

"Hmm that is a worrying prospect. Soames has been making noises about wanting to examine it scientifically, and Freddy metaphysically. I've been resisting this, frankly because I'm afraid of a reaction from it. I think they haven't pushed their case for the same reason, but we have to establish your dominance over it. It would be dreadful if we manage to defeat Afsoon, only to find our real enemy is the very symbol and foundation of your church. Our new converts are testimony to the power of it. Whoever wields that blade will win the hearts of both the good and the evil in this world. That person must be you, and the blade itself must accept you as its mistress, or we may all be doomed. I think it is time to examine Sophia, under both the microscope and the third eye, but very cautiously and with compassion. If she assumes command, we had better make damn sure we haven't upset her."

Eve was silent for a long time, and was indulging her habit of rubbing her thumb up and down each side of her nose. Matt knew better than to press her for a response before she was ready. Finally she focussed her attention outwards and on him. Despite his stated logic he was relieved by her response, and on reflection examined his own gut feelings, and saw it as the only realistic way forward. "No Matt, I think this is a time for faith. If she proves to be the Alpha in this relationship, then I think we have to trust that she has the best interests of our place in creation at heart."

The following months were catastrophic. Except for the most shielded and isolated, the world's computers died, power grids went down, electronic communications and components failed. It seemed from Matt and Freddy's investigations, that an encrypted viral attack had been piggy backed onto electric current. It transferred like a cancer into any device capable of receiving electronic instruction with which it came into contact. Any attempt at repair or reboot met with violent reaction from the equipment. If capable of movement, it was a physical attack on its would-be technical re-pair teams, otherwise full discharge of power in the form of high voltage current. Any robotics were lethal to approach until power sources ran down or were discharged. Transport was brought to its knees, often suddenly and with fatal outcomes. Food was diminishing fast. Looting and rioting around the world resulted (in many instances) in martial law being implemented.

Prior to, and in preparation for this foreseen eventuality, Eve's intelligence machine, under Matt's guidance, had managed to approach and win over original thinkers in government and community departments all over the world. These cells had co-operated in secret to form contingency plans and had waited in readiness for just such a crisis. On the go ahead from Jackie, small sleeper groups and units swung into action, to muster local security forces at short notice. And to arrange distribution of the food and supplies that she had been stockpiling from the container warehouses in which they had been stored. Shipping arrangements were in place via road, rail, sea, rivers, canals and air, and where these failed, use was made of any non-electrical or mechanical means, such as steam, airships, balloons, and animal carriers. Makeshift medical centres were ready to go, and non-computerised or electrical alternatives, and maintenance and repair crews were also in readiness to downgrade to pre-"hi tech" systems. Of course it wasn't enough. Some governments and communities had rejected any approach. And some were in any case already in the control of Afsoon's forces. The world quickly became a chaotic and extremely dangerous place, but a degree of order and stability had been achieved, despite local rebellions, civil unrest, and a high death toll.

Eve's organisations, and those few enlightened governments who had been willing to listen, had completely closed and shielded their computer systems (both technically and metaphysically). But sooner or later, even these were expected to be breached. Soames and Jackie had ensured that kill and back up procedures were in place, but communication was anticipated to be the greatest problem. Everything was being utilised to achieve this, from animal carriers such as pigeons and dolphins, to pony express type dispatches, and shielded fibre and wire radio communications. Freddy had set up a "priest" worldwide network of adepts, capable of communicating in the metaphysical realm. Eve of course, had proved herself well able to travel and communicate wherever she wished in these realms, although there were inherent dangers in doing so, for her, or anyone going along for the ride.

Eve's people had struck back at Afsoon's technical interests on Earth, with similar devastating effect. Soames, however, had been unable to locate or track the pod carrying Afsoon's body. And neither Freddy's adepts, nor Eve herself, could sense its whereabouts. They had to conclude that it had made another jump, and that the "Sleeping God" could soon be very much awake, and manifest at the head of his church, and in the full mantle of his power. Skirmishes and small wars had broken out all over the world between Eve's and Afsoon's forces, and territorial borders were being established. One welcome side effect of this was that when either side gained a territory, it quickly set about establishing order, although it also went about recruiting the populace to its cause, and swelling the ranks of its war machine. A huge positive was that nuclear, or any high-grade technical attack, had been effectively neutralised. Intelligence suggested that if the disablement of technology continued at its current rate, in a matter of months at most, the best that could be hoped for to achieve, would be an equivalent to Roman technical ability; with, perhaps, unpowered flight, steam power, and mechanical or manually operated weaponry and explosives. And even that would take time to establish. A dark age was descending.

Warrior Queen

Eve stood in full battle gear. The design was more than a little eye catching. Jackie had noted that Sophia had an affinity with iron-based products. On touching them, it seemed to extend itself into them in some way. When Sophia was active, they exuded that same sinister, white shadowed, black and gold dripping vapour. Eve's steel scabbard and Fem-Roman styled armour was a sight to behold, whilst the black, skin hugging, impact hardening under suit, was both supple and extremely difficult to cut or breach. Jackie herself tightened the obsidian jewelled sword belt about Eve's waist and stood back to assess the result.

"Wow Eve, you won't have to lift a finger. Our enemies will drop to their knees at the mere sight of you." She made a few minor adjustments then held a mirror to show Eve the result. "All very good Eve, appearances really are half the battle, but only if you can back them up with lethal action, so I'm afraid it's back to business. Afsoon has thrown everything at the Turkish border. He either sees it as a highly significant strategic prize, or he is distracting us from some other action he has so far managed to keep from us. Or of course, he could be trying to lure you out into the open. But fuck it! The Turks are falling back under the onslaught of his mechanised tanks and ballistics. Our own forces have been insufficient to adequately support them, and stem the slaughter being meted out by his fanatics. They are currently fighting a failing rear guard action through the border foothills, and are outflanked by guerrilla fighters, who are also waiting on their retreat through the river valley. We need a victory in this first major confrontation, to win hearts and minds. It's time for them to see their Queen in action.

"Freddy's guys have divined that further enemy forces are waiting in the high pass above the waterfall that our allied army is being pressed into. Surprise is the mother of conquest, so if you can turn the Turks back on Afsoon's corralling force and gain a victory, the guerrillas will find themselves inside the Turkish border, having to retreat into either Turkish territory, or face a returning and victorious Turk army. Going horseback was an interesting choice, but I have to concede those demon horses you brought out of the half reality, will certainly enhance the fear factor, and I'm glad you are taking Ben and Janie for back up. Shame you couldn't manage more of our people through the half realm dream paths. First sign of any thing going wrong though, tune into the shard and jump back here, even if it means losing the whole army. That would be a source of deep regret, but without you, humanity is lost." She stood on tiptoe and kissed Eve. "Good luck. Be careful passing through the half realms, Afsoon could be lying in wait."

Helen was pacing anxiously on the terrace to their apartments. "I'm worried sick Freddy. I don't like her putting herself at risk like this. Afsoon could be anywhere."

"We've been through all this Helen. Eve would have it no other way. It has always been hers, and our policy, to have her lead from the front. She must light the way."

"Light the way? Like Jesus you mean? Don't you see the parallel? What if she picks up another bloody disciple? That would make twelve. I know what you're thinking, but John doesn't count. He and Eve are one. Twelve would be just too much like Jesus. And look what happened to him when he chose to confront his enemies in Jerusalem. Have we already had our last supper Freddy?"

Eve had found that since her encounter at the chapel, she could move with relative ease into the half realities. But for her to come back, elsewhere than from where she had departed, required a more tortuous process. It meant dragging the physical self, and the space surrounding it, into the metaphysical realm, then passing through the intervening domains, to a world near the focal point of egress desired. Every realm traversed wanted to capture the light passing through it. Escape and re-entry into fully created space, could only be achieved by ripping through the matrix of their combined resistance. Any lapse of concentrated effort would be fatal. To do this quickly was hellishly difficult, but she could manage it. To take others was monumental, maybe impossible, and she was relying on Sophia to provide the power she needed.

The horses were for speed. Being half created creatures they moved easier in the metaphysical, and she had chosen monstrously powerful beasts with wicked teeth and clawed forelegs. They were vicious, murderous and untameable to any but Eve. The huge effort of bringing such creatures into created space, she felt would reap rewards in projecting both the psychological fear factor, and as the lethal weapons they obviously were. Currently they were extremely skittish. This reality was painful for them. Everyone had stepped well away from their raking hooves, and the acid drool they slobbered, that melted solid furnishings in the common area leading to the terrace some way below Eve's apartments. Eve described a pattern of complex cuts in the air with Sophia, and a watery reality of swamp and rotting trees melted into the empty space, that had previously hung over the drop to the valley floor. Just then, the door to the common room crashed inwards under the force of Helen's boot. Before any could stop her, she had mounted a nearby table, and vaulted onto the back of Eve's mount, just as it was kicked forward to leap through to that other place. The arch folded behind them with a subdued and ominous plop.

The wind and hail battered the riders, and lightning strikes split trees with ever increasing regularity and proximity. Eve wanted to be mad at Helen, and rail against her stupidity, but the storm, and her need to concentrate defeated her efforts to give voice to her rage. After struggling for what seemed hours, to navigate them into a calmer realm of clouded forest, hard ground and soft rain, she realised that having Helen there, clinging to her waist, filled her with a sense of warmth and strength. And as there was no changing things now, she patted Helen's thigh and drew her hands tighter about her waist. The beasts galloped on tirelessly. After passing through freezing mountain trails and scorching desert, they re-entered woodland, and a series of sunny glades that ran alongside a shallow, crystal clear river. Eve began scanning the area, looking and listening. The river joined another, faster flowing, deeper river, and sometime after, Eve and the others heard the thunder, and saw the mist of what could only be the head of a mighty waterfall. Except for Ben, they all voiced their fears when Eve urged her mount into the swiftly flowing water.

Eve shouted back at them. "Come, our reality lies ahead. Our troops are close to the base of a waterfall, and we need something violent to assist our return into our world. Be ready. We will emerge into a war zone."

As their hair and bodies became slick from the dense mist being thrown up from the approaching water drop, a great churning and heaving, in the basin before the fall caused a back flow that impeded their progress. But their mounts were tireless and swam on into the maelstrom. Something was rising from below. A flesh-coloured hillock broke the surface water, which could have been traversed by steps of bony vertebrae rising between two large flat shoulder blades. The giant's hunched back, now flattened, as the creature unfolded from the depths, and stood from its kneeling position fully sixty feet tall. A giant Afsoon looked down on them and swung a mighty war hammer upon the mount on which Eve and Helen rode. Eve's voice carried clearly through the cacophony of noise generated by the turbulent waters. "Really Afsoon? We have no time for your childish theatrics. Stand aside or be consumed."

She drew Sophia and blew a puff of air at the tip. A black claw reached for and crushed Afsoon into its grasp, before whipping back into the blade from which it had exuded.

"What the hell was that?" Helen shouted in her ear. "Is it that easy? Is Afsoon vanquished?"

"No! He is just playing with illusion and testing our defences, but his efforts will reveal nothing to him. He cannot observe what transpires here while Sophia confines his influence, although he will know his little subterfuge has been foiled."

Before anything further could be said they were swept over the fall. Helen screamed, Janie trembled and Ben sweated. They all tumbled into a sickening vortex, and rode calmly out from under the roiling pool at the bottom of the fall, straight into the vanguard of the retreating Turkish army. A warrior queen with her escort, and accompanied by the banshee scream that had issued from Helen during the fall. The cacophony of gunfire and whistling missiles hesitated and held their breath to give access to this extraordinary apparition that trailed its white shadowed aura like a witch bride's train.

Eve's voice punched, with earth shattering volume, into the settling dust and dusk of the early evening rout. "DESIST!"

Tired soldiers dropped to their knees, in both the retreating army, and that of the leading attack force, amongst whom, many were already turning to flee, whilst others prostrated themselves in pleas and prayer. A lone leviathan tank continued to roll forward, aiming and firing shells directly at Eve. She patted them aside with Sophia and gave a crackling war cry as she spurred her mount to spring forward. Swinging her blade in blurring sweeps, she carved the tank, and any who rode in it, into a pile of twisted metal and blood. The attackers ran or laid down their weapons, or exited their vehicles. Eve accepted many allegiances, and placed them in the care of her own regiments (those who had been supporting the Turks) for induction into her purpose, and her faith. Then she called for a war council. Walking back along the riverbank to the hastily erected command tent with the Turk general and her companions, she suddenly stopped and requested privacy for a call of nature. She waded into the water and retrieved the two eels that had wrapped themselves around her ankles as she had trudged along the muddied bank. The water now boiled with them, and shaped into the rough outline of a face, and they communed.

After a war council with the general and a very few select officers, Eve requested private council with her companions. As soon as they were alone, Eve stripped off her armour, sword belt and scabbard, and dumped them into Helen's lap. "I have to go. It is important that you take my place and establish order here. I will take the mounts. They are unhappy in this realm, and in pain. Any prolonged time here will kill them. Ben will have your back, but I will take Janie home before I go where I am needed. This whole episode has been a distraction on many fronts. I will give Janie the intelligence she needs to help her counter Afsoon's other attacks around the world."

"But where are you going? You must take someone with you."

"No! Where I am going no one can come, I have spoken with the eels. Afsoon is communing with the worm in person. That was his real gambit all along. I must stop him. Now go and be me. They need a messiah."

"At least take Sophia with you. Please, you will need her."

"No, she is the symbol they will follow. She must stay with you. She will be in my hand when I need her. She is never beyond my reach."

"And what of Afsoon? Is she beyond his?"

"That is something we will soon know."

Having returned the mounts to their home world, Eve placed Janie back in the enclave, with a full brief on the activities of Afsoon's war machine. Exhausted she reached for Sophia, stepped into yet another place, and paused to look up from the bottom of a watery midnight chasm. She could feel the slithering touch of the monsters that crawled around her feet and swam nearby. But they were as nothing against the malignant power that occupied the gateway into the void. At the pinch point of the crevasse ahead of her, a whirling black and blood red vortex ripped and churned into a grizzly funnel, which seemed to be made of the gnawed and shredded remains of all manner of part dead creatures, from the nightmares of the dammed.

Once beautiful, half dead, and rotted faces swirled past. Their defeated efforts to scream their despair, lost in the gurgling spouts of blood that exploded from the gnawed and ripped tendons of their infinitely stretched throats. One such pitiful creature turned a terrified eye to watch what was left of itself spiralling into the depths of an ever-darkening funnel, and the gore-filled throat, of a monstrous serpent. As Eve watched, it became apparent that the vortex was flattening and reversing as the creature struck once more, and surged its gigantic bulk against the weight of the ocean deeps, that had so long imprisoned it, and forced it from this earthly plain. Such was the ferocity of its frenzied attack, that its head entered through the vortex, and ripped a crater in the walls of the chasm, before being forced back with whatever poor creatures were sucked into the tearing and gnashing void with it. No sooner had the vortex reasserted itself, than it became manifest, that the crazed serpent was already renewing its attack. A calm but equally unwelcome presence stood in the narrow space on the other side of this pit of living death, bargaining with, and antagonising the creature that occupied it.

Eve hadn't known what would happen to her, when she manifested so deep into the enormous pressures at the bottom of the Sargasso trench. Her faith in Sophia had proved well-founded however. She had appeared in Eve's reaching hand as she materialised in the watery deep. Enfolded in a shroud of white shadowed black, Eve walked unharmed through the necrotic remains of the countless unfortunate denizens of the sea. They seemed to rise from their slumber on puffs of disturbed silt, only to lay down again as she passed, as though in supplication. At her approach, the thing in the void became subdued. Its gigantic head turned ponderously. It swam close, lazily lifting a heavy lid from its one malevolent red eye, and it looked directly into Eve's paralysed gaze. The slitted pupil dilated, as though to offer Eve a doorway into its bottomless world.

Afsoon spoke into her mind. "Ah you found me. And just how did you manage that so quickly? No matter, you are here now, and I am afraid you are too late. I had better introduce you, as you may only know him for a few moments, unless I am able to prevent him from consuming you. Please meet my friend and partner, Ouroboros." Afsoon bowed deeply, with a cavalier wave in the direction of the red eye. "Between you and me, he is totally insane. He is barely capable of coherent thought, since you re-forged that blade, and stole most of the essence with which he held the forces of entropy and decay at bay. He is after all a creature of chaos, and they do not usually last long. And now here you are, with the means to re-stabilise his missing intellect, and although his thoughts are slow," Afsoon tapped his own temple with a finger, "dementia poor thing, he is beginning to sense what you hold. He is likely to strike at any moment. You are as good as dead really.

Tell you what, give the blade to me, and I will hide it for you, and who knows, if I put in a good word, you may just get out of here alive."

"You are seriously going to release that thing Afsoon? Do you know what it is capable of? There will be nothing left. You will have no world, no universe to live in, let alone to rule. None of us will." Eve was edging closer to the void in which Ouroboros, slowly, but with increasing agitation, swam. "By what means do you hope to release it? An ocean of pressure, both physical and metaphysical, keeps this portal shut."

"Ah Eve, you made a cataclysmic mistake when you trapped me in that pod. I have learned so much, and I command all of its metaphysical properties. Closing down a shard for a moment is no big deal."

Afsoon too, was edging closer to the portal. Ouroboros swam up to it, and his eye filled it, while his roving pupil searched. It focussed on Eve again, and on what she held, then it was gone, swimming away in endless other-world murk, trailing a vast cone of turbulent sludge. "You are quite right of course, he will consume everything. This universe will be a dead thing, but he will be trapped this side of the portal. Whilst what he has been protecting against, and keeping from seepage and contamination into the source of creation, is the multiverse. Who wants a puny universe when the whole multiverse is out there to be conquered? Hand over the blade now Eve, quickly! Orouboros is coming, and I will release him. You are alone Eve. Even with that blade you cannot oppose both him and me."

"What makes you think I am alone?" She waved Sophia and a blinding light revealed Eve in a boiling endless mass of eels. She spoke to them in ringing tones. "You have been true to your word. Now be true to your promise, as I am to mine!" She waved it again, and leagues of shining angels were at her back. The void burst into a trillion watery shards as the head of the serpent broke through. At that same moment, Eve stabbed with a double handed grip at the malevolent eye. And also at that same moment, Afsoon grabbed for the cross piece of Sophia, levelling blows at Eve's face. And the watchers attacked Ouroboros, hacking with flaming swords at the vast body of the thrashing creature, forcing it back from whence it came, and Afsoon and Eve with it. The blade was still deeply embedded in the eye of Ouroboros, yet still did Afsoon and Eve fight each other for control of it. Finally, with a mighty thrash. Ouroboros shook them loose. Both maintained hold of a sword, Afsoon's of glowing gold, and Eve's, of dripping, light consuming, black. And they were flung far out into the multiverse. Now blind and subdued, Ouroboros slunk back to the safety of what he knew and took up his guard against the incursion of the multitudinous lesser realities. The portal wreckage drew magically back to reform the stopper against the beast.

As Eve floated off into oblivion, she maintained her grip on Sophia, but it writhed and formed in her grip, like a vase on a potter's wheel, into a dark and beautiful maiden, who spoke with soft and musical tones that resounded in her skull like a struck bell. "Dear child, thank you. You have freed me to return to my greater self, of which I am but the faintest of echoes, yet unlike that demon worm, a universe will not confine me." She waved a hand and a plateau of rock appeared in the void, bearing a dining table set for two, a bottle of good wine on ice, and several steaming tureens. She indicated they should sit. As they did so, galaxies sprung into view around them. Sophia cocked her head to one side, and a soulful smile played on her lips, while she assessed Eve's current mental state ...

"You have been told that I often appear, but have no true cognisance because I am forever being unmade. There is some truth in that ... do try the food. I really am an excellent cook, and it may be an eternity before we can do this again." She poured wine for them both. "In fact I span, and I am coherent, in the whole of the multiverse. My mind and my thoughts are always present in one part of the eternal cosmos or another, and my awareness is infinite. Omnipotence however is lonely, and vastly overrated, so I accept independent opposition, and intrusion into the fabric of my perfect oblivion. After all, an undisturbed ocean contains little of interest ... You should know that Elohim is my only fully sustained creation and is the only true creator in existence. He can manipulate chaos and contain spiritual essence. He is a maker and artificer, but he cannot unmake, that is for me, and now for you, alone. Although your power is very small, there is a need within creation, for another to possess the ability to both make and unmake. This you will understand if you can find your way back.

"Elohim was very clever when he discovered Lucifer's little project, he recognised you for what you are, and became fearful. He could not destroy you, so he separated you into maker and unmaker, and bled off my power to protect his creation from incursion, by creating Ouroboros. Then he placed your bodies where he hoped you might be destroyed, but from which he believed, that at least you could never return. There was no room in his house for another maker, and certainly not an unmaker. Cream with your strawberries?" She poured. "He understands now that when he formed the world from the stuff of chaos, and peopled it with free thinking souls, many other entities were also swept up in his making. You might know them as demons, or frailties, or diseases and such. You see, Lucifer is wrong. Elohim's humans were not designed imperfect, but they were contaminated by those entities, osmosed, or possessed if you will. Of course he could not admit that, even to himself. After all, despite all the evidence to the contrary, he thinks himself perfect. In his mind, it is all just part of the unfolding of his eternal plan, and who knows? Perhaps there is something in that.

"The true self always tries to surface of course, but the demons keep it subdued, so that they too can have existence in creation. But it is a creation not to their liking, and one which they always try to corrupt. They diminish your kind and are the cause of most of the ills in the world. It is also the reason why those close to you heal and rejuvenate, because you, either consciously or unconsciously, unmake their demons. You are the only created entity able to do that. But for now you are banished from the centre of creation and must roam the multiverse and the aprons of chaos. First you will forget, and must learn to know yourself again. You too can achieve freedom, but only when you have consumed the entity you know as Afsoon. You two are 'one,' and should never have been divided, but you were 'first,' and it was you, this body that you wear, who was grazed by my greater self. You are my daughter. It is your birthright to be made whole. Consume him. But be careful, the soul that occupies him is strong. Do not let his will subsume your own, or you may never return. You will be bladeless in this wilderness, but some magic will still reside in the blade I will return to Helen against the day you reclaim it. Look hard Eve, there will be echoes of it in every reality, that only you may wield."

Who Am I?

Eve awoke but she was no longer Eve. Nor was she female. Nor was he clothed. Nor did he remember anything before waking into a damp and misty woodland glade. He was laid prone on cold earth. Sharp stones prodded into his back, causing him to shiver and shift in discomfort. Gritting his teeth, he sat up slowly and stiffly, and hugged his knees for warmth. Twigs and leaf mould stuck to his back and chafed at his anus and genitalia. His head swam, and a strong woody smell, mixed with earthy animal scents, pervaded the chill air. He was too confused to recognise or react to the fear and sense of imminent doom that wobbled impotently in his thighs and crotch. Nor could he overcome the weakness in his body which kept him dangerously immobile, yet maintained sufficient strength to punch bile up through an objecting gut, and a heaving chest, for unwilling ejection in a vile smelling torrent of lumpy slime. Eventually there was nothing left to expel, and the gut-heaving slowly and painfully abated. Exhausted, he lay curled in a foetal ball for several minutes. Then, with great caution, he looked around, abruptly certain that another presence occupied the glade.

A large stag stood knee deep in the mist across the clearing, looking directly at him. He did not feel threatened, just thankful that he was no longer alone. He rocked gently onto his knees and inched towards it. It backed off a pace, but neither looked to run or to attack. Slowly he crawled his way to it and reached out a hand. It then did something strange and lay down. It had been running hard. He could see the steam rising from its hide. Without thought or fear he lay alongside it to share the comfort of its warmth and the soothing pounding of its heartbeat. He pushed into the stag's side, and began to drift into a pleasant daze, then, thwack! Thwack! Thwack! The stag kicked and bucked, shook violently, shivered, and was still. He looked with bewilderment at the three arrows, one in the throat, one in the eye and one in the ear, then he watched the light of life die in its sad eye, and he began to weep.

"Well, will you look at that? If I hadn't seen it with my own eyes I would never have believed it. Still, he did us a favour. I thought we'd lost the bugger. We'll feast well tonight lads. Tie his hands and slip a collar on him Jack. One of the dog collars will do for now, until Smith can fix a better one. Two prizes for the price of one. Looks like a bit of a simpleton, but he seems strong and appears to have a way with animals. I reckon his lordship will give us a bonus for him; and along with the safe delivery of his niece, there might even be a promotion in it. Gerard! Conrad! Get the stag back to camp and have it prepared for later." Jack did as he was ordered, and once the man was secured, spoke to him. "You're the property of Lord Banham now m'lad. Got that? Do you speak, or just grunt with the animals? Got a name?" He understood none of this. This language was unknown to him. He just stared vacantly, and complied with being pushed and tied, and followed when the lead to his collar was jerked. "Ah well, guess we'll just call you Stag then."

Helen sat in the meeting hall at the enclave, looking up at the apparition in front of her. Fully eight feet tall with golden hair cascading down its back, and fucking wings! Wings it had flown in on from the terrace over the valley, with its two companions, one equally proportioned, and the other smaller, maybe six and a half feet, but even more beautiful. "So what the fuck are you? You look like angels, but you scare the shit out of me, especially when you fly in here and call on me by name."

"I am Baliel, and these are Cariel, my sister, and Fariel, my cousin, and no, we are not angels, at least not anymore. Recently, and for ages past, we were bound in the form of mud dwelling serpents, or as you know them eels, and long ago, we were watchers. The Lady Eve has freed us from the domination of Ouroboros, but many were lost in the fight to banish that creature from this world. I am sad to say that Lady Eve was amongst them."

Helen's legs buckled, but she was caught up by Cariel and laid on a couch before any of her companions could move. Helen's head reeled. She floundered in a black tide of grief, and in those dark moments of despair, she found the bright spark of her absolute faith in Eve. Shaking off the kindly administrations of her friends, she sat upright, and determined to confront this new situation head on. "No! I don't accept this. Did you see her die? What is that body language you are exhibiting? Is it a shrug or a shudder? You didn't see her die, did you? And how do you explain the reappearance of Sophia at my side? She lives somewhere, I know it! We will find her. We must get her back. We cannot defeat Afsoon without her. You will help us."

"No one saw her die Lady Helen, but nevertheless, she is lost. If it is a comfort to you, so is Afsoon. They were last seen being shaken into oblivion by Ouroboros. Even as she met the great emptiness, yet she fought on. It was a fitting end, and we honour her courage, but there can be no coming back from the dark place into which they were both hurled."

"You are wrong! She has defeated death before and will do so again. If Afsoon is gone too, then we can still win. We will win, for Eve, for our messiah. We will fight on until she returns. She risked all for you Baliel, will you stand with us?"

"No Lady Helen! We cannot. Our history has been one of betrayal to the creator himself. Lady Eve knew this, and rightfully bound us with the most sacred oaths, to defend the portal. In return she gave us the Sargasso Sea as our domain, but forbade us to leave its confines until such time as we have proved ourselves worthy. We will not betray her trust. We will regain our honour."

"But you believe her dead. Surely that changes everything."

"We believe her lost, not dead, and until we know different, we will honour the oaths made to our Lady. Nor can we share our knowledge with you, but even though we risk hope of redemption and reconciliation with our father, for our Lady's sake, we will guide you when we can. And I do not think it will detract from our honour to leave an adviser with you. My sister Cariel has requested that she be our envoy among you. We will keep the Sargasso safe from your enemies, and it will be a place of sanctuary for you should things not go as you would wish; at least for as long as we can make it so. May the Lady Eve be always with you, in spirit if not in form." He turned and leapt. In a single wing beat, he was gone.

Helen looked at Cariel, then at her companions. Matt just shrugged and sighed mournfully, Janie stared at Cariel in bemusement, and Freddy scratched his head in a distracted daze. "How the fuck do we accommodate an ex-angel?"

Before she could say more, Cariel had swept her up, and flew out and up to, what in Eve's absence, was now the terrace to Helen's apartments. "I will be happy for a space on this terrace. I may thus stay close to you, and I like the open air, and this lofty position above the valley. Good health Lady Helen. No harm will befall you while I live. You should rest and conserve your strength, for you are now regent and steward of an empire, and of a great and wonderful cause."

Afsoon awoke, but he was no longer Afsoon. His knees buckled, but he did not fall. Instead, to regain balance, he stepped forward in two great strides from beneath the arch of the standing stones that were cloaking him in shadow. Finding himself at the head of an altar, he looked out into a circle of masked supplicants. All fell to their knees in submissive ecstasy. He stood naked and glistening in the torchlight. He had no memory of his past, nor did he understand in what mumbling language he was being worshipped, but the opened and bloody chest of the beautiful young boy on the altar gave testimony to his status as their deity. He plucked the still steaming heart from the earthen bowl into which it had been placed, and bit from it as one would from an apple, and then turned to face his unholy flock with blood congealing on his chin. Arrogantly, he paraded his engorging and disproportionate manhood. Without stopping to consider its sex, he reached for the nearest naked form and forced his seed into the unresisting but terror-stricken creature, before moving onto the next, as was his right as God and Master.

Stag was manhandled to the back of a cart and his lead was made secure to it. Jack called to a young squire. "Oy Jorge, Get over here boy! This is Stag. He is a gift for Lord Banham. Have a proper collar fixed and his feet manacled, and wash him down before the stink makes me vomit. You can beat him if he resists, but don't damage him in any way that can be seen. I'm going down to the brook to get some of this muck off my hands."

When he'd gone, Jorge grabbed a younger lad by the ear. "You're with me Mickel. Get a bucket and wash that fucking simpleton down, and get the smith over here to put manacles on him." He complained to Mickel rhetorically. "I'll be a knight before long, and Jack will eat shit." Then realising he was on dangerous ground, he addressed Mickel with threats. "Repeat that you little turd, and I'll cut your balls off. Got that boy?"

With Mickel hastening away to obey instructions, Jorge decided to amuse himself by venting his spite on the dumb creature in his care. He broke a stout branch from a tree and wandered over to where Stag stood, just as he had been left, still with a vacant look on his face. As Jorge drew close, he pinched his nose and turned his head to the side. "My god you stink! You been lying in pig shit or something? Answer me boy." After repeating himself several times with no response, he swung the branch at Stag's head, but Stag grabbed and held it before it got anywhere near him, and however much Jorge tried to pull it back, he couldn't move it an inch. In a rage of frustration, he kicked out at Stag's groin, but found his foot held equally firmly. Struggling achieved nothing. On seeing Mickel returning with a bucket and the smith in tow, he was shocked from his efforts and stopped his struggles. Stag let him go.

"What were you doing with the slave Jorge? Looked like you two were dancing?" As he spoke, he bent to put the manacles onto Stag's ankles, and hammered in and flattened the ends of the pins.

Jorge was red faced but quick with an excuse. "The dolt would not obey my instructions, so I had him kiss my boot." And then with a sly grin, "I think Jack wanted his hands manacled too, with a short chain behind his back."

"Really, is he that dangerous then? He seems pretty docile to me."

"Don't argue or you'll have Jack and Master Bernard to answer to." He stomped off.

Smith turned to Stag and his tone was not unkindly. "He's a bit of a shit that one, but I had best do what he says. I'll give you a bit of slack though. Too short a chain will be damned uncomfortable when you are running behind the cart, and there's a good half pace of chain twixt your ankles. Run with short strides, and you should be able to avoid a fall." He replaced the collar too, and then with his finger, he tapped the hollow just below where Stag's collar bones met. What's that tattoo under the dirt, some sort of pentagram maybe? The devil's sign!" He crossed himself. "Keep it covered if you can. It will not be well received around here. Are you mute?" Receiving no response of any kind, he addressed Mickel. "Wash him down Mickel. Get him a jerkin to keep him warm and to cover that sign, and a cloth to cover his manhood. Fix it securely, so it doesn't come off when he's running."

Mickel finished his chore as soon as he could, and raced off for the items smith had demanded, and a piece of cord. By the time he returned, some clarity had started to glow in Stag's eyes, and he was looking around curiously. After Mickel had quite expertly secured his makeshift loin cloth, Stag demonstrated that he could already use some basic vocabulary in this alien language. "Thank you Mickel. that is a good job."

"Blimey Sir, you speak with the air and accent of a high knight. How came you to be a slave? Were you on some quest, and robbed and injured in the head? Master Bernard who found you, said you were a simpleton. You look and act like one, even if you do speak like a nobleman." Stag did not respond. Something had caught his interest in the trees. When he looked back to answer, Mickel had already become disinterested, and had gone back to the main camp.

After a long day of Stag tirelessly half running behind it, the cart was at last, brought in to help form the outer circle of the encampment, close enough to clearly see the fire and the stag roasting over it, but too far to benefit from any of its warmth. Stag sat and looked, and listened to the comings and goings of the camp, but again his attention was diverted to something in the trees. A noise brought his awareness back to the campground. A girl of about fourteen was leading a young horse, a fine looking grey, in his direction, but it was faltering on its front right leg. She was meandering to and fro, but ever closer to where he sat on the ground behind the cart. When she was close she spoke to him without looking at him. "Are you hungry?" He said nothing. She threw him a hunk of meat, which he deftly caught in his teeth, and laying his head back, managed to bite off pieces and chew them without losing the larger piece, all this without the use of his hands. He wasn't sure whether she was looking at him with curiosity or disgust. She started to make off.

"Thank you my lady. What is wrong with your horse?"

She stopped, keeping her back to him, checked that no one was looking, and turned to face him. "It's true then? The boy Mickel said you spoke like a nobleman, how have you come so low?"

"Your horse my lady, is it hurt?"

"I am not a lady, at least not one of any import. I am my lady's maid and this is her horse, or it was. It is lame and was due to be our meal tonight, until Master Bernard killed the stag. A stay of execution, but not for long, a lame horse will slow us down, and Master Bernard is in a terrible hurry. He says this forest is unsafe, and we must get through it fast. My lady has argued with him, but an injured horse is useless. It will be killed tomorrow. I wanted to let him wander and graze on his last night."

"I think he is not so injured. Bring him here where I can see him."

"I am not a fool sir. I would not place myself within your reach."

"Then release him. He will come to me."

"He will not sir. He will try to return to my mistress."

"Show me then. What can be the harm?"

She hesitated. "Master Bernard said he found you laid alongside with the stag. Is it true?" He inclined his head. She wrung her fingers and licked her lips in thought. "Very well then." She released the lead rein. The horse nodded, hobbled to Stag and put its nose into his lap. Stag twisted around so that he could clasp the horse's foreleg with both hands. He felt up and down the leg, and then gave a sharp twist. The horse reared, neighed, and turned away, trotted a few paces, stopped, turned back, dipped its head at Stag, and then trotted off back to its mistress, with the girl in hot pursuit. As she passed between two carts she stopped, and he heard a loudly whispered "thank you," before she took off again to the far side of the fire, where her mistress's coach was positioned.

As the first rays of a cool red sun filtered through the leaves, a small delegation made its way to him from the clearing around the fire: Master Bernard, the smith, the girl of the night before, and another, maybe two years older, who was presumably the girl's mistress. They were leading the grey with them. Master Bernard strode ahead. As he approached, he spoke to Stag. "The Lady Elaine says you talk, so why haven't you spoken to me or my men? Speak now or it will not go well for you."

"The only one who spoke to me was your man Jack, and I was confused. I still can't remember what happened, or anything else."

"No memory you say? Seems like a tall tale to me. The sort of thing a man might say if he had run away and left his lord or his friends in danger. Is it true you fixed Lady Catherine's horse?"

"Yes."

"Then I have work for you. We are transporting the Lady Catherine to be the ward of her uncle, Lord Banham. Her father has also sent a gift, a mighty stallion war horse, for stud purposes. It is a monster. None can ride it. And those who approach it risk life and limb. It will not be led, so we have tried to keep it boxed in a high cart. It has fair ruined it, and trying to contain the beast has slowed our progress considerably. If you can calm it, and tend to the injuries it has inflicted on itself trying to escape, and you promise to behave, I will have you un-manacled. You will continue to wear the collar until we get to our destination. Your future status will be decided by Lord Banham, if you survive your encounter with Titan that is."

Lady Elaine arrived in time to hear this last. She addressed her mistress. "My lady, it is not right to put this man in with Titan. The horse is mad. It will kill him, and did he not save your wonderful Dancer?" She turned to Master Bernard. "Good sir this man has proven skills. Surely they can be put to better use. To send him to his death would be a terrible waste."

"Contain your maid Lady Catherine. The only waste here is the time we delay in continuing our journey. If this man can help, well and good, if not, then he would probably have been dead anyway, had we not rescued him from this forest. Unchain him smith, and let's see what he is capable of."

The horse had somehow got free. The cart was wrecked. A man lay unmoving close to it, and several others were nursing injuries. Its front legs were hobbled, and the horse was rearing and dashing its hooves on the ground, trying to shake loose the chain. One of the men at arms was aiming a cocked crossbow at the creature. Bernard shouted at him. "If you release that bolt Conrad, the next will be in your head, and that would be a mercy. What do you think Lord Banham would do to you if you harmed his stud horse? Now step back. We will see what our Stag man can do. As Stag approached Titan, it came down heavily with its hooves either side of a rock, and the chain snapped. It ran back and forth looking for its escape. Everyone scattered except Stag. He stood between it and the woodland trail it had decided on. He walked forward.

Titan reared on its hind legs and pawed the air, readying to dash Stag's skull. There was a scream from Elaine. At the same moment the air went black with arrows and crossbow bolts. Three columns of horses crashed into the clearing, their riders slashing with swords and axes at anyone with a weapon.

As Titan's hooves came down, Stag leapt sideways with incredible speed, and grabbed Titan's mane to swing around in an arc and land squarely on its back. Without so much as a kick, he directed the enraged creature straight into the melee. Two armoured horsemen blocked his path. Titan smashed through the first, knocking horse and rider to the ground. The second got alongside and swung a broadsword in a decapitating blow at Stag's neck. Stag wasn't there. Somehow he had dropped off on the opposite side and slithered under Titan's belly, to come up under his assailant's sword arm. Stag wrenched him from his horse in an arm breaking throw, retaining the man's sword in the process, before remounting Titan, and driving him on towards the Lady Elaine. He grabbed the scruff of her gown and heaved her up in front of him, then made for the trees. But she fought with him, screaming for her mistress. Exasperated, he turned back into the fray, cutting down two more armoured men, the one on foot lost the arm with which he had grabbed and torn Lady Catherine's gown. She was slung up in a similar fashion to her maid, and laid over Elaine's struggling body, before Titan bolted into the forest. Stag managed to direct them to the brook, using it as a shallow path to make good speed away from their aggressors, before cutting back into the forest, through an intricate lacework of criss-crossing trails. The two ladies had managed to get into position astride Titan, and in front of Stag, despite the difficulty of hitching up their gowns. Catherine had yet to stop berating Stag for his cowardice in leaving the rest of the party to their fate.

Eventually, when he thought they had placed enough forest behind them, Stag called for a rest and set about removing the arrow from Titan's shoulder. Catherine came to his side with a peace offering of some water that she had managed to fetch from a nearby stream in a large piece of silk ripped from her gown, and which she had fashioned into a bag. "I am sorry for calling you a coward. You risked your life for us, when you had every reason to hate us. I just had to shout at someone. My father says I am always ready to lay blame. You were very brave and very selfless. If any remain alive, they are slaves to their captors now, and god knows what fate they had in store for Elaine and me.

"Elaine has pointed out that any normal man would have looked after himself, and she asked me to remember that you saved Dancer. He is probably in their hands now, but they will look after him. He is a valuable asset since you cured him. Thank you. My uncle will reward you I am sure, if you can get us to him." Stag cleaned Titan's wounds, spitting on leaf mould to form a paste, and rubbing it into the cuts he had made when he had withdrawn the arrow, then he found some grasses for him to chew on, and in the uncanny way he had with animals, bid the beast to stay and rest awhile. Titan settled down trustingly. Elaine had collected wood and tinder and was trying to start a fire by rubbing sticks. Her hands were raw with the effort. Stag didn't know what made him do it, but he ripped a nail from his little finger and threw it into the wood, causing it to burst into flames. Elaine and Catherine both looked at him in puzzlement, but said nothing.

When morning came, Catherine was startled from her huddle with Elaine by a wet tongue raking the side of her face. She screeched bringing the others scrabbling to their feet. "Oh my darling, my darling Dancer. However did you find us? Were you following all the time?" By now she was sitting and hugging its neck with tears in her eyes. She looked up and mouthed another thank you at Stag. Stag broke camp quickly, fearing that if Dancer could find them, so could others. Breaking again at midday, Stag asked the girls if they had any idea how to get to Lord Banham's keep. Elaine had some knowledge of the route, and said that they had been on a well-broken trail, and that another two days' journey on horseback would have seen them there. The next substantial landmark was to have been a lake, about a day's ride, but from where they now were, she had no idea how to regain the trail. Stag thought about this and wandered off into the woods. He sat on a fallen tree to contemplate a course of action.

A raven flew down, perched on a branch, and looked at him with curiosity. He gazed back into the depths of its eye and slid off into a reverie. He was gliding through the air above the forest and could see a lake in the distance. The raven's cawing as it flew away brought him back to his surroundings. It circled above for a bit, then flew back to its perch, then did it again, cocking its head as if to say, "your turn." Stag wandered back to camp, and the bird branch hopped above, cawing every minute or so, and alighting on a large bough close to where the girls were tending the horses, although in Titan's case, this consisted of pushing grasses in his direction with a very long stick. "I think we have a guide …" The raven took them on. By dusk they were hungry, having eaten nothing but berries, and a few raw mushrooms gathered by Elaine, but they had reached the lake, and several large trout were no match for the quick reactions of Stag, which Elaine and Catherine set about preparing for the fire. Stag's sword, although awkward, was sharp enough to gut the fish. Elaine had also managed to get some eggs, by robbing nests in some of the smaller trees. This time she started the fire on her own by striking a flint stone against the sword.

Seeing all was in hand, Stag decided to clean up. He swam out to the centre of the lake and dived. He descended fast but felt no inclination to arrest his progress. His eyes quickly adjusted to the diminishing gloom, and soon he found himself coming to rest on the bottom. His hands and knees sank several inches into the silt, and his pedalling feet caused a murky cloud to engulf him. As he flexed his knees to push for the surface, his toes splayed over something hard and cylindrical. Instead of springing up, he tumbled in the water and searched with his hands. After a few moments of panning the bottom, he located it. The rest of it seemed embedded in the bedrock, or maybe between rocks. He pulled at it but it would not shift. He was sure he would never find it again if he left it. Placing his feet either side of his hands, he heaved. It seemed to move a little. He exerted every muscle of his body and every ounce of his immense strength. It wobbled a little but remained wedged. He relaxed and decided he would have to leave it. And then it seemed to writhe in his grasp. He attempted to withdraw his hand, but it stuck to his fingers, and his reaction pulled it cleanly from its rocky grip. It was a sword, complete with belt and scabbard. Stag passed it over his head and shoulder and swam for the daylight above.

When he returned to the fire, there was a welcome aroma of cooked fish, which the girls were wrapping in large leaves, and Stag noted some men's clothes, staked out with rocks to dry on the pebble beach. "Where did those come from?"

"Elaine found a body back in the trees. It was vile. The worms had already started on it, and the stink was gagging when we moved it, but you needed some clothes, so we stripped it and washed them in the lake, as best we could. We threw some leaves and branches over the corpse, but that smell stays with you. We have both rubbed our hands raw with gravel from the lake trying to get it off of them. There was a dagger nearby too. We will bathe and wash our own clothes after our food, if you will keep watch. What have you got there?"

"It seems we are all finding treasures. It is a sword. I found it at the bottom of the lake. I will examine it after our meal, and perhaps you will then show me where you found the body. There may be more, and they may not be dead. He looked around, chose the tallest tree, and deftly shinnied up to the topmost branches, where his keen eyesight could survey their surroundings. There was a thin wisp of smoke in the remote distance, but nothing of any immediate concern that he could see. Where was a friendly raven when you needed one?

After the meal, he left the girls to go and sit on a rock on the beach and examined the sword. The belt was more of a harness and was designed to be worn on the back. It was woven from black wire and was as supple as silk, with a hefty silver clasp. The pommel was composed of five black oval stones and was of a shape to perfectly fit his hand. They remained cool to the touch despite his handling of them for some time. He knew somehow, that even in the heat of battle, it would not become slippery with sweat. The scabbard was similar to the harness except that it was rigid. Finally he drew the sword. It whispered from the scabbard with a tone that seemed to silence the world. It was light swallowing black and had an edge that might cut through granite. Stag decided to test its edge and walked over to where Titan was grazing. The girls, who had joined him on the beach and were watching, now followed to see what he was about. He wasn't sure how, but he knew he had the skill. Elaine, realising his intent screamed "no!" He cut down, in two rapid cross strokes, and sliced through the metal cuffs that had been used to hobble Titan's front feet. They fell clear, without harm to Titan, who remained uninterrupted in his grazing. Stag cut the collar from his own neck then quickly re-sheathed the sword. The girls just looked at each other fearfully.

"Come show me where you found the body. Then it will be time to move on." Stag did a quick search and found a discarded bow, and a few paces on a quiver of arrows, as though someone who was being pursued was shedding weight to increase the speed of his flight. Another day's ride took them through less dense woodland, and finally to the edge of the forest, from the cover of which they looked out at Lord Banham's castle, a forbidding edifice some five miles distant, on a rocky prominence.

Catherine stepped forward, but Stag held his ground. "My apologies Lady Catherine, but from what I have heard of your uncle, I would sooner not meet him. Are you sure you cannot return to your father? I feel your life there would be better than here."

"That is a decision I have no part in. My father must keep his allies on board. A year from now I will be wed to Lord Banham's son. I will be treated well enough, and you need not fret for Lady Elaine. Her father is old, and otherwise childless. She will inherit his estate and will have more suitors than enough."

"And what do you have to say about that? Should you not both marry for love?" The girls exchanged glances.

"You are a strange one Sir Stag. I call you that for clearly you are a great knight, but you are also very naïve, and more than a little frightening, demonic even in some part. Possibly it is your loss of memory, and the injury that must surely have befallen you, which causes your unusual behaviour. Yet you have been a good friend and guardian. Call on me if ever you have need, and I will try to help. Take Titan. He is yours now. I hope that you soon regain your memory and find your people."

Elaine stepped forward and raised herself on tiptoes to quickly kiss him. "Thank you Sir Stag. I will always remember you, and our time on the road. There is a town some five miles from here, built around an abbey. You can find lodgings there." She pointed. "Just follow that road." She slipped the dagger into his belt. "This dagger has a jewel in the hilt. You can trade it for your keep."

He handed it back and folded her fingers around it. "Keep it. I can get money. Hide it. One day you may need to defend yourself. I wish you well Lady Elaine, and you too Lady Catherine." He swung up onto Titan and headed back into the woods. He knew that unwelcome followers were not far behind.

A small group from the bandit force had tracked them and would probably have caught them had their journey been longer. They still represented a danger to the girls, if they were fool enough to pursue them into Lord Banham's lands. Stag decided to remove that danger. His keen senses alerted him to their presence far before they were aware of him, and then it was too late. He bore down on them while they were at rest, one with his pants down relieving himself, and another returning with water from the stream. There were only four, and becoming victims was far from the forefront of their minds. He felt justified in killing them, but it was too easy. He settled for beating them senseless, stripping them, and leaving with their horses and possessions. He had had a very enlightening conversation with one who had regained consciousness before Stag rabbit punched him back into oblivion. And this seemed to confirm much of what he had divined from his talks with the girls. The King's resources were stretched to breaking point in financing and resourcing crusades across the sea. He had become so weakened by this, that many of the aristocracy had broken ranks, risking ex-communication in order to expand their own domains here. Some were emboldened to conspire for the throne. The kingdom was at breaking point. There was a usurper on every corner. Robber barons ruled and increased their lands wherever they could. The raiding party that had attacked Catherine's encampment were Lord Taggard's men, a powerful neighbour of Lord Banham's, who had recently decided to double the size of his estates, and counted the forest through which they travelled as part of his new domain. Lord Banham disputed this claim and saw the forest as his own.

Arrowfen

Apart from a change of clothes, a good cloak, and a stout pair of boots, Stag sold everything (including the newly acquired horses) on the way to the town that Elaine had mentioned. Once there he found a tavern, took a seat by the fire, and ordered food and a beer. A middle-aged and tired looking tavern wench served him. She was nevertheless quite good looking, and was grabbed and molested by a few of the patrons, as she made her way through the throng to where he sat. Apparently resigned to their raucous attentions, she placed a tankard and a pasty on the table before him. He asked her if there was a room to be had for the night, preferably something clean and airy, and for sole occupation. The landlord was shouting at her to clear the tables and help out in the kitchens, but she came back a few minutes later, and said a room was available for two silver coins. She leaned forward and whispered. "Don't pay more than one, and that is too much. Insist on looking at the rooms and take the one at the front. It is his, but for silver he will give it up."

The landlord was calling again. He barged his way through the crowd, jostling a young serving lad, causing him to drop a tray of food. Grabbing the lad by the ankle as he tried to scurry away, he beat him viciously with the tray. The wench grabbed his arm, and he turned on her, cuffed her hard around the ear, and shouted at her to shift her lazy arse, and get the rest of the patrons their orders, and she had better be nice to them. "I'll be dealing with you later my lady." The last was said with broad sarcasm and got cruel laughs from many of the patrons.

Stag took her advice, and got a barely acceptable room, which after his insistence, the landlord got the wench to clean, and then, leaning so close that his cabbage breath made Stag turn away and grimace, he whispered breathily that for another silver she could be hired to perform other services. Stag found this distasteful but paid the coin, deciding this would be the best way to provide her with some time to rest from her onerous chores. She finished the room and said she would return shortly.

She came back, clearly having washed herself and brushed her hair, and wearing a fresh homespun dress, which she started to unbutton and pull over her head. Stag stopped her. "I don't need those sorts of services."

She looked fearful. "Then what? Do you want to punish me? Have I displeased you? What would you have me do?"

"You are out of place here. You walk like a lady, and your voice is cultured. I think your story is not a happy one, but I do not want to pry. Please, just take a rest and keep me company. Perhaps you can tell me something of the land around here. I am displaced from my homeland and would like somewhere to call my own. Is there perhaps a parcel of land I could purchase?"

The tension left her a little. She sighed and sat on the bed. "Land? Have you got an army? All the good land has been grabbed by the powerful. My husband held a keep by the sea some ten leagues from here. Lord Fearos demanded fealty. My husband was a baron in his own right and refused. He was a brave and battle-hardened warrior, and our keep was well defended, but we were no match for the might of the mercenary army sent against us. We were besides betrayed, and the siege did not last long. They butchered my husband, plundered, raped and murdered my household, and when they had finished with me, they threw me onto the streets to beg for food and succour. I had no choice but to sell myself into service to survive. No one wanted me. I was an object of ridicule. The grand lady brought low.

"I was spat at, kicked, and refused food. Perhaps I had been too proud and remote from the people. The owner of this establishment," she spread her hands indicating their surroundings, "had been a stable hand. He had come into a small inheritance and left our service just before the keep was attacked. He was the only one who would take me in, and he seemed to relish being able to pay a pittance for my pledge of service. He paid a lawyer far more to make it legally binding. He is a weasel, but I am his property now ... Even if you had an army Sir, unless it was a very big one, you can forget land. All good land is gone." She shrugged dejectedly and looked at the floor.

"What is your name?"

"Anne."

"Anne, you said good land is gone. Is there any bad land, land that perhaps is not wanted, where I might hide and be left alone?"

"Are you sporting with me Sir? Who would pay for, or even want, bad land?"

"Please, just tell me if you know of any such."

She looked at the ceiling for a time, then started to speak. "I suppose there is ... but no, you couldn't even build a house there. It would be ridiculous ..."

"Please finish what you were going to say."

"Very well, but you won't thank me for it. There are the bog lands, ten days on horseback from here. They sit in a bowl-like dip that is below sea level. If you could negotiate the boggy wetlands, and I am not sure that anyone ever has, although many have perished in the swamp, that have been fool enough to try, you might find a small area of hard ground, where the land rises high on the other side, to form a half circle of sheer cliffs rising from the sea ... In time the sea will probably break through to form a crescent island," she mused.

"One more question. You said your master employed a good lawyer when he bought you. I may have need of such a one. Does he still practise in this locale?"

"Yes, he often helps the Abbey with deeds of purchase and such like."

After calming, exercising and tending to Titan in the stable, Stag was gone for most of the day. He returned with a young black mare, and had it placed in the stable, several stalls up from Titan. He spent some time in the afternoon with the landlord of the tavern, negotiating terms for the keep of the extra horse, and other matters, then went about further business. In the evening he returned with the lawyer and two eminent towns persons in tow. They took a table by the fire, where Anne waited on them. A deed of purchase was drawn up and appropriately signed. Four gold crowns were exchanged, one each for the towns persons and two to the landlord, for pledge papers. Stag ordered drinks all round and one extra, and invited Anne to sit and drink with them. She looked at her master and shook her head. "I have chores to do."

"You will do no more chores for this man." He handed her the deed of purchase and her pledge papers. "Do with them as you will. You are a free woman."

She looked nonplussed. "But where will I go? I have no money."

"I have little knowledge of this land and its ways. If you will be my guide and assistant I will see you well provided for."

"What choice do I have?"

"I'm sure our good landlord here would keep you on for a small wage." Stag raised his eyebrows at him. He nodded far too readily. "I could perhaps look in from time to time to see you are well treated." He looked significantly at the landlord. "Or I could buy a small cottage. I would not be here very often and would need a housekeeper."

She sat and drained her drink. "No! I want to be as far away as I can from this town, and this tavern, and this fat smelly excuse for a man, and never come back, if you can make that happen, I will be your guide and assistant good Sir, for as long as you will have me."

"Well said Anne. Then you will need to earn your keep, and I am afraid I am going to charge you with your first chore. Take these riding clothes." He pushed a package towards her. "I am assured they will fit you. Go to the stable. There is a black mare in one of the stalls that needs to be named, and to get to know its new mistress. I take it you do ride? We leave at sunrise."

She jumped to her feet in a high flush and staggered. Stag grabbed her elbow to arrest her fall and pointed her towards the door. She came back sometime later, still flushed, and in a light sweat, but looking stunning in her new riding gear, having apparently just exercised her new mount. Stag was alone by the fire with a tankard of ale and waved her over to join him.

Before she was halfway, the door crashed open behind her, and four brutish and heavily armed men walked in, the lead man shouting. "Your best ale Master Brewer, and we will have a place by the fire!" Seeing Anne, he grabbed her shoulder. "You! You will serve us. Our master may want to get to know you better." He looked her up and down lasciviously, then more closely at her face. "Do I know you?" He shook his head. "Be about it woman." He shoved her so hard she fell to her knees, but she was up and off without breaking stride. "Perhaps it will come back to me."

A heavy hand came down onto Stag's shoulder, "Move!" Most of the patrons had already left, and others were trying to follow without drawing attention to themselves. Stag rose, gave a courteous bow to the brute, and backed off. Another of the foursome tried to shove him on his way, but Stag just walked on with no noticeable acceleration in his stride, and took a seat in a shady corner. The landlord remained out of sight in the kitchen, but shoved Anne back out with the drinks. Stag thought he heard him say "Fearos."

Anne placed the drinks and went to leave, but was grabbed by the thigh and hair, and spun around, the hand shifting from thigh to breast, and she was forced to face a bearded giant of a man.

"Does she look familiar to you Gaunt? You were at the Beaumont siege, weren't you?"

Gaunt took hold of her chin and looked close. A broad smile creased his rough features. "Oh yes, I remember you. Thought I'd split you in two. Oh well, I think we can rectify that oversight right now." He started to fumble at his waist. Anne spat at him and tried to struggle in vain.

A voice saturated with quiet menace cut the air. "Put the lady down, make your apologies and leave." The man holding Anne responded with a guffaw, but could not entirely eliminate a slight quiver in his laugh. Anne was vigorously shaking her head at Stag.

"This is no lady. Half the men at Fearos castle have left her ruined flower dripping with their spent seed. And you Sir are a dead man." There was a whisper that seemed to cloak the room in silence as Stag drew his fearsome blade, and four fingers were struck from the hand that had been holding Anne's breast. The giant Gaunt lunged at Stag with a drawn dagger and was thrown ten feet across the room to land in a heap in the corner, where he struggled to rise. The other two had drawn their swords and attacked together. Stag cut both their blades off near the handle, tripped and rabbit punched one as he tried to escape, leaving him motionless on the floor, and caught the other with a right hook to the jaw that left him similarly indisposed. The giant was back up and threw a war axe at Stag's head. Stag plucked it from the air and threw it back, pinning the hood of Gaunt's cloak to the wooden beam he was trying to duck behind for cover. He looked around for the fingerless man, just in time to see Anne thrusting a dagger up between his legs.

"I think it's time we left." They rode hard, and Stag took them into the forest he had lately travelled.

"This is the wrong direction Sir. We are going inland. The land you seek is seaward."

"The forest will give us good cover and there is something I need to collect." Daybreak had them back at the lake. Stag left Anne with a roaring fire and several fish and went swimming again. He returned with a small chest brimming with gold coin. On his previous swim he had dived several more times after finding the sword, thinking it unlikely that it would be the only treasure, and he was right. He had taken several coins on the first occasion to establish their value, and made sure he could find the chest again when he returned. His guess was that the owner of the body Elaine had found had probably ditched it there in his haste to escape his pursuers, and in the hope of returning later to collect. They took a roundabout route to the bog land Anne had told him of and arrived there two weeks later.

Stag seemed to have an uncanny knack for negotiating the treacherous swamp, and arrived with a shaking mud-covered Anne, and their two horses, on a broad flat area, some forty feet down from the land side edge of the up-thrusting cliffs. He investigated the ground thoroughly, and then produced a bottle of wine to accompany the produce they had brought with them. They set about having a picnic, in what was an incredibly beautiful and unspoilt spot, sheltered from the sea breeze, and full of diverse flora and fauna. A crystal-clear spring sprouted from a fissure in the rocks to complete this mini paradise setting. Anne took the opportunity to clean herself and lay in the hot sun to let her garments dry.

"This is perfect Anne. Do you think we will really be able to purchase it?"

She couldn't help smiling. "I think they will throw it at you. Do not pay too much for it."

"Will you help me to negotiate for it Anne?"

"Why you would want me to is beyond me, but of course I will help you. How could I not?"

"We will build a beautiful house here and make this place a haven of safety. I have a mission Anne. I know it in my soul, and I know I need a safe and private place from which to launch it, and good people around me to help and support me. I just don't know what it is yet. But my memory will return don't you think? And then I will know. I must be ready."

Anne patted his shoulder and lied, reassuring him that she thought all would turn out for the best. In her heart she was confused. How could such a formidable, and (in some ways) frightening man, be so naïve and childlike, and yet so endearing, and damn it, so believable and convincing? If anyone could achieve such fantastical and unlikely dreams as his, she guessed that maybe, it might just possibly be him. She realised that she did indeed feel safe for the first time in many years, and lay back in the grass, to fall into a deep and dreamless sleep.

As Sir Stag's negotiator, Anne had been clever. She had made a bid for the entire peninsula in the name of the man she now referred to as her master. This included a large area of good grazing land on the landward side of the swamp, and made the offer seem not to be insane. Especially when she explained that her master wanted it for a stud farm, using Titan to start a new line of war horses. One look at Titan was enough to convince anyone of the validity of this proposition. The swamp lands were seen as nothing more than an otherwise useless boundary and barrier, between the grazing lands and the treacherous currents, and stormy winds of the sea. The local skinflint baron who owned the lands drove a hard bargain. Anne just negotiated away the size of the grazing land, until they were left with a thin strip, roughly half a mile wide that she made sure included the road that wound into and across the peninsula base line, and led directly to nearby coastal towns in both directions. She still felt though, that they had paid too much.

In the months that followed, stone masons, miners, engineers, and others were employed. Sir Stag had devised a system of consecutive drawbridges and watch towers across the marsh. His knowledge of where to find bedrock highpoints, for the cantilevered foundation columns of the bridges, confounded the engineers. Dykes were built and water drained, to increase the area of stable land, and to create river canals on the seaward side of the Fen. Finally, a tower was built that rose above cliff height to give a view of the sea, and a turreted keep with a courtyard, large dining hall, separate dwellings, plus an armoury and barracks. Some craftsmen from each discipline who wanted to settle, and had earned his and Anne's trust, were retained and given accommodation for their families. Viewed from the heights of Giants Tor some ten miles inland, the tower and keep resembled an arrow, and the peninsula became known locally as Arrowfen. Its reputation grew, and many of those dispossessed in the local land-grab wars, came to beg sanctuary. A small but industrious village developed some distance from the keep, but still seaward of the fen itself. Little was asked of its inhabitants other than loyalty and tolerance.

Crusading knights returning from the holy wars overseas with what men were left of their fighting retinues, were being waylaid and murdered on the road before they could reach and reclaim their lands. One such large group, whittled from forty to twenty-five, and fighting a rear-guard action, with their backs against Arrowfen's swamp, entered the treacherous bog as their only recourse for escape, and were either being cut down, or drowned in the sucking mud. Sir Arrowfen Stag (a name suggested by Anne until he could remember his own) ordered a band of villagers he had been attempting to train in rudimentary fighting skills, to attack from swamp paths only he knew. They drove back the aggressors, and created time for the remaining defenders to be guided through the bog, onto the lowered bridges further back, and then into Arrowfen proper. The beleaguered knights managed to bring the body of their lord with them. A lapsed priest from the village performed the necessary rights and burial service. Arrowfen asked Anne to arrange for medical attention for the wounded, and to invite those who were able to dine with them in the great hall. His offer of hospitality was extended to include shelter until they had recovered, and the road was safe.

At dinner Anne asked their captain Michael the name of their lord and explained that she knew of him. His estate was not very far from her husband's. She informed him, that during his long absence, their Lord Edward had been deemed likely dead, and having no male heirs, his estate had been taken in forfeit to Lord Fearos. Resistance to the claim led to the household being put to the sword, and Edward's daughter Loraine was forced to marry Stephen, Lord Fearos's son, to legitimise the seizure. "What will you do now master Michael? You and your men have no house-hold to return to. Perhaps you have family who can give you succour or employment."

He shook his head. "It is unlikely we will find employment in this god-forsaken land. We will have to take our chances on the road until the king calls us to arms my lady."

Anne continued. "My master Sir Arrowfen has need of a master at arms, and would happily employ, and provide accommodation for you and such of your men as would wish to stay."

Arrowfen, slightly surprised by Anne's offer, nodded his assent, and Michael addressed him. "I must tell you Sir Arrowfen, that the crusade has gone badly. A new witch leader has risen amongst our enemies, since which time they have grown vastly in numbers, and in fanatic zeal. We have been chased across the sea, and an invasion is being prepared. Our lord believed we have at most two summers, before they build enough ships to bring their savage army to our shores. He was returning to inform and support the king, in preparing for the defence of the realm. It is likely that all good men will be called to rally to his aid, so our time here may be short lived. Perhaps through necessity this broken kingdom will unite against a common foe. But it is hard to believe that even then we can be victorious. I have seen fearful magic at work. The witch king's armies bring war engines and monstrous creatures with them, the like of which I have never seen, nor should they walk on this earth. But if I may form a force to protect and escort those, who like ourselves travel this road, and there will soon be many, and if I can send word to our king then until we are called, I think I can speak for my men and accept your gracious offer."

Of those returning soldiers supported on the road, some stayed, and Arrowfen soon supported a strong garrison of a hundred men. Although in the process, Arrowfenites had become unpopular with land owners in the surrounding territories, many of whom were now facing mounting claims for the return of lands, and for damages, from a growing number of armed veterans, often acting as one to display a formidable fighting force. Villagers and off duty soldiers alike were being set about by gangs of thugs and bullies, whenever they were away from the confines of the fen, or visiting local towns. An armed presence was becoming increasingly necessary. Michael had proved a skilled captain however, and the garrison was a well-disciplined and feared fighting force.

Sir Arrowfen, for the most part, allowed him to handle all defence and military matters, with Anne in charge of the house and lands, and also having ultimate authority under himself. Anne was worried about him though. He had been having nightmares, and had become increasingly insular, taking up sole residence in the keep's tower room that overlooked the sea. He spent much time up there in his alchemic laboratory and seemed to be practising what some were concluding to be dark arts into the late hours. She had heard unearthly screams more than once, but could not investigate as he always locked himself in. She was thankful that Michael was in command of the soldiers. She felt some of them might have challenged the conduct and authority of Arrowfen had

Michael not been held in such high esteem. If she didn't have good reason to know better, she might herself, have taken him for a weak man.

His sword had been laid in a chest since their arrival at Arrowfen. His manner had become mild and distant, sometimes even seeming cowardly, when he was offered disrespect, either here, in the village, or on rare occasions, when he visited town, except for once. Anne had accompanied him there to shop for supplies. He had ignored insults and jeers, and even being pushed aside by a gang of thugs, until they had turned their attentions to her, calling her a tavern whore and lifting her skirt. She was quick, but she knew him to be infinitely quicker. He seemed to watch and wait for her reaction. Her dagger was already arcing towards her aggressor's throat, but she was tripped from behind, her wrist grabbed by her tormentor, and a hand thrust up between her legs. It never got past her knees. In a blur of movement, the hand was cut off at the wrist by the man's own dagger, which Arrowfen had lifted from his belt. The others suffered broken limbs and jaws, and were left to limp away, nursing their wounds and supporting their comrade.

His face white with suppressed rage, Arrowfen addressed the crowd that had formed about them. "You all saw what happened. This was mercy, and it is the last time you will see it, should the person or virtue of Lady Anne ever again be violated by word or deed. She is mistress of my lands, and I will defend her honour and authority to my death." He stomped off and never mentioned the incident again.

Whilst loyal to a fault, she was sure, despite the widespread telling of the incident, that even Michael doubted his courage. The miners, masons and engineers however, held him in high respect. He had overseen the digging of a copper mine and seemed to know exactly where the rich seams were. Under his instruction the seaward side of the fen had been drained into a network of dykes and canals and the bridges built to designs that confounded the engineers. Anne herself had received much benefit from this. He was a healer of uncanny skill, and had dealt with many an injury or illness that anywhere else would have been permanent or terminal. Just being in his company for any prolonged period seemed to invigorate and rejuvenate one. She felt and looked ten years younger since being with him, and had eventually entrusted him to look at, and to heal, the physical damage that had been done to her immediately after, and since, the brutal siege of her household. Today an envoy from the king had arrived, and Michael had brought him to the keep to give his message. Arrowfen insisted that both he and Anne remained to hear what he had to say. It was a call to arms. In the building of his war machine, it seemed the Witch King had been more industrious with his exploitation of the resources and manpower of his subjugated enemies than anyone could have anticipated. "The invasion force will be on our shores in the spring, three months hence." Neither the messenger nor Michael was best pleased with Arrowfen's response. He asked Anne to offer hospitality to the messenger while he considered the king's request, then gave his apologies and retired to the tower.

He looked across the sea to where he knew the Witch King's forces were amassing, and, as on so many other occasions over these last months, he prepared to send out his soul to observe the entity orchestrating the invasion of these lands. Several times now it had become aware of him and had attacked his essence with devastating force. On the last occasion it had entrapped him in a psychic prison of white-hot fire. With a superhuman effort he had created an opening and escaped, but had nearly perished in the process. Exhausted, he was left to lie on the cold tower floor, unable to move, until daylight had flooded the tower. He had avoided any further observational excursions since. Now though, more than ever, he needed to know what the creature was planning. Somehow, he knew that he was the only one who could stand against him, except that he did not think he could.

Reluctantly, he dropped to a cross-legged position, and released his soul into the meta-psychic wind that always blew towards the Witch King. It was hungrily waiting and sucked him out before he was ready. Almost instantly, he was in the tent of his enemy. This was the first time he had seen him in the flesh. His back was towards Arrowfen, and he was pouring over the maps and plans of his invasion. Arrowfen glimpsed the landing sites before the creature suddenly folded them and started to turn. The demon, for this was surely what he must be, was aware of being observed. His aura leapt from him, contorting and expanding, and reforming into a deluge of searing black pitch to engulf and bind his enemy where he stood. Panic stricken, Arrowfen hastily dove back into the blasting wind, that was now trying to prevent him leaving, and projected with all the energy he had against the psychic back-flow, but the creature was already on his tail, clawing pieces off of his aura.

He saw himself cross-legged in the tower room and reached like a man in quicksand for that which might haul him to safety. His aura stretched, one end entering and holding place in his physical form, and the other gripped in the tearing talons of the demonic creature outside of himself who was now being pulled in like a shark on a fishing line. Arrowfen struggled for what seemed like hours in the effort to kick it free. Finally his essence snapped, leaving a piece to be consumed by the beast. His heart was pounding at his chest like a battering ram. He was fitting and drooling, and was certain he was going to die. He had lost the power of speech. Fen knew somewhere inside himself, that he needed a strong soul to draw sustenance from. He reached out in his mind and whispered desperately into the mind of another.

Minutes later the door to his tower room crashed in, and as though far away, he could hear Anne issuing orders. "Get him to my chamber. Now! Hurry and be careful. Secure the door. None must enter here. Set guards at the tower base."

"He's heavy. We can't lift him down these narrow stairs. We need more men Lady Anne."

"No!" Anne knelt beside him and gripped his face in her hands. "Fen can you hear me?" Only Anne ever addressed him so, and he responded. He felt the strength in her soul seeping into him from her slender fingers. "Can you stand Fen?" With her help, and that of the two trusted men she had brought with her, he managed the stairs and the passageway to her chamber, where he was laid on her bed. The men were despatched with instructions to say nothing to anyone.

Fen managed a croaked whisper. "Hold me Anne?"

She was beside him in an instant, holding him close and stroking his hair. He trembled violently for half an hour. At last, he was still. He tried to speak but choked. She dripped water between his lips. "You heard my call."

"I have heard you many times Fen, but before now it was in my dreams, and I could only observe. You were always unaware of me. I know you have been battling with the Witch King and trying to protect us. I just didn't know until now that it wasn't my own fanciful thinking."

"Thank you Anne. You are a true friend."

"I am more than that, and you know this for truth. I have seen the looks you try to hide. I know what you need, even if you do not. You would not take it, or let me give it, but you are helpless now."

In the pale light of a full and extraordinarily bright moon, she rose to stand on the bed, stepped over his face and pulled her gown over her head. From her inverted position, she dropped slowly to her knees and removed his clothes. He tried to resist, but pressing her knees onto his shoulders, she effortlessly pushed his flailing hands back onto the bed. Having stripped him bare, she rested on her haunches and looked down at his body. Her face twitched into a slow smile. "Hmmm, I might have guessed. It's a good thing I am on top." She stood again and turned to face him. Her lips parted, as she lowered herself, reaching between her legs to guide him in. He tried once more to rise. She placed her hands on his shoulders and pushed him irresistibly down, then rocked fully back onto him. He knew then that even in full strength, he would have been unable to resist her. Each bobbing thrust poured energy into his weakened soul and then ... "Oh God." Unbearably draining expulsions were interspersed with ecstatic inrushes of energy, and every orgasmic wriggle from Anne, both drained him to physical exhaustion, and filled him to over-spill with spiritual vigour and vitality. In another reality, Helen awoke from her dreams and cried out in borrowed ecstasy.

"Am I like Helen?"

Fen murmured a reply in his sleep. "You are Helen ..." He sat groggily upright, as a cloud of image-filled bubbles riffled through his consciousness, to burst randomly, in soap splash memories, of romantic interludes. His identity stayed hidden, but Helen and his love of her, he remembered. He reached achingly for more complete recall and tried to convey to Anne what he saw. "You are ... a version of her ... but how do you know of her?"

"You have called me by her name often when you have been distracted, and you were never more so than you were last night ... How am I a version of her?"

"She is ... a singularity ... a soul ... a stone dropped into the water of reality. You … you are the ripple and vortex, created by the stone's plunge, as it wobbles its way into the watery depths of her created being. But … you are possibility too … matter from which creation is drawn, near formed reality, less dense, more malleable.

"Without you Helen could not be created or clothed in form. Without her you would be formless chaos. Together you exist, she the centre, and you an extremity, like a hand or fingertip. Further out are more insubstantial extremities, which you in turn draw from, and give existence to, until primal chaos asserts its infinite reign." He stepped from the bed and Anne saw him shimmer into the form of a beautiful woman, before stabilising back into Fen. "In knowing me you solidify and begin to merge with her. I need to see the king's messenger. The Witch King must be defeated …" his voice faded to near absence, but she heard his last words nonetheless. "Must be … absorbed."

It hadn't been so hard to persuade Michael to stay at Arrowfen, with twenty picked men, as protector of the land and its lady. Michael had asked for Anne's hand several times now and would not leave her open to danger. Anne had been more of a problem, until he had explained that he would be hampered by his need to protect her from the Witch King's forces, who were likely aware of her importance to him, and would surely move against her. Arrowfen's defences would afford much protection from them. He also needed her and Michael to prepare, and to stock the lands and the keep, for the king's army, which he was sure, would need to retreat to a better stronghold than the king currently occupied following, what Fen was sure would be, a defeat at the hands of their enemies. Fen intended to inflict as much damage as possible on the Witch King's army before that defeat. Then bring the king's forces in a rearguard action to Arrowfen, where a siege could be weathered indefinitely. The revealing of these strategies did much to assuage Michael's pangs of guilt and regret at handing over the leadership of his men to Fen's charge.

Fen had also built a fleet of shallow draft boats, of Viking longboat design which were currently moored at the bottom of a mine shaft, terminating in a large cave (now a hidden harbour behind the small beach, at the base of Arrowfen's cliffs). These were capable of manoeuvring over and around the many sand bars and rocky reefs that surrounded the cliffs. Under his navigational leadership, they would also be able to negotiate the treacherous currents; currents which had wrecked many an unwary ship that had sailed too close. He knew from his observations, and his glimpse of the Witch King's plans and landing sites, that after his attack on the king's stronghold, the Witch King intended to put the king's forces to the sword, and then lay siege, by land and sea, to Arrowfen.

Witch King

The Witch King listened with half an ear to the mindless chatter of his junior priest, as the grovelling little creature hobbled and tripped his way over the sharp volcanic rocks. A sickly-sweet odour emanated from his sweat soaked body, but he made sure to keep his face averted from the king while he spoke. He did not think he had the strength to rise from another backhand blow from his master who objected profusely to the even fouler odour of the breath that was expelled when Copus croaked words through his dry and cracked lips. Copus knew his continued existence was relatively assured for now, because of his knowledge of where to find the sword key, and of the dangers associated with attempting to use or retrieve it.

The heat was becoming unbearable, but the king had insisted on continuing, despite the sun having reached its zenith. The king of course was unaffected by the heat. Nevertheless, when Copus saw him wipe his lips, he gave him the last of his own share of the water. This seemed to amuse the king, but he took it and drained most of the canteen. Tipping the dregs onto the ground, he told Copus to stop his tears as he was wasting valuable fluids. Copus could take no more and fell to the ground weeping at his master's feet. The king waited until his protestations abated, then began to chuckle. "I wondered how long you would last. Try to do better next time little man. I expect far more from my followers than only their best." The king placed his own unused flask next to the man.

"Keep it. I don't think I would want to touch it after your stinking flesh has been in contact with it."

As the sun finally set, they reached the upper third of the volcano, and followed a horizontal path around a small bluff. On reaching the far side, a shock of cold wind seemed to exhale from a man-sized fissure in the rock face. Much recovered, Copus indicated the opening with an attempt at a flourish. "The gateway to the higher plane my king."

"Yes, yes. Stop your childish posturing and take me to the fucking sword."

Deep within the subterranean passage, the lamp revealed a slight widening of the walls that had pressed so claustrophobically close for the past hour or so. A blank perfectly flat rock face now barred further progress. One third of the way up the rock wall, at about shoulder height for a tall man, protruded the magnificently worked hilt and jewelled pommel of a sword. Skeletal hands still enclosed the hilt in a grizzly double handed grip. Half a torso hung from the reaching arms, above a litter of broken bones, and scattered knightly accoutrements. "The fate of the many, who have tried to avail themselves of the sword's power these past centuries lie before you my king. But for all their skill and arcane knowledge, none were true deities as you are my Lord, my God. Only a true deity can use the power of the sword to cut asunder the rock face and enter the source world, or use its power as a weapon superior to all others. Will you take the sword My King? Should I begin the opening ritual?"

He let Copus prepare his dark ritual and used the man's monotonous chant to focus his own seer senses. The sword was not only an object of power in itself. He thought he could feel through ethereal substrates that seemed to connect him to its power flow, that the thing had robbed power from those who had tried to wield it. Their deaths seemed to give it sustenance and life. "Stop your prattling man and grasp the sword!"

"But Master, I am unworthy. It will kill me and take my sullied and unclean soul! And who then will prepare the way for you with the necessary ritual. I say this not for myself you understand My King, but only so that you may be unobstructed in swiftly inheriting what has waited so long for you to take."

"What am I Copus?"

"You are my King, my God, and ruler of the universe."

"And yet you defy me. Grasp the fucking sword!"

Weeping and shaking uncontrollably, Copus defecated as he reached for the sword, then screamed. The king watched his flesh wither and slough from his bones. Copus had served his purpose. The king understood now how to shut off the power draw and subdue it to his command. Swiping Copus aside, he reached for the sword and sliced it easily down through the rock face, which peeled open into a gothic arch, wide enough to admit a man. He stepped forward and was thrown violently back several feet. He summoned his power and reached into the barring spell with his spirit mind. Although powerful, it seemed to be of a simple construct. The king extended himself into its matrix and carefully picked it apart.

It was irksome and time consuming, but he was sure it would be worth the effort. Cautiously he stepped forward again. This time he was thrown some thirty feet back along the passage, bouncing off both walls before coming to a sliding and skin grazing rest. The droplets of blood from his palms and knees burst into flames. He studied this phenomenon with interest, before resuming his efforts. A day and a night passed, and still he could not pass through the portal. Finally, he settled down in front of the opening, and reached through with his mind. It was like writhing through sharp sand, but he persisted for many hours. As he was about to give up, something from the other side tugged at his thoughts. A picture of a metallic sphere opened into his mind, and conveyed distorted images of a past he had been unable to penetrate, since his being summoned into this world at the ritual of the standing stones. It was incomplete and sketchy, but he gleaned enough to know that he belonged to another world. A world that could be accessed through this opening, but that he was somehow physically barred from ever entering, no matter how successful he was in breaking the spell and opening the way.

He meditated on the memories and information that had been transferred to him from the strange artefact on the other side. A name presented itself ... Afsoon ... and with the name, a little cache of half memories splashed into his musings. He needed a proxy, and another name promptly rose up in his mind ... Anabel. He had divined, that the intricate structure of the sword, somehow held and contained spiritual power filaments that imbued it with a kind of subliminal mind, and a near sentience. And, that being other worldly, none from this world could use its power, which meant that as far as he knew, he was the only one who could. Therefore he concluded: No thing living in this world could pass into that other place. His "Anabel" was not living, and never had been. She was a construct of past memories from a man and a woman in that other realm. With the power of the sword, and the trapped and undying agonies of those it had consumed, from which it drew its strength, he believed he could bring her into a fleshly existence. She would have no soul of course, and would be merely an extension of himself, perfect for his purposes. She would do his bidding, and being composed from the sword itself, she would be able to come and go, into and from that other realm, and bring him all that he needed, to place the focus of power here, in this world. The pod like artefact that had communicated with him, was somewhat large to bring through such a small opening, but he would find a way. For now he had a world to conquer, and a mysterious presence across the sea to investigate.

Uther

Fen rode through the gates of the king's keep with a force of eighty veteran crusaders. They had been unhappy at him assuming leadership in place of Michael. But gratitude for the shelter and protection he had given them, had earned their loyalty, if not their respect. In the dining hall that night, Fen was unsurprised by the small number of landed nobility represented. Although in truth, the king had amassed a sizeable army, mainly of disinherited nobles returned from the crusades. But also, some would be pretenders for the throne, fighting for pride of place in the dining hall, close to the king. To their disgust, Fen had allowed his captains and himself to be jostled to one of the low tables. A burly latecomer knight had jostled Fen further and was all elbows and shoulders in creating room for himself and his men, all of whom were equally bullying and aggressive.

Fen gave a start when he observed the Lady Elaine sitting near the king. She had grown into a beautiful young woman. He enquired after her from one of the serving women. It seemed that through the ill-timed deaths of several of her relatives, she was now a lady, soon to be rich in lands and wealth. And that the king had taken her and her lands under his protection lest she should meet with a similar fate as many other such inheritors. This may in part have been due to the fact that her lands bordered his own. During the course of the meal, Fen's burly neighbour and his retinue had several times taken food intended for Fen and his men, and he had helped himself from Fen's trencher more than once. But for now, Fen's attention was focussed elsewhere on a disturbance.

Side doors near the king's table crashed in, and a rider on a war horse rode into the dining hall, flanked by twenty fully armed men. The king was on his feet, and swords were drawn by those close to him. The rider dismounted and saluted the king whilst addressing him and the hall, in a booming and arrogant voice. "My King! I claim the hand of the Lady Elaine. It is my right as second lord of the realm, and protector of the Western marches. My champion will fight any who dispute my claim." He waved a hand and a huge giant of a man stepped forward. "You all know Sir Guy Felland, and of his prowess with the sword, lance, and any weapon of war or chivalry. He has twenty kills to his name and has won honours in many battles. If none will meet my challenge, then the lady and all her estates will fall to me."

One of the king's aids stepped forward to respond. "Lord Fcaros! Have a care. You presume too much. You are perilously close to overstepping your authority. You know full well that the only person who might stand against your man is the king's own champion, recovering now from wounds earned in the king's service, and incapable of meeting any current challenge. Your demands are unbecoming of a lord of this realm."

"Still your craven tongue, I have the right and the might to secure my claim, and if none will accept my challenge, I will take what is rightfully mine. What say you my king?" Wearily King Uther looked around the hall of subdued knights and warriors. None would meet his gaze. Sir Guy plunged his sword two handedly into the earth in front of the king and stood behind it, glowering into the hall. Fearos smiled mockingly. Fen had been whispering to his captains. His burly neighbour was in the process of helping himself from Fen's trencher again. Fen turned from his captains, snatched up his dagger and plunged it through the man's hand, pinning it to the table. Before he could scream, Fen wedged an apple deep into his opened mouth, and broke the jaw of the man's captain, who had made a grab for Fen's throat. Fen's captains, both shocked and awed, hurried to do his bidding, whilst Fen himself leapt the table, strode up to and snatched the sword from Sir Guy's grasp, and broke it over his knee. Incensed, Sir Guy lunged at Fen who simply side stepped and tripped him, sending him floundering to the floor. There was a collective gasp and silence as Sir Guy rose with swift and fluid menace from the floor.

King Uther's voice filled the silence with a booming command. "Hold still Sir Guy, or lose your head. If this knight has accepted your challenge, you will meet him with honour on the field, tomorrow." Turning to Fen he demanded: "Your name Sir Knight?"

Fen dropped to one knee. "Arrowfen Stag, My King."

The king looked to his adviser, who shrugged and shook his head in ignorance. "If it would please you My King, I feel you should not waste time with preparations for a contest. You have an enemy at your door. If there must be a contest, it should be here and now in this hall, so we can get back to business."

Uther looked at him assessingly. "Do you know who you fight Sir Arrowfen? He is perhaps the greatest warrior in the land. You will likely die at his hand."

Fen gave a short nod.

"Very well, prepare a space in the hall. Lord Fearos! If this man is willing to lose his life to meet your challenge, then there must be gain should he by some happenstance defeat your champion. Your house and stables within my estate, together with all livestock, your warhorse and that of your champion, and the armour and horse of all of your men who have entered the peace of my hall in battle attire, will be forfeit and passed to the victor. Do you agree?"

"It matters little what you put in the pot, his head will adorn my gates by this evening's end, and as victor I will lay claim to his lands and possessions. I agree."

"And Sir Arrowfen! I am advised that your heritage is unknown.

From where do you hail? Are you indeed a knight?"

"In my own land I am a knight, but my birthplace is far from here."

"No matter, you will probably soon be dead, and as no other came forward, you will be my proxy champion, and will fight for the hand of Lady Elaine. Kneel and be knighted. Should you by some unlikely twist of fate survive, you can tell me more. Shocked by this outcome, Fen's knees almost gave out of their own accord, as in a subdued and distracted whisper, he paraphrased part of the king's statement, "El … aine's … hand?"

Whilst still on his knees, Elaine strode to stand before him. Brazenly placing her hands on his shoulders she leaned forward, and with great deliberation kissed both cheeks. There was an awkward hush in the hall as Lord Fearos glowered at her. "Sir Stag 'Arrowfen' is it now? Is your memory healed then? It seems you are destined always to be my champion." As her lips brushed his ear she whispered. "You are a great warrior, but Sir Guy is skilled, battle hardened and brutal. He will attack fast, with a lunging up-thrust slash to your groin. It is a feint to bring your head down as you retreat. The true blow will come off a complete rotation, with enough momentum to cleave it from your neck. His skill is such that it will land where he or his master wills: at the king's feet, or more likely in my lap. Do not think to attack whilst his back is to you. Others have lost an arm from his daggered back hand cut, by so doing. Nor should you be fooled by his size. He is fearsome, fast and supple as a cat. She stuffed a satin favour into the neck of his tunic and withdrew. There were only a few other ladies in the hall, but Sir Guy was awash with their favours.

Elaine's prediction of Sir Guy's tactics was accurate, but all his sword edge found was empty space. Fen had somehow rolled around with him, copying his rotational movement and delivering a back-hand fist, with the handle of his borrowed sword, to the side of Sir Guy's head, which dented his helm. He seemed unaffected by the blow however, and now looked twice as dangerous. Adopting a low fighting stance, he almost danced in his sword swirling advance. Instead of dodging, Fen met each testing sword slash, allowing them to almost touch his flesh before he parried them to slide harmlessly away. He hoped to trick his opponent into believing more power would be enough to get through his guard, and fool him into putting too much weight behind his cuts, thus providing Fen with an opening whilst Sir Guy was off balance. But his opponent was too wily, and began to slash at odd angles, and stab at eyes and feet, constantly circling to move outside of Fen's fighting arc. Fen, meanwhile, mirrored his opponent, and was now meeting every slash or stab, and stopping them dead, or sliding them off his blade, meeting force with exact and precise opposing force. When, out of nowhere, a mighty two handed over arcing cut came down like a guillotine from above, and must have cleaved any normal man from crown to crotch.

Fen knew his borrowed blade would be insufficient to withstand such a blow and would surely shatter. Whilst vainly wishing for his own sword, he realised that he had been playing to the audience, and decided to let reflexes do what force could not. Stabbing upward, he caught the edge of Sir Guy's sword on the tip edge of his own and used the deflected force to give momentum to his own sideways kick and roll onto Sir Guy's braced knee. From there he threw his weight forward, and grasped both of Sir Guy's downward slashing wrists, forcing them on and into the earth. He then kicked back with both feet, snapping back his adversary's head, and dropping him to the ground like a felled ox. He sprang up with Sir Guy's sword in his hand, placed a foot on his neck and spoke to the king. "My King, this man is unconscious and, although I am sure he would not ask for mercy, I feel such a great champion should be granted it, while he has no will of his own to dispute the decision. You will have need of such fighters in the war to come with the Witch King."

Fearos secretly signalled his crossbow man to release a bolt at Fen. As Fen dodged the bolt, an arrow from one of Fen's captains took the man through the shoulder. Fearos's men were surrounded by Fen's own fully armed soldiers (who had received and acted on his earlier whispered instructions, to arm and be prepared). They were forced to give up the promised weapons, armour and livestock. Fearos saved face as best he could, by cutting the throat of his own crossbow man for his "dishonourable behaviour," and by making his apologies to the king. The king now spoke to Fen. "Sir Arrowfen. You have amazed us all with your battle prowess, and your unorthodox tactics. You will amaze us further if you can find a way to get Sir Guy to fight for us, for surely you have broken his neck. It is cruel to keep him alive. He will not thank you for sparing him. Nor will he want life if he cannot fight. It would be far kinder to show mercy and kill him now."

"Nevertheless, I would like to try My King. I think his injuries will heal. I have some skill in these matters."

Elaine whispered into the king's ear. "It seems the Lady Elaine has knowledge of your healing craft. I cannot say I am not sceptical, but you have done great service today, so I will allow you your request. He is your property now. He will surely die anyway, but if not, when you find, as I am sure you will, that you are unable to heal him. Please do not let him live as the cripple he will undoubtedly be. Swift death would be both honourable and preferable."

Fen's men took, occupied, and made secure, the house and parcel of land and possessions that were forfeit to him. Fen was commanded by the king to attend a war counsel this night, but he was given leave to escort his betrothed to her apartments, see to her comforts, and do whatever it was he thought he could do for the stricken Sir Guy. Elaine kissed him at the door to her bower, and told him to go and attend to his patient. "There will be time for us later Sir Stag of … 'Arrowfen'? My Lord." Her hands were still resting light on his shoulders. She stepped closer and looked up at him with wide eyes. "My Master?" Elaine held his gaze for a moment then gave him a gentle shove. "Now be off and about your business. Heal Sir Guy and serve your king."

The entire counsel of lords and newly promoted commanders of the king's forces went silent when he walked in. This was due less to the new-found respect he had earned after his defeat of Sir Guy, than to the presence of the two men who accompanied him: his captain Sir Benedict De'ath, nephew to one of the lords butchered for his lands by Lord Fearos, and a subdued and morose Sir Guy, who although pale, and rubbing a swollen and sore neck, was fully mobile and able to take his place in the assembled gathering.

Fen gave them cursory and barbed introductions. "My commander in chief gentlemen, Sir Benedict, recently returned from the crusades, and soon to be the inheritor of lands currently held in stewardship by Lord Fearos, following the previous Lord De'ath's demise at the hands of brigands and thieves."

Most lowered their eyes but some angry stares were directed at Fearos, of which Fen, and no doubt Fearos, took note. "And Sir

Guy, whom you all know and respect, and for whom I have yet to decide an appointment, but whose knowledge and counsel I feel will be invaluable."

Fearos's composure was admirable. Apart from a few dark and menacing looks at Fen, he soon established himself as the loudest voice, and was in favour of a quick and decisive victory, using the king's armoured battalions in a frontal assault. "Let them land and assemble their troops on the beach, then hit them with the full might of our heavy horse and armoured foot soldiers, before they have time to organise themselves. Our navy can pick off their anchored and skeleton manned ships at the same time, cutting off any retreat. Then we can get back to the business of rebuilding our fractured kingdom to its former glory."

Sir Edmund Court, the king's wounded champion, who had been carried in and seated at the head of the table near to the king, spoke quietly and in evident pain, but everyone paused to listen. "Such a plan would be suicide. I have seen and fought the forces of the Witch King in the lands across the sea. I have never seen the like of his army. It is vast, well equipped and well organised. He could easily make multiple landings, and each would still outnumber and outmatch our capabilities. The war ships are sleek, fast and heavily armed. We should instead harry them at sea and on land, in rear guard actions, and retreat into fortifications prepared for siege. Even then I fear the worst. He has monsters in his control that would make short work of breaching our walls. If we can bring these creatures down, then maybe, if we also strip and burn the fields and crops in their path, and cut off their supply lines, it might be possible to defend ourselves long enough to outlast their diminishing resources. This is the best plan but I fear it is not enough."

No one liked this plan, especially Fearos, but such was their reverence for the man that they had to give it some credence. And when Sir Guy went against his old master and gave support to the plan, also pointing out that the larger part of Fearos's dangerously vast mercenary army languished on his estates, the inference of a correspondingly depleted royal army, and a weak throne, was evident, it divided opinion almost equally.

Fen remained tight lipped, other than revealing the exact landing site that he had gleaned from the Witch King's battle maps. He had to cloak this knowledge as skilful deduction, laying out strategic reasons why the Witch King would choose such a landing, and revealing a knowledge of the sea and coastline so detailed that he was unsure himself of where his information came from. It aroused some suspicions of how he had acquired such knowledge. The king settled matters by commanding that Fen ride at his side, in the second wave of the advance forces. Fen felt neither plan feasible, but knew his own ideas would be rejected, until there was no other alternative. A compromise was eventually conceived. Word would be sent to the navy to harry and run, but not until the attacking fleet reached the treacherous currents and reefs of the near coast, where the king's naval commander's knowledge would level the balance of the inferior speed and fewer numbers of defending warships. Half of the land forces would ride to meet the attackers on the beach, as Fearos had suggested, but would also be prepared for rearguard action if necessary, only bringing up heavy forces after receiving word from the vanguard that frontal assault stood good chance of success.

With the assistance of Elaine, who was a relative and friend of Sir Edmund, Fen secured an interview with him, and after some skilful persuasion by Elaine, agreement to let him attempt a healing ritual. When he left, Sir Edmund, although still weak, was on his feet, and capable of moving around and giving orders for the siege preparations of the castle. Fen suggested that Sir Guy could assist with defences, and Sir Edmund put him in command of the wall.

Finally, Fen and Elaine retired to her apartments. When she pushed the heavy door closed the sounds of the castle faded to near silence. She turned in a fluid rustle of satin, and raised downcast eyes to look fully into the black on blue of his. Moistening parted lips with the tip of her tongue, she spoke breathlessly. The trace of a flush highlighted her cheeks. "So, Lord Arrowfen … We are betrothed … And we are alone ... What is your pleasure? In such circumstances as these, when you are about to risk your life in battle, I am sure the king would marry us tomorrow … Or if your ardour is such that you cannot wait, he might be prevailed upon to do it tonight …" Seeing him struggle to formulate words of response, she took impish delight in moving close, and expanding her ample chest to expel a heavy sigh … "Or yet still, if you really cannot wait …" she ran a finger across the back of a chair, "we could consummate our union now and marry tomorrow. Any issue that might inadvertently arise from my deflowering would be within an acceptable time frame." She looked down and bit her bottom lip. "Oh Sir Knight! Such a large and dangerous weapon pointed in my direction … It must needs soon be sheathed, before some mishap occurs. But command me my lord and I will happily obey and assist you, in that regard."

Fen could feel the air around her crackling with spiritual energy and imperative portent. Ethereal fingers seemed to reach out from her to caress, enfold, tug and pull, dragging him into the churning vortex of her centre. Her gown whispered from her shoulders to drop in folds at her feet. She stood naked before him, and the unsettling wisps of conscience from his subdued identity puffed away into the ether with a feeble groan. When he broke her carefully preserved maidenhood, they both gasped, she in orgasmic release, and he in a sexually charged surge of transformative energy that threatened to overwhelm him. Spiritually, he became a writhing bucking dragon that expanded and grew in density until, with a final mighty thrust, it tore free of its earthly form, leaving the lovers twitching and helpless, in a tidal expulsion of bodily fluids that drained them into blissful oblivion.

Fully cognizant now of who she was, and her purpose for being here, she remembered from her encounter in the temple with Freddy, that virginal sex was a source of great power, but this was of a different magnitude. There was no time to waste on speculation however. Eve flexed mighty wings and burst into the sky, racing for the western sea. She realised that in her amnesia, she had dwelt too long in this realm. Her presence and her actions here had given it a density of substance it should never have achieved. She realised too, that her unconscious maintenance of a male form, whilst useful in disguising her from he who would seek her out, had sapped her energy enormously. It was time to bring her business here to a close.

From a great height, Eve spied the Witch King's fleet and felt him stir to her probing thoughts. She folded her wings and dropped from the sky like a meteor. She could feel him transforming and expanding his spiritual aspect. Filling her lungs with the fire of her passing, Eve hit him with a burst of searing hellfire, and buried poisonous talons into his flesh, before he had time to transition.

She used her mass and momentum to push him, in an explosion of splintered beams and ships' planking, through the bottom of his ship. Transforming into a giant squid, she dragged him ever deeper into the murky depths. Eve could feel him changing and knew it would be a giant sperm whale. She was already wrapping around his new form, in the shape of an even bigger sea serpent, and was crushing the breath from him. They broke the surface and decimated a quarter of the fleet with their struggles, before Eve resumed a hybrid of her former dragon self, entangling him with poison tipped tentacles, and dragging him into the air. Eve clamped shut his mouth and smothered the blowhole with her bulk. Having achieved a great height where the air was thin, she felt his form shift again. And again she plummeted, taking out several more ships. She could feel the waters boil, with the release from the wreckage of thrashing monstrosities, which were dragged down in their titanic wake. She was a serpent once more, and now he mimicked her form but bigger, with crushing muscles and gaping razor teeth.

This was what Eve had been waiting for. She had felt his lack of density, but she needed the simple form he had now adopted, to put her plan into action. Eve became thinner and infinitely longer, and denser. In seconds she had him wrapped in a constricting and tightening cocoon of diamond scales. "Absorb him," Sophia had said. Eve didn't know what that meant or how to do it, but this was as near as she could get for now. She could work out the rest later. Eve injected threads of herself into all of his vital organs, and individually wrapped and crushed them down until they stopped functioning, but there was nothing she could do to extinguish the essence of him, that lurked deep in the pits of his soul. And now she had other things to worry about. Eve could feel the ebb tide of the unnatural power surge she had experienced on piercing Elaine's maidenhood. If Eve did not soon return to her earthly body and home ground, she would be trapped out here in spiritual aspect, in the midst of a nightmare of thrashing demons, and with the malignant spirit of a monster inside of her. As quick as the thought, a momentary sensation of rushing wind whipped her across the sea and poured her back into the body of Arrowfen Stag. Eve found herself sitting upright next to the blissfully sleeping Lady Elaine. Despite the extra effort, for Elaine's sake, she would maintain this form a little longer.

With his face a metaphor of bewilderment and emotional up-heaval, Fen bent to kiss Elaine, and strode from her apartments calling for Benedict. "Beg an audience with the king and have someone bring me my sword. Prepare and arrange passage for Lady Elaine, and all she would bring with her, to Arrowfen. Also, honour my promise to Sir Guy, and remove his lady and child from Fearos's house. Send them with the Lady Elaine. Say nothing to anyone else. If Fearos hears of it, he is sure to have them waylaid on route. I will move for the king to set out immediately for the coast, and endeavour to ensure Fearos and his men are with us in the second wave, where I can keep an eye on them. I know you want to fight Benedict, but I need you to lead our ladies to safety. Do not take the main road, and travel by night. You may see a Merlin falcon following you. Don't ask me more, but if you encounter any danger you cannot overcome, speak to it. I will know and will endeavour to help. Act fast, act now. If the king can be prevailed upon, I will wed this morn, and you will be ready to leave immediately after the ceremony."

The king took a lot of convincing. Fen constructed a tale of a spy network within the Witch King's army, explaining that he and the Witch King hailed from the same land, and were old enemies. Afsoon, as he now named him, having destroyed and laid waste to Fen's lands and estates. He related that Afsoon was currently indisposed, and that his army was being led by one of his mutant commanders. With both Sir Edmund and Sir Guy backing him, and several others, who would back anyone who seemed able to contain Lord Fearos, the king cautiously agreed to move on the morrow and to strike whilst their enemies lacked the leadership of their king. The wedding went ahead in the king's own chapel. It was a small affair, and the ladies and their retinues were spirited away by Sir Benedict. Fen could feel Afsoon restless within him. He was communing with his commander, on a subliminal level, using the power contained within his own version of the sword, which he must have left in the creature's keeping. Fen somehow had to keep Afsoon's spirit separate from his body, and imprisoned within his own, but it seemed he also needed to capture and find a way to contain Afsoon's sword to truly hold him. Fen's own sword arrived on a cart, still in its chest. The two men at arms, who brought it said none could lift it from the chest, and feared it was useless as a weapon. When Fen leaned from Titan's back and casually threw the scabbard and the harness containing it over his back, they dropped to their knees and, embarrassingly, kissed his stirrup.

The vanguard had reached the landing site in the dark hours before dawn, and before the arrival of their enemies. They had set up defences out of sight from the sea, on the other side of a pebble strewn rocky ridge. On Fen's suggestion they had littered the approach ground with sharp rocks and debris, and covered them in a deep layer of foot binding pebbles. A massive black sailed fleet had been spied, but had been seen to divide out at sea, the greater part heading up along the western straits, where there was a consistent current. Fen knew their destination was Arrowfen, but his attention was required here for now. When Fen arrived with the king's cavalry, they took up flanking positions behind the ridge, and awaited the heavy foot soldiers to take the centre, backed by archers, and such war engines as had been sufficiently mobile to be horse drawn. The road to this shore was good and straight, so they had been able to move quickly, reversing the Witch King's own tactics for speed to his disadvantage.

Afsoon's intent had been to strike without warning, and to wipe out resistance and support inland, with minimum losses. His demon army would then continue its unstoppable march through a land unprepared for war and ripe for plunder. Arrowfen would thus find itself pinched in the grip of well fed and resourced siege forces on its landward side, and an equally well supplied and supported blockade on the sea. Fen's intentions were to inflict as much damage as possible on every mile from here to Arrowfen, to lessen the potency of Afsoon's army, and to keep the king safe, with sufficient resources and men to rebuild the future stability of the kingdom.

The battle was bloody, with heavy losses on both sides. Initially, Uther's forces fared better, until a monster was released from one of the warships. Fen, in the reserve cavalry with the king, spotted it from the ridge, and drew his sword. For one tiny moment the world went quiet, and all looked in his direction. He led a charge that cut through the ranks of Afsoon's army to meet the creature while it was still scuttling from the sea. Twice the size of a war horse and with eight legs, she was fast almost eluding Fen, with all his speed, but he had leapt from Titan and had reached and was on her neck hacking at her with his deadly sword. Equally fast, her front legs were behind her neck, manipulating a web and entwining him, hampering his attack and slowing his movements. Suddenly to all observers, he was gone. The thing had consumed him, but was now seen to be fitting, rolling and hopping, its legs cramping and spreading alternately, as it spun this way and that, and then a mighty spout of blood gushed from its abdomen. Fen's sword thrust through, and slashed a great gaping wound from the inside. Slimy and awash with boiling blood, Fen tore his way out from the wound, slashing this way and that at the tiny creatures attempting to flee the death throes of their gruesome mother. Wiping and spitting the creature's entrails from his mouth and nose, he bellowed at his followers, "Kill them all! Not one must survive!" His men were on them before they left their mother's back, and Fen continued with his awful frenzy, until all were dead. Wasting no time he re-grouped his men, and led the retreat through a mass of awed enemies, who were in fear and disarray, and parted like wheat before the scythe, affording him the chance to join with the king's overrun and departing forces. A fiercely fought rearguard action brought them to the open gates of the king's castle. Sir Guy ushered them in, drew up the drawbridge, dropped the portcullis and secured the gates behind them. They made straight for the king's hall, where a hasty war council commenced. Fen, still covered in stinking gore, presented his plan.

"The castle will fall, so let us use it to our advantage. A skeleton force, which I am perfectly happy to supply and lead, can, with the war machines and defences at this castle's disposal, inflict much damage on a besieging army. Then, when maximum damage has been achieved, let it be taken, but with a booby trap in every inch of it, and when occupied by our enemies, fire the lot, and get the hell out. The king, and any who wish, can go to Arrowfen where my intelligence tells me is the destination of the main body of the fleet. Its natural defences are virtually impenetrable from both land and sea, and with its onsite resources, it can withstand a siege indefinitely. You landed lords will doubtless want to return to your own castles and your domestic armies. You are unlikely to suffer a heavy direct attack until, and if, we fall. The Witch King's forces will attempt to support the attacking fleet making for Arrowfen. It would be strategic and useful if you would harry them on route, and be a supporting force in the land at large." He knew this strategy would suit Fearos and the landed lords well, as it put them out of harm's way, and left the king, his army, and claimants to the stolen lands, isolated and under attack; the hope being that the armies would weaken or destroy each other, leaving the land and the throne up for grabs, and rich pickings to squabble over. Uther, of course, was indignant and insulted until he saw the several monsters coming over the horizon. His advisers persuaded him that it was likely that this plan was his only chance of holding the throne, and suspicions over where Fen got his information from, and why Arrowfen should be so prized by the Witch King, were brushed aside for now.

Sir Guy had followed Fen's instructions, given before the king's army had left for the coast. The castle was booby trapped and ready for firing. Fen took command. The castle siege engines had carefully avoided harming one of the monsters, although in the event, the other two also suffered small injury from these devices. The walls were soon breached, and Fen's plan was put into action. Fen suffered a serious injury dispatching one of the monsters as it clambered over the rubble of the outer wall. The besieging army also took heavy losses during their advance through the traps in the castle precincts. Fen and his men fired the castle as they fled. Another of the creatures, and much of the advance attack force, were near wiped out in the ensuing inferno. Nevertheless, a single monster, and the still larger part of the army that remained, was soon in pursuit of Fen's retreating war party. Just as they reached the cover of the withered forest it happened. The constant killing had spiritually invigorated Fen, and was probably the reason he was already showing strong signs of recovery. Unfortunately, it had also invigorated the presence within. Afsoon chose now to strike, launching a mental attack, and stretching the invisible bonds imprisoning him beyond Fen's ability to contain him. To his men's astonishment, Fen's disguise dropped away. He returned to his female form. Eve was seen to be wrestling with a huge serpent, gouging at its eyes and clawing runnels into its scaly skin. Both antagonists seemed to grow in size and stature, and to rise off the ground. The serpent wrapped Eve in its coils and squeezed. The air shimmered, and then imploded with a "whumpf" and they were gone.

Benedict and Oblivion

Benedict fought fiercely against the onslaught of the outlaws. They were outnumbered. He didn't think he and his men could hold them off for much longer. He feared deeply for the ladies in his charge. A mighty blow from a cudgel brought him to his knees. With his head swimming, he looked up to see the weapon descending again. Just then he spotted the Merlin that had dogged their steps for the entire journey, and he cried out, "Merlin help us!" The weapon never descended. The cudgel wielder screamed in agony as his arm burst into flames, and then an eerie humming filled the air. Swarms of hornets descended on the outlaws. And in the air above the whole scene a ghostly woman wrestled with a serpent. Freeing an arm, she extended her fingernails, transforming them into savage talons. She gouged into the writhing creature's eyes and squeezed. Afsoon twisted in agony and began to transform, throwing out a dozen new heads to replace the one that she had disabled. Eve maintained her grip and rolled. Sprouting fiery wings, she tore through the attackers, ripping off heads and incinerating flesh, as they scattered and fled. With each new kill, she grew in vigour and strength. The serpent felt her burgeoning power, but realisation of her strategy came too late. It struck out with its many heads for its own kills, but was swallowed up in another "whumpf," and clap of in-rushing air as Eve snatched them from this shadow reality.

Eve had risked everything when she'd expended nearly all of her fast-depleting energy to respond to Benedict's call, but the gambit had paid dividends in giving her the opportunity to drink power from the departing souls of her enemies, before Afsoon had realised what she was up to. With her new strength her mind sharpened, and she knew she had to get Afsoon and herself away from here. Away from this world that was fast becoming the true centre of reality, a reality that Afsoon was largely in control of. She couldn't go back to her world. That was barred to her. Instead, she summoned all of her recently acquired strength and flexed her powerful wings. Flapping them in mighty gusts against the resistance of the void, she flew into the ether on a journey into chaos, where she would either defeat Afsoon, or drag him with her into the great unmaking, to destroy them both. Sensing his danger, Afsoon fought wildly, biting at her chest and face, but Eve held true. Out through the orbit of Pluto and the ninth layer of the multiverse, and on into deep space and timelessness, and finally ... There it was. The boiling void, dark explosions and implosions, unheard rustlings, screams and shrieks, sudden creations eaten from within, skitterings and chitterings: probing invisible grasping tendrils of nothingness, reaching ... and waiting, to consume, and to unmake or remake, or part make. Love, hate, cruelty or fear, joy or beauty, could emerge or die, or be reborn here. Here was heaven and earth and hell, seething into and through an unholy intercourse of entwining endless void.

She was exhausted. With drooping wings, she hung at the edge of uncreation, not knowing whether or when it would reach out to take her, and the thing that was writhing within her slackening grip. Then she spied her, but where? Above, below, near, or out there? A figment perhaps, but she so needed someone. Yes, it was her. "Sophia" with a plate of sticky buns, drinking tea, and seated at a table on a veranda, that was on a travellator that was constantly moving away from the boiling oblivion consuming its other end. She was waving and gesturing for Eve to come to her. Eve fell hard onto the veranda next to her. Sophia produced a cat box from under the table, took Afsoon by the scruff of his scaly necks, then shoved him into it, and locked the door.

"There now, we can have our tea in peace. Sticky bun?" She offered the plate. In a daze, Eve flopped into the other chair at the table, and took one of the proffered pastries, then shook her head, to get some perspective back into her thoughts.

"What the fuck!?" She leaned over, anxiously peering through the cage front. Is he still in there? Is he dead? I can't see him." Pulling the cage back from Eve's reaching hand and placing it under the table, Sophia spoke around a mouthful of sticky mess. "Ah now ... that is one of the great unanswered questions. Is the cat, or in this case, the serpent in the box, dead or alive? Or is he both dead and alive, or is he even in there at all? We won't know until we open it. Schrödinger never knew either, bit like creation really, not there until you observe it. Let's just have our tea and ponder that one later, shall we? It's a beautiful morning, and I so rarely get a chance to spend time with my lovely daughter. You are always off gallivanting around the multiverse."

"Whereas you just spend all your time in the black hole of fuck all."

"Touché. You are right of course. I really should get out more; take some 'time … and some space …' for me … for us. Tell you what, when you sort your life out and put this current mess behind you, I promise we will take a holiday together. How does that sound? Some quality time. Just the two of us." She reached over and ran her fingertips down Eve's cheek. "Perhaps later, once we have had some time to get to know one another better, Helen could even join us. How is she by the way?"

"What the hell are you talking about Sophia? How the fuck should I know? I have been kicked out of my world, left stark naked in another gender, with no memory of who the fuck I am, in a world on the other side of insanity, with a crazy lunatic hunting me down. And you are the sick bitch who put me there! I have once again betrayed the woman I love, twice, and have no idea whether one or both of them, now have a monster growing in their womb."

"That is far too many fucks Eve, verbally, and perhaps literally too. Can we please begin to talk like grown-ups now? I do so want us to be friends. First let me put your mind at rest about one thing at least. You are a woman, you cannot father a child, even a monstrous one."

"Shows you know shit you mad bitch! I ejaculated Sophia. My fucking God did I ejaculate. I thought my soul was going to drain out. You can't tell me that there is no chance one of them might be pregnant." Eve's eyes began to well up, and she started to stutter and shudder, and spoke on quietly, in halting gasps. Wh … what will that do to Helen … Dear God we were childless …" Gripping the table edge with blood drained fingers; she rose to her feet and shouted at Sophia. "And even Anabel died before she had a … a … a …" She couldn't articulate any more. Turning her head away, eyes squeezed tight shut, she tried to stop the tears. "L… life. Oh shit!"

She felt warm arms gently enfold her, and allowed Sophia to pull her head onto her shoulder, and stroke her hair, while she continued to shed silent tears that dissolved into the cashmere of Sophia's sweater. After a time, Sophia spoke again, quietly, soothingly, with a voice as soft as a lullaby. "It doesn't matter what shape you adopt Eve, or how much seminal fluid you ejaculate, it is only a disguise. You have eggs Eve, not sperm. And, truth be told, you should never conceive as the woman you are either, it could be disastrous on a scale you could not imagine. But I feel you already suspect that. Nor will it happen, unless you let it, even if Afsoon were to have his way with you every day throughout eternity. You are not like other women. Unless you decide to conceive, it just won't happen. You control that outcome. It is in your DNA to deny it, or allow it."

Eve looked up, calm now, into the soft perfect blue of Sophia's eyes, so nearly on a level with her own, and saw love, and … what? Recognition perhaps; something indefinable at any rate, before it slipped away into nothingness. "And what now of Afsoon? Clearly you have the power to destroy him. Are you going to throw him into the void, or re-open Pandora's Box?"

Sophia released Eve's arms and gripped her shoulders reassuringly for a moment, before dropping her hands. "That is for you to decide. Come, sit. Let's talk." They sat silent for a time. Eve watched universes form and fade, oceans pour from the sky into the funnel of a volcano, then erupt as an exodus of the damned. All fighting for the chance to climb a ladder into heaven, where dwelt the Kraken, who was scooped into the cupped hands of a horned Goddess, bleeding a trillion suns/sons from a gothic arch, where her vagina should be. And a black whirlpool swallowed them all. Seeing her pre-occupation, Sophia waved a hand, and they sat on a beautiful plateau floating in space, with rivers and streams, and a warm sun resting on the horizon. Soft grass was beneath their feet, lounging woodland creatures, soothing bird song, and the steady rasping beat of a grasshopper chorus befuddled her senses. The smell of new mown hay wafted on a light warm breeze. Eve did not realise for a long time that the breeze was the breath of Sophia's words.

"The enigma you need to understand Eve, is that creation requires 'free will' in order to exist. If you have no free will, then you are not a person. You are merely an extension of someone, or something, else. Elohim understands this in a limited sort of a way. He doesn't like it, but he understands that some independent 'someone' must observe him and his creation, in order for him, or it, to have any substance. If they are not independent of him, then he, and it, are just a passing thought in his own mind, and it will fade as surely as it came. It will in fact return to chaos. Just as your dreams and fantasies, or even your sense of self, are nothing until you speak them, or write them, or record and communicate them in some way, to some independent other. Only then can they have a chance to be made into reality. Adam and your namesake were only very well constructed and obsessive thought, until they defied God. Creation burst forth from their union, dragging a multitude of half formed demons in its wake, all desperate to have substance and power in this new formed existence. Multiply 'He' said, and this command they chose to obey, increasing the substance of a very imperfect and malformed creation with every generation, each new human heavy with the weight of its parasitic demon horde. It is now in danger of gaining so much substance and density that it will stagnate and implode under its own weight, and may separate from its origins altogether. It has poison at its centre. And the hell that has formed in everyone's dreams since the beginning of space and time may well be a premonition of this state of stagnation and hellish imprisoned torment.

"In short, God is creation. A creation realised by the recognition of the independent souls that exist in the hinterland between 'Him' and oblivion. Earth is the penumbra of 'Him,' the first ring, or layer if you like. 'He' shines through it, and through humanity with ever weakening force until his light is swallowed up in the chaos and oblivion, from which he sucks his power in order to maintain and grow reality. Whilst this is all in perfect balance, both states support each other, and in the thin slice of shadow lands between the two there exists self-determining time and space. The two vastnesses of creation and oblivion where lie eternity and infinity rely for their existence on the linchpin of your Earth, and its echoes of reality throughout the cosmos and the multiverse. But Earth is becoming too heavy. If nothing arrests its gravity, it will become hard and opaque, and will collapse in on itself, dragging universes with it. Then it will sink into the dark of oblivion and chaos. Ultimately, without the dynamic disturbance and irritation of creation's insertion into the void, the void too will settle back into nothingness. It will calm and flatten, and external reality will cease to be."

"Are you saying that God and creation are not eternal and infinite?"

"Eternal yes, if all goes bad, He will remain a blind boil in the skin of oblivion, but infinite? No! He exists in my infinity, and at present, we all exist in his eternity, but time is not infinite and can be brought to a stop." Sophia let her eyelids drop and said nothing more for what seemed like an age, and Eve could not find anything to say either. And then, opening beautiful eyes that shone with inner light, Sophia looked deep into Eve's eyes, and that look carried a sigh that washed into her being like a refreshing breeze.

"I touched you Eve. I touched and flowed through that magnificent body you wear. You are my offspring, my progeny. And only you, in all of creation, can 'unmake,' and, by doing so, can restore balance and maintain creation at its optimum. When you heal Eve, it is not really healing. It is the unmaking of the disease or affliction, the demon that is the cause of the malady affecting the host soul. Although you are by comparison very small in power, minute even, you are an anathema to God. And you are the fulfilment of Lucifer. You can also be the saviour of humanity and reality, and indeed, of God himself, but I urge you, do not breed. To do so would increase the substance of chaos and oblivion, and ironically, all would again be unmade. It may take forever for you to maintain creation, and the work will be hard. You will face temptation and opposition, but it really is the only worthwhile goal, and the rewards are the heavens we all so desperately seek and hope for."

"Even you?"

"Especially me, do you really think I want to go back into that endless sleep of nothingness? I want to be awake and alive and vibrant. I want to be proud and to see you succeed. I want to love my beautiful daughter. I am vast Eve, vast beyond the imaginings of anything that exists. And I must become so small, like a spark, a tiny leap of static electricity from a vast intellect, just to be able to commune with you. And yet to me, this is the most important moment in existence. You are the embodiment of all my hopes and dreams ..."

"Do you know you have just grown horns and a tail, and your nails are growing at an alarming rate? Your eyes have become black slits. And ... and your back is dissolving."

"Really? Shit! I've let us get too close to the pit. Dammed travellator, nothing ever stays constant in this place." She blinked. There was a jolt and a judder, and the pit began to recede as her form returned to *normal*? If such a thing as normal could any longer be thought to exist.

"Now to business. Sticky bun? Tea?" Naturally, being mum she poured, and just for a moment, looking over Sophia's shoulder, Eve thought she saw a mad hatter materialise from the pit, before four demons in white coats grabbed him, and dragged him screaming back into the void.

"What are you going to do about Afsoon?"

"Can't I open the box and find him gone?"

"That's a gamble, and it might work ... But ..."

"But?"

"But you might be gone too. You two are connected, two parts of a whole."

"Would that be so bad? Perhaps it would be better if neither of us existed."

"I think you would have to put that question to God, to all of creation, and to every soul within it. It tears my very essence to hear you voice it to me Eve. It would be like removing the supporting piece of Jenga from a very precarious tower. And of course, there is the possibility he might not be gone. He might come out twice as big and twice as scary."

"You say you are my mother, so be a parent, and help me decide what to do."

"No. This has to be your choice. I interfered too much already when I suggested you absorb him. Your will is free Eve. Without it you are just an echo of something else. You need to understand something about parenthood Eve. A good parent passes free will onto her children. Some accept it and some don't. Those who don't are non-persons, non-souls; those who do create and sustain the future." She reached down and lifted the cat box back onto the table, pushing it towards Eve. "It's time for you to create the future Eve." She stood and turned to leave, stepping out into the pit. Eve was shocked to immobility, and called out involuntarily, as Sophia was quickly absorbed and unmade.

"Wait! Please don't leave me. I ... I'm frightened. Mother, pleeease!" A crab scuttled across the table and pinched her hand. Eve snatched it away, and saw she had a letter in it. After inspecting the envelope this way and that, smelling it, and lifting it to the light, she finally opened it, and a crowd of alphabet letters poured out onto the table to form words. Eve read the message that was doing little squat jumps on the table before her.

Dearest Eve
Whatever you decide, I will always be proud of you.
Love
Mum x.
PS: It's all there for the making. Go get it Eve.

Meanwhile, the crab had been busily folding the envelope in on itself, and kept folding it until it reached a point of density, and with a pop, became a faceted ruby that shone from within. The crab dropped it into her palm and scuttled off again. Eve absently pocketed it.

The words dissolved into memory, and Eve sat looking through the grill of the cat box, into the dark within, and wondered ... what to do ... and where to go. The chaos settled back into an endless sea of nothing. When she could stand the emptiness no longer, Eve came to a decision. Tucking the box under her arm, she walked back into creation ... and kept walking. A black marble path formed in front of each footfall. Until in a day, or a year, where a footstep could span countless light years, galaxies and eons; she reached the orbit beyond Jupiter, and the ring domain of the insane blind worm that barred her path to the steadily hardening core, of the reality within.

A meeting with a blind worm

A deafening whisper riffled and caressed, clawed and gouged at her innermost fears and speculations. She stood in a vast ivory arch, formed by the carved and bloodied fangs of the blinded one, and could feel its forked tongue slithering out behind to encircle her. "Fool hardy creature. You dare to confront me again, and alone. Death is too good for you, witch. You will be my mate, my slave, and my plaything. I will gouge out your eyes, as you have done to mine. Perhaps I can graft them to my own empty socket and see through them the ugly and cringing creature that I will make of you."

"Then serpent, you would never know of the wonderful gifts that I bring." The light was fading as its coils slowly encircled her space.

"What possible gift could you bring to me? I encircle reality and will one day consume it. I take whatever I want from the half worlds. Do not think that lack of sight inhibits my power."

"And yet it does limit your pleasure, what if I could restore it?"

"Restore it? There is no eye in existence that can restore the sight you stole from me. It did not just see light as other creatures do. It saw into and through all of existence. Nothing was hidden from it. It was a jewel that fell out of the rift between chaos and creation at the dawn of time, and it was placed into my forming skull by the creator himself. There is no other like it anywhere in the cosmos, nor can there be. And even if there was ..." The darkness was almost complete now, as the body of the great serpent slowly constricted, and rasped into the space around her ... "Its magical abilities were in the soul that was entrapped within it, the soul that you sapped power from, when you re-forged your blade, and released when you drove the burning length of it into my eye, the soul that filled me and gave me sanity and life. My thoughts contract now. Her anguished intellect that gave shape to my consciousness, and the life force I drew from her torment slowly die now. But that will be no comfort for you, because you will be a part of my insanity and my death, which will creep on through many millennia."

"And what if I said I also had a soul, a soul that would not be trapped, but that would share your space with you? Be as you are. Guard as you guard, a mate to reinvigorate you, and be with you in eternity."

Eve could feel that the constricting had halted. "You sense it don't you? You sense the truth in my words. You can take your revenge if you wish, but dementia and death will eventually take you. But these things are really just mighty demons that afflict you until you can take no more. And death watches, and waits to invade you with its silent and eternal cold. I can unmake those demons. I can release back to you your vigour, arrest and restore the intellect you are already losing. I can give you back your sight and grant you the means to fulfil the purpose for which you were made."

"And what would you have in return witch?"

"Nothing but free passage and protection when I come and go through the boundary you guard and protect."

The coils relaxed a little, and light filtered in. "The soul is in that box?"

"Yes, and no."

"Do not toy with me witch." The light faded as its coils bunched.

"It is Schrödinger's box. You know of what I talk?"

"Then it is a gamble you offer me."

"Normally that would be true yes, but this will be no gamble. It will be a battle. You are already observing in me the half reality of its existence. It can do no other than seek completion of its reality in me. It will come into being when the box is opened. The rest depends on my ability to unmake what it has become, and on yours, to contain it, and parent it to full growth."

"So you are attempting to divide yourself, so that half of you can spend eternity with me?"

"In a way yes, but to me this other half is like a cancer waiting to attach itself to me, but when I break free of it, I will also unmake it, and heal it of its demons. It will be as a suckling babe, awaiting a parent to nurture it to full growth."

Time contracted to a single point, while its reptilian intellect ruminated on this. Eve's thoughts became a stagnant pool, until

the pebbles of an answer dropped into the torpidity of her somno-
lence ...

"Then begin, and let us see what transpires."

"First constrict your scales and pile your coils to make a deep
murk, so black that no light can penetrate. Make for me a dark
temple in which I can work. This thing I am about to release is a
thing of light. I know now that I am a creature of darkness. In a
limited way 'it' is able to create, whilst most of my ability is to
un-create. I would not have it in an environment from which it can
draw comfort and strength."

A mighty undulating shuffle of tightening coils snuffed out the
light, and all of the physical senses with it, and a wondrous thing
happened. Eve shone star bright in the darkness, but it was the light
of oblivion, only observable by, and in, one who has looked into
the fire of transcendent chaos. Within the box a dim glow could
now be seen. Eve opened it, and Afsoon's essence poured out, its
leviathan head sniffing, searching, and snorting fire, and dripping
molten drool ... It spoke.

"So this is it then, Eve. Finally we do battle." He was extending
his senses, and trying to locate her. "Do not think that by hiding in
the dark you can escape me, nor should you have any hope that
you will find release in death. I will possess and use you Eve. And
I will quite literally bend you to my will and destroy everything
and everyone you value and love." So saying, he became a ball of
incandescent fire, flinging out spirals of whiplash plasma to scour
the void. His intent, to slash, lacerate, and shred her ethereal form
wherever it was hidden in this dark tomb. Eve moved her consciousness into the heart of the fire like a black proboscis, feeling it
burn and score runnels into her soul as she did so. She clapped her
hands to either side of his searching gaze and looked into the
burning glare of his eyes. Her darkness thrust into the depths of his
being, and spread like a cloud of doom, slithering and oozing
through every private fear and thought of the one creature, they
had both now conjoined to become. Punching a mental fist
through the wall of his solar body, she reached down and clawed
into his sexual psyche. With slow and erotic rhythm, she began to
manipulate and massage the highways through which his seminal
essence would flow, enticing pineal desire. In unity and unison,
they screamed with the exquisite agony of her ministrations. Tor-

turous pain was now emanating from the vastly engorged and wraithlike phallus, into which his essence and life-force unwillingly pumped and pulsed. Realising too late, her intent, Afsoon panicked and managed to rip his upper torso away from her. "Leave me be whore. You cannot do this!"

Eve crooned at him with sarcastic venom. "What's wrong Afsoon. This is what you wanted, isn't it? To ram your oversized manhood inside of me, to spill your mighty seed over and over throughout eternity, well I am going to make you spill all of it! All at once! In one orgasmic explosion that I hope is excruciatingly painful for the both of us. Though I will know the pain, the orgasm will be yours alone. You are a disgusting and vile creature Afsoon. You have always made my skin creep."

His doom fell on him and tightened around his will like a winding sheet. He knew he was to be disassembled. "You know, don't you? You have always known. I finally worked it out. Your obsession with sex, always trying to force it on me in one way or another, or more specifically, the uncontrolled orgasmic release in which it culminates. Helen was never in any danger from you, was she? Just so long as she was my active lover."

"Really John? Helen is nothing. She could never give you the ecstasy that I have, and I could do it again, and again. You took me beneath the moon John. You lusted for me in the habitat. You want me Eve. You know you do, but not like this ..." He was starting to lose coherent thought, but through sheer willpower, managed to re-focus. "Please Eve, don't. I was wrong. We can rule together ... as equals. I will tease your lust to heights you never thought possible. You can't do this. You are insane Eve. Everything I have done has been for you. You are living in a dream fantasy. Do you really believe all that has happened to you is anything other than the ravings of a madman, strapped to a bed in a lunatic asylum? I can help you, nurture you, and bring you back to health. It's all I ever really wanted ... It was just shock therapy ... Eve pleeease. I'm begging you to stop. You will destroy us both."

For a moment she faltered, then looked inside of herself, and knew truth. "It's too late for you Afsoon. You know that the power I will take from this union will be enough to unmake you." She wrapped her thighs around his pelvis.

Suddenly he contracted. "Or it can empower me and destroy you! You crazy bitch!" And with a greedy look of triumph on his twisted features, he exploded into a super nova of white-hot energy that blasted into her pelvic tract, and thrust outwards with almost unstoppable force ... "almost."

With a vast clutching contraction she pulled back the shattered pieces of her ethereal self, and thrust back at him, with "truly irresistible" and enveloping counter force, piercing herself to the midnight depths of her being, on the lance of his erupting spiritual manhood. She felt him weakening and dissipating with each unbearable surge and expulsion. At the same time, she knew herself to expand with godlike power, riding on the storm of a writhing and flailing serpent that continued to pump unbearable jolts of thigh crunching potency into her hungry spirit. She would not spill and waste most of her essence in the deceit of orgasmic overspill this time, nor surf in her ignorance on the turbulent wave-front of her sex drive, and lose herself in the abandonment of personal ecstasy.

This time, she would become the wave itself, and control the creative power that was released from between her thighs, directing the fullness of it to serve her purpose. Afsoon saw his imminent doom and began to weep pitifully. She could feel the structure of his soul dissipating and reforming into the blank canvas she had sought to bring about, but also she could feel herself absorbing his creative ability, and the memory and essence of all that he was. These things cannot be destroyed and must always exist somewhere. She realised now what Sophia had meant when she said "absorb him." It had been sage advice and had led her to this catalytic moment. At the last ... as the very last drop of him drizzled out, to become osmosed into her consciousness, his face shone with angelic composure, and he said simply, and with paradoxical clarity. "I love you Eve."

She would ponder that for many years, but not now. She let the phrase sink into the depths of her mind. After a time, she squatted and urinated, spat on her hands, and scrubbed vigorously with clawed fingers at her genitalia to remove the contamination of him. Looking down at the eel-like creature writhing at her feet she called out. "Ouroboros! Come and accept my gift." She reached down and lifted and cradled the writhing creature over the palms of her two hands. "Let it have light to help it grow strong and vast like its parent and spouse." There was a surge and rush, like the emptying of an underground river, and light flooded onto the black marble plateau beneath her feet. She found herself facing the arch she had previously stood within, and the serpent's eyeless face above it.

"And my eye? You promised I would see. Let me see my child. Let me see my mate."

Eve withdrew the ruby from her pocket, and it unfolded and expanded in her grasp to the size of her fist. Ouroboros dipped his massive head, and she placed it into his skull, where it continued to expand, until the cavity of his empty socket was full. Immediately his head writhed away, and ducked into a myriad of realities, to see what had been unseen for so long. He then flicked out his tongue, lifted the creature from her hands and scrutinised it. Finally he dipped his mighty head to the floor, and placed the creature before her.

"And what of my demons? You said you would heal me of my coming death."

"I will indeed heal you. But I should tell you that you will be changed. I don't know what form that change will take, but I believe in my heart that you will be better for it. Should I continue?"

He looked at her with his ruby eye, blinked slowly, and continued to stare into and through her with his all-seeing gaze. Eve knew this for acceptance. Reaching her hands into his eye socket, she spread her arms to encompass as much as she could of the shining jewel. A lance of ruby light blasted through her abdomen, and refracted outwards from her extremities into a spectrum of a thousand blinding colours. Eve could feel the malevolence of the many parasitic and destructive essences. Essences that had clung to and formed the body of the serpent these many millennia, desperately trying to cling to existence, seeping through her mind, screaming offers of servitude, and promising power. Anything to retain their parasitic hold on reality, and to resist expulsion. It was like trying to pump out sludge from her arterial and vascular systems, but at last it was over; and she dropped, and lay drooping and exhausted. The creature, quite tenderly, laid her onto the floor and bowed its mighty head to rest it before her. In a booming voice, strident with renewed power, he spoke. "Pass Friend! You are welcome, always."

Semyaza

Helen looked out from the city through a rift in the cloud basin, which had parted when Cariel blew upon it. In the grey depths below, a US navy war ship was powering through the sea lane that the watchers had kept open through the Sargasso. A military spy plane was shadowing the ship on a level with the cloud city, and a submarine was at an equal depth below. All were using experimental types of quasi paranormal technology to try to gauge what had caused cloud to hang on the surface, and murk to billow below, on the whole of the Sargasso. With the exception that is, of the six-mile-wide shipping lane that since its formation two years before, had enjoyed constant sunshine. Cariel assured her that nothing of the city could be detected or observed, and that any incursion into the cloud or murk would be hopeless to navigate, and would always lead the craft back to the shipping and air lanes.

Helen sighed. "Three years Cariel! I know she's out there somewhere trying to return. I feel her." She seemed to look into another place and her hand absently strayed to her inner thigh, whilst her other hand gripped the sword Sophia which seemed to have adopted her since Eve's departure. "Sometimes she is in me Cariel, in my dreams anyway. God knows we need her. The war hasn't gone well."

She shivered, and Cariel drew her into the shelter of a wing. "You control two thirds of the globe Helen. You are the icon of millions. I think you are over harsh on yourself."

"But my grip is loose. Terrorism is barely under control. There are food riots in every city. Despite the efforts of Jackie, Ben and Fadil, and the rest of the disciples, our church is losing followers by the thousands. America and Europe tolerate us because we are the only ones who have maintained sufficient technology to keep the world economy functioning, or who have the means to combat the many complex biological threats. The Vatican has reacted against us, excommunicating all who follow us ... Poor Soames ... He hides it well but it chews him up. Eve is denounced as a false prophet, and the rest of us as dangerous heretics. I am sure the pope is behind half the riots. They gnaw at our strength from within, whilst Afsoon's followers seem to have tight control of the areas within their territories and borders, and far more consistent loyalty. And now we have reports of the 'Awoken Messiah' having descended into hell to raise a demonic army who will destroy and enslave us all, 'the abusers of his kingdom.' Indeed, there has been evidence of demonic beings both sighted and active in many of the random attacks on our borders. We know they will strike with full force soon, but when, where, and how, we have been unable to divine."

She turned to look into Cariel's impossible ultra-violet eyes, took a deep breath and paused pensively ... "Why do you think Semyaza wants to see me Cariel? Do you think he may relent and help, or at least share knowledge with us to help us defeat our enemies?"

Cariel responded slowly. "Be careful Helen. His will is all enveloping, and his motives are unknown and often questionable."

Cariel escorted Helen onto the terrace where Semyaza waited with his back to them, looking down through the clouds as Helen had lately done. She indicated that Helen should approach him and left. He turned at her tread. Fully nine feet tall with liquid mercury eyes and silver hair cascading over his shoulders and back, he was a daunting sight, but Helen did not break stride. She walked up boldly, sat on the stone slab next to where he stood, looked up into his bottomless orbs, and waited.

"Not many would hold my gaze as you do Helen, or dare to sit in my company without my invitation."

"Are we not friends Semyaza, bound to a common cause? Friends do not show deference or awkwardness in each other's company."

Semyaza sat down next to her. "Friends? That is something we shall establish." His eyes seemed to cloud over for a moment, and then to focus on her. "I think I like your familiarity Helen, but I should make it plain that even the creator could not bind me ... Do you find it beautiful here? Has Cariel shown you our gardens?"

"Why am I here Semyaza?"

Semyaza cocked his head to one side and looked long at Helen. "Your incisiveness is refreshing, if a little abrupt, one might even say rude, but yes perhaps we should save our overtures of friendship until our business here is out of the way." He sat in thought for several minutes, before taking her hands into both of his, and revealing what was causing him such consternation. "I have summoned you here because it has lately become known to me that Eve is attempting to return."

Shocked and stunned, Helen abandoned her studied relaxation. All attempts at disrupting his propensity to dominate forgotten. She was on her feet, eyes blazing on a level with his, and facing him. "You are in contact with her? Where is she? What is preventing her from coming back to us? Why aren't you helping her?"

The trace of a smile flitted over his features. "Will you interrogate me Helen? Only you have ever been so bold." Again he gave her an assessing look, this time casting his gaze up and down the full length of her body. In her eagerness to know more, she was oblivious. He would not be hurried, however, and remained thoughtful for what seemed to Helen like an eternity ... he finally responded with sober, but somewhat disconcerting brusqueness. "I think perhaps we shall be somewhat more than friends, but in order to pursue our 'common cause,' it is only right that you possess all of the facts. To answer your question, no I am not in contact, but I am aware of her and her current difficulties, and I will try to help."

"Is she hurt or in trouble? Can I go to her? Do you know where she can be found?"

"She is unhurt but ..." Again his tone and demeanour changed. His voice became softer, conspiratorial, and supportive. "When have you ever known Eve to not be in trouble? No, you cannot go to her. Nor can I, or any of the watchers."

"Then what is there to be done? Can she get here by herself?"

"She could get here by herself, but it requires tremendous effort, knowledge she has yet to discover, and skills she does not have, and ... it may all come too late ... if ever, unless ..." He spoke no more, and infuriatingly, waited on her reaction.

"Unless what? Spit it the fuck out Semyaza! What are you holding back?"

Now he did smile, and it was as of the sunrise banishing the shadows of a lingering dawn. "Spit it the fuck out," he mused, and there was something indefinable and unsettling in his melodious chuckle. With the fading of his smile, the light paled once more, and foreboding mingled disconcertingly with his earnest words. "There are ways that she could be brought here sooner, but you would have to open your mind, your soul, and ... well, to be blunt ... certain parts of your anatomy, to achieve it."

The inference prodded at her uncomfortably. Helen's bravado was being crowded and jostled. She had become well versed in scriptural knowledge and knew of the fall of Semyaza and the Grigori. Fear nibbled at her, and her legs slid sweaty and cold against each other, as she started to back away. "What ...?" She took a quavering breath, looking around for a path of retreat. "What do you mean?"

"Oh come now Helen, you know the power of sex magic by now, and of that moment of conception that can produce either great power, or a life. I am suggesting that in order to speed Eve's return, we do both. Eve is trapped outside of this densest of realities. To enter here, not in the future when it may be too late, but now, she needs a vessel in this place. If that vessel is powerful enough, and the bond of Eve with its mother strong enough, we can draw her essence to us, like a salmon to the source of the river that gave it birth."

"What are you saying? You want to fuck me to bring Eve here. Is that it? How the hell does that work? And how does it help us having a nine month wait to produce a mewling new-born in our midst? In any case, you must know that I am barren. Thank you, but no to that one."

"Don't be so naïve Helen. You have been the close companion of Eve. You and all the disciples have been touched by her sanctity. You have attained a higher level of humanity. Do you really think you remain barren? Haven't you always wanted a child? Eve could never give you one."

She hadn't seen him move, but somehow he was much closer. Helen tried to subdue the fear and rage simmering within her. "You want me to mother my own husband? Haven't you interfered enough in humanity? Isn't that what brought you and your followers to your downfall, writhing as serpents for thousands of years in the mud of the earth?"

There was a slight hesitation, while something ugly flitted across his features. She continued to back away but seemed to be creating no space. "Things have changed Helen. You can probably number your years in millennia, and you are genetically close to perfection. With such longevity, the loyalties and moral foibles of those with short lives no longer apply. You would die of boredom, or kill your lover, if you had no variety. You will find open and diverse relationships are a necessity, if you are to maintain interest and excitement, and even ... enduring love. The being we would create would be half angelic Helen, and would grow to maturity in days. What a vehicle that would be for Eve to inhabit. We could make her male. Then you could have a lover of a complimentary sex to share your bed with."

His will was consuming her, and despite her efforts to resist, she was dropping into the well of a deep and enfolding trance. She could see actual images of the years rolling off into eternity, feel the boredom and frustration of a seemingly infinite and repetitive life and love pattern, and the tensions between her and Eve turning to hatred. She was trembling at the thought of the excitement and delights, of sampling the forbidden and the taboo. Her heart began to pound and her head to spin.

His voice rumbled on in low hypnotic tones, running a strong undercurrent, to her now excited, heavy and rapid breathing. His voice became soothing, masterful and thrilling. "I would be failing in my debt and my gratitude to Lady Eve, to you, and to all of creation, if I did not create this opportunity for her immediate return. Eve and humanity will revere you for it."

A soft breeze riffling over her revealed her unexplained nudity. Her every nerve jangled with pent erotic tension. Having been so long denied the stroke and thrust of a lover, she responded, aching with sexual need to be fulfilled. In that moment an image of Eve standing in the contracting coils of a gargantuan serpent rushed through her mind like a high-speed train. She was abruptly transported back into the present, but too late, and to no avail. Finger slaps to her flailing arms left them dead, bruised and useless. His vice-like grip on her hair immobilised her. He was already thrusting and bucking inside of her. In a self-loathing state of orgasmic disgust, she feebly began to claw and bite. This just seemed to excite him. He became rough and animalistic and would not stop.

An awful scream filled with anger and hatred exploded unbidden from her bloodied lips.

Cariel heard her distress, and in a winged and violent blur, she swept in to rip her from him. An anguished howl of impending retribution followed the turbulent and obscuring speed of their departure. Descending in a stoop and a tight spiral through the thick cloud cover, they landed onto the deck of the navy ship below. They were swiftly surrounded by a group of armed marines. Cariel's wing shielded Helen's nakedness, and her voice rang out clear and commanding. "This is the Lady Helen Wolfe. You all know of her ... We spotted a dog on your ship that previously belonged to her consort, Eve Gabriel, and so must assume your master to be Captain Baker. Please inform him we are on board, and that we require a place of refuge and safety."

"I am informed you are Eve Gabriel's ..." He raised his eyebrows in question. "Consort?" He did not wait for an answer. "Doctor Gabriel is still registered with the US authorities as a suicide, but it was pretty damn obvious that your lunatic nut of a tyrant goddess of the same name were one and the same. Now, I know I am going to regret asking this, but how the hell did you get onto my ship? What kind of creature is the companion who came with you? And if it's not too much to ask at this early stage of our acquaintance, what trouble has Doctor Gabriel gotten herself, and you and your friend here, into now?"

Helen looked towards Cariel who shrugged her wings and sat down cross legged in the corner. She gave an exasperated sigh and dropped heavily into the only chair, deeply grateful for the shower and loan of military fatigues that had been afforded to her, but sorely missing the comfort of Sophia hanging at her side. "What would you say Captain Baker, if I said we had pissed off an extremely powerful angel? Who is likely to be looking for me right now, with a view to ..." She looked again at Cariel, who simply inclined her head. Helen finished her sentence, "impregnating me, if he hasn't already, with ..." She clawed her hands in a frustrated attempt to rip a description from the air around her.

"Well, I don't know what the fuck it would be. Scripture suggests it would be a human hating giant demon. Semyaza insists it would be the essence and very soul of Eve, and that would make me ..." She shuddered. "My husband's mother, wife and ..." Shaking with the foiled effort to complete her sentence she finally settled for, "Lesbian, fucking paedophile lover." She let her hands drop to dangle loosely on the floor, a visual echo of her emotional exhaustion.

Captain Baker spread his arms and looked at each of his hands in turn, as though looking for the nails that had crucified his hold on any sense of normality or reason left in the universe. Finding none, he dropped them dejectedly to his sides, and started to speak. "Who? What?" He walked purposefully to the door, hesitated, then turned, strode back, and punched the palm of his hand several times, finally gripping the punching fist as though to quell any reckless outburst ... "Of course, what other explanation could there be?" He seemed to be speaking to himself, and Helen was in any case, too exhausted to respond. He paced some more. "I fucking knew it! I have suspected it for some time, of course. In the years in fact since meeting your ..." He stopped, and turned to her, addressing her directly. "Did you say husband?" Shaking his head, he turned his eyes up to the ceiling in exasperation. "I am actually in hell, aren't I? And you two are the latest of my tormentors." He paced up and down, stopping at every third turn to huff out a breath and gesticulate, start to speak, shake his head, and continue pacing.

Finally, he gave a long slow sigh and got control of his rapid breathing, stopped pacing, and looked calmly and resignedly to the door frame that his dog had been blocking the daylight from ... "Here Zeus!" He dropped onto his heels and petted the grizzled looking animal affectionately. Zeus licked his face and sat looking at him adoringly. "What do you say boy? Do we help these two mental fucking harpies, or throw them into the sea? No one would know, and we could just go on our way. Live our lives in relative normality. Not that anything is normal anymore. The world now seems to belong to fantasy creatures like these two here. It seems we have become the oddities in this universe." His eyes took on a vacant look, as he stared into some past memory of how life once was. Zeus cocked his head to one side with a look that seemed to sympathise with his master, then padded over to Helen and put his head in her lap.

Captain Steven Baker of the USS *Fairweather* stood, clapped his arms around his ribs several times, as though to ward off cold, and restore circulation. He muttered some more words under his breath. "Fuck it! When reality disintegrates, all we can do is find a pattern somewhere, and try to follow it. It's not as though I have much choice anyway. The crew will probably fucking mutiny if I refuse to help." He looked at Cariel, then at Helen. "What do you want from me Helen Wolfe? What will it take for you and your demon clan, to stop dragging me through the shit-filled swamps of purgatory?"

Helen looked to Cariel for an answer. Cariel slowly unfolded to her full height, her head almost grazing the ceiling of the small cabin. She shook, and braced back her shoulders, as though she would take flight, looked down on them both, and burned bright in the dismal light of the cabin. "I have been communing with my brother Baliel. Semyaza is oldest and strongest among us. He has always been unquestioned as our leader. He will suffer no opposition to his will, and his wrath will be both terrible and swift, but I have been shielding our presence here. Nor will he suspect that we are so close, but he will break my shielding or figure out our whereabouts soon enough. Many of our number have come to distrust him however. Also, we are bound in gratitude to Eve for releasing us, and by the strong oaths and obligations with which she wisely tethered us to her cause. We have suffered much in the past by the breaking of such trusts. If my brother can convince enough of our number to act with honour, and to rally in defence of Helen, we may be able to force him to comply with his promises. But he must, in the meantime, be diverted from finding us, and of having his lustful intent further consummated with Helen. Any creature of such a union would, I promise you, have no resemblance to Eve. Also we must give my brother time to gain the support we need to oppose Semyaza. We need your men captain Baker, armed with whatever weaponry you have at your disposal. Pitiful fighting force though they will be, under my direction and with surprise on our side, it may divert his attention long enough for our purposes. You wanted to know what was in the clouds Captain Baker. Will you let me take you there, to our city in the sky? I must make this clear though, it is likely that many of you will not return."

Eve's Intrusion

Eve paced back and forth across the black marble plateau, and tried, for the hundredth time, to walk into Earth reality, to pass through the ring and sphere that was "Ouroboros." It was like walking into glue. A few feet of penetration was the best she had managed so far. With a mighty cry she screamed out into the star filled space that surrounded her. "Ouroboros! What treachery have you wrought, that after inviting me to pass, you put a barrier in my path? Did you not call me friend? What friendship is this?"

A beautiful, but distinctly reptilian woman, with dark hair that fanned out like a cobra's hood, writhed onto the edge of the plateau, and walked sinuously towards her. When she spoke, a forked tongue flicked from parted lips, to reveal glimpses of barbed fangs, stained black with poison. Eve braced for battle. As the she snake weaved a wary course towards her, a sun baked rock between two ornately carved wooden chairs, materialised between them. The creature slithered into one, and in hissing tones, invited Eve to occupy the other.

"Pleas-sss-e sss-sit. 'Friend' was perhaps the wrong word. I think I must acknowledge you as my sss…is-sss…ter. Were we not both created long after genesis, and your power used to create me? I have put no barrier in your way 'sissster.' The barrier is of your own making. Before your whorish battle with Afsssoon, you reached into a transcendent state, but not as the Christ. For you are his opposite. The light you shed is the light of oblivion. Nevertheless, your difficulty in returning to created space is similar. Condensing a transcending spirit is not an easy thing. It is like trying to force all the clouds in the sky into a thimble. Even Jesus could only sustain it for a limited time." She spoke slowly and with many prolonged and contemplative pauses which Eve found both infuriating and frustrating to her eagerness to return to Helen and the rest of her friends. Also, it was flesh creepingly repulsive and frightening because during the pauses she looked as though she was resisting an overwhelming compulsion to rip open Eve's throat with those venom dripping fangs.

Eve tried to guide her to the point. "It can be done though?"

"Yes-sss … with much study, many trials, and learned, and experienced disciplines, but I agree with what I sense in your troubled and prophetic ssspirit, that intervention is required now! Sssomething portentousss is building in the den-sss-ity of Earth. Something dangerous that threatens usss all, perhaps exissstencsse itself."

"What can be done?" A vacant stare crept into the creature's ruby eyes. "I am looking now … Helen is embroiled in a dangerous circumstance that could have an apocalyptic outcome."

Eve was instantly on her feet, and finding it hard not to give pace to Ouroboros's words by ringing them out of the foul creature's neck. Somehow she kept herself in check. "What? What danger is she in?"

"SSS-Semyaza! He would father a beast with her! Quickly ssister! Give me permission to fetch your sword!"

Eve did not hesitate. "Granted."

"You must let me ride your power. Kiss-sss me. Take care not to puncture your tongue or inhale my pois-ssson. You will find it … un…pleas…sss…ant."

Eve felt sick at the thought, but Helen's predicament precluded argument. She almost choked on the smell of decay and retched on the flicking tongue that probed the back of her throat. Eve was unable to suppress a shudder, at the apparent relish the creature seemed to get from the intrusion, but Ouroboros soon faded to insubstantiality … then came back into full focus, holding Sophia reverently in her hands. Reluctantly, she offered it to Eve.

"Take the sss-sword. Call on our mother for the power to condense into the Earthly realm. A battle with the angels is upon usss. Helen and her current consort cannot win, and losing may be the end for us all. You will need help. Take me with you, for I cannot enter without your permission and your as-siss-tance. Nor will you win, without mine. We can ride on Afsoon, whom I name 'Black Death' in your honour." Eve winced at that. "He has grown large and strong and will be of great assistance in our battle."

A flood of misgivings writhed through the depths of Eve's soul. Hadn't she fought to near death, and the extinction of all she knew, to keep Ouroboros out of Earth reality? And now she was being manipulated into bringing Afsoon along for the ride. She hoped "Black Death" was not a prophetic naming for any but their enemies, but her overriding concern for now, was to save Helen from whatever catastrophe had befallen her, and … and … her … "consort?" The rest she would deal with later. "Promise to our mother Sophia, and on the eye I have lately returned to you that you will return here when we are done, and never again cross into my reality without my permission."

"You must learn to trussst sissster but for now I will promise."

They rode a huge black-winged serpent and Jörmungandr, as she now renamed herself, had summoned three winged demons of her own likeness, claiming them for her offspring, to follow in their wake. She whispered incantations into Eve's ear, which Eve repeated. A hole wobbled into existence in the glue that separated her from her home world. Pointing the way with the unsheathed Sophia, they flew into the soup of a dangerously unstable reality. When "Black Death" surged forward, Eve felt the crushing arms of Jörmungandr constrict and tighten unbearably around her waist and chest.

End of Book 2

www.ingramcontent.com/pod-product-compliance
Lightning Source LLC
Chambersburg PA
CBHW050356030726
47503CB00006B/1888